AN UNEXPECTED KISS

"Mrs. Hanson is in no need of your money."

His gaze narrowed. "Then she desires a position in society? No doubt the mother of an earl could see a number of doors previously closed suddenly thrown wide open."

"Mrs. Hanson has never possessed the least interest in society."

"I am not the gullible fool you have marked me, Miss Smith. There is something that she wants."

"Yes. To know the son she has not seen in twenty-two years. Is that so terrible?"

"Why would she wait twenty-two years to seek me out?"

"I suppose she feared your reaction to her return."

"But she managed to overcome her fear after discovering the news of my inheritance?"

"Your inheritance had nothing to do with her decision."

"Of course not. And I suppose her decision to bring along a young, extraordinarily lovely maiden was coincidence as well?"

"You are a very disagreeable man."

"Forgive me. But if you desire me to be bewitched, who am I to quibble?" he mocked, his hand lifting without warning to cup the back of her neck. "I discover I have an unexpected taste for treacherous beauties."

"Sir . . ." she began to protest, only to be effectively silenced when he abruptly angled his head downward and claimed her lips in a bold, seeking kiss. . . .

From "A Mother at Heart," by Debbie Raleigh

A HUSBAND FOR MAMA

Mary Blayney
Julia Parks
Debbie Raleigh

ZEBRA BOOKS
Kensington Publishing Corp.
http://www.kensingtonbooks.com

Kensington Publishing Corp.
850 Third Avenue
New York, NY 10022

All Kensington titles, imprints and distributed lines are available at special quantity discounts for bulk purchases for sales promotion, premiums, fund-raising, educational or institutional use.

Special book excerpts or customized printings can also be created to fit specific needs. For details, write or phone the office of the Kensington Special Sales Manager: Kensington Publishing Corp., 850 Third Avenue, New York, NY 10022. Attn. Special Sales Department. Phone: 1-800-221-2647.

First printing: April 2003
10 9 8 7 6 5 4 3 2 1

Printed in the United States of America

CONTENTS

Child of Her Heart

Mary Blayney

One

"Are we almost there, Miss Morton? Are we in Yorkshire?" In that odd way she had, the child passed from sleep to restless energy in an instant, awakened as the momentum of the coach changed. The rough lurch of open road gave way to the staccato rumble of cobbled streets that meant a town. The ten-year-old clambered up from her seat to lean at the window. She turned from it for a moment to ask, *"Combien de temps jusqu'a l'arrivée?"*

"Speak English, please, Marguerite. Yes, we are indeed in Yorkshire and will stop very soon." Caroline Morton ignored the disapproval radiating from the woman seated across from them. "We are coming into Thirsk now."

The child flashed her a grin and spun back to the window.

As much as Caroline envied Marguerite's ability to sleep in the uncomfortable carriage, she envied her energy more. They had been traveling for weeks, months if you counted from the day they had abandoned Marguerite's home and had begun their journey to Calais. From Calais to Dover by boat, then coach for another two hundred miles.

Caroline thought she had been tired when they left Amiens. It was as nothing compared to the weariness that held her now. Her body was stiff with it. Her breath came in deep drawn sighs as if summoning strength from a miserly storehouse in a secret part of her body. Perhaps if they were able to find a decent supper, her energy would be renewed. A decent supper and a few hours rest.

"Sit down, my dear. We will be stopping soon enough."

Caroline reached over and pulled the little girl away from the window and settled her next to her on the seat.

But Marguerite could not contain her excitement. "We have done it, Miss Morton. We have done it!"

She knelt and threw her arms around Caroline's neck and Caroline pulled the tiny fairy of a child into her arms. They hugged each other, a long rocking embrace. It was the only show of emotion that Caroline would allow herself. Their years in war-torn France had taught her to guard her expression, her sensibilities, her fear. They had both learned to communicate their deepest feelings with no more than a touch. But they were almost home now. Soon they could cry their happiness, their relief, from the rooftops. Soon, but not quite yet.

The three other passengers looked on with varying degrees of approval and Caroline smiled at them over the head of her armful.

Marguerite's enthusiasm was contagious. It was as fine a tonic for her fatigue as anything a physician could prescribe. The aching exhaustion faded to a tolerable weariness.

The weariness gave way to a thrill of pleasure as Caroline recognized the stretch of buildings that marked the main street of Thirsk. The spire of the church came into view even as the bell began to toll the hour with the same reassuring resonance she had grown up hearing.

How she longed for the scent of May blossoms, a dinner of steak and kidney pie and some cream cakes. There were distressing memories here, too, but right now they could not compete with the welcome of home.

As the coach entered the inn yard, Marguerite pulled away from her, climbed on the seat yet again, and looked from the coach door. Her face was expectant, filled with the high hopes she brought to every new experience. Marguerite looked back at her governess and announced for everyone to hear, "Our troubles are over."

Ah, but she spoke too soon.

The very moment that Caroline leaned forward to pull her back, the coachman opened the door from the other side and Marguerite lost her balance. It happened slowly, so slowly that Caroline was able to grab the sash around the girl's waist. With a surge of triumph, she knew that if she had strength enough she would be able to arrest her fall and save her from injury.

Before Caroline could test her strength, the material gave way with a slow certain ripping sound and Marguerite tumbled into the mud. That was upset enough, but the look of surprised pain on the child's face was more cause for concern.

"Oh, my dear, what have you done? You are hurt?" For two years they had faced danger and discovery in a France driven mad by revolution. They had made their way to England without a scratch. How could this happen now when safety was at hand?

Caroline turned to the ostler, a familiar face though his name escaped her. "Is Mr. Osgood still the surgeon here?"

"Yes, miss, the best there is."

Relief, anxiety, confusion, and a wave of misery came on the heels of the ostler's words. Who would have thought such a commonplace answer could induce such emotions, could push concern for Marguerite aside? Caroline denied them all. If Marguerite needed help she would not hesitate to call on Reynaud Osgood even if it was the one meeting she had hoped to avoid indefinitely.

"And he is still in the old part of town near St. James Green?"

The man nodded and Caroline turned to Marguerite.

The child looked up at her, eyes wide, and shook her head. "Oh no, Miss Morton, I have no need of the surgeon.

I am not hurt, only surprised." She made to stand, then smiled a little. Caroline turned to ease the hubbub caused by the small accident.

"It weren't my fault, miss. It weren't."

Caroline gave him a long hard look and he had the grace to look embarrassed. She was not about to waste time on a pointless argument in a public place, not when it would keep them, even for a few moments, from the bed and food they both longed for.

A man stepped out from the doorway of the Golden Fleece into the courtyard, then hurried over to help. This face was unfamiliar. When Caroline asked for a room, he shook his head with casual regret.

"I'm that sorry, miss, but every inn is full, at least until tomorrow night, or even the next day. Besides the market, there be a prizefight as well."

Marguerite pulled on her hand and Caroline bent down. "We have slept in the stable before, Miss Morton."

Yes, they had slept in a stable and a miserable experience it had been for both of them. Now that they were home there was no need for that.

Taking Marguerite's hand, she nodded to the man. "Where is Mr. Pettigrew?"

The man bobbed his head. "He retired two years ago and went to York to be with his children. My name is Roster. I own the Golden Fleece now."

No help from that quarter, she thought. Even in Thirsk life does go on. "Thank you then, Mr. Roster. We will go elsewhere."

As she moved toward the main road, Roster spoke one more time. "Shall I send your boxes and trunks along or hold them for you?"

She looked over her shoulder. "We have no baggage." She turned away, not caring what ideas he and their audience drew from her bald statement. She had more pressing concerns.

All the inns were filled? Where to go? What to do? Her head was all a muddle as she tried to find a solution to this latest problem. She would do what she had for the last two years. Rely on herself. Only a little longer. Only a little farther.

She turned back again and found the ostler, innkeeper, and her fellow travelers at a standstill watching them as they left the courtyard. Had they never seen anyone penniless before?

"Are the Landrys in residence at Landreau?"

The innkeeper shook his head, his face sober. "They're in London, miss."

Her heart fell. "Is Miss Landry with them?"

"No, she's at home." He emphasized the "she" as though pleased that he could give her some good news.

Relief huge and welcome eased her anxiety. Susan was home! With a nod of thanks, Caroline turned and caught up with a stumbling Marguerite.

They turned from the main street onto one of the wider side roads. "We will walk to Landreau tonight, my dear. I had hoped to have some time to rest and tidy ourselves, to send a message to Miss Landry before we appear on her doorstep. But she has been my friend since childhood. It will not matter that we arrive late and travel-stained." *And without baggage.*

Marguerite nodded.

The ownership of the Golden Fleece might have changed, but five years was not long enough for much else to be different.

A string of genteel residences still edged this side of the town, bordering the new grass of the green, but close enough for easy intimacy with the townspeople.

She would wager that she still knew the inhabitants of most. The house they passed now, the Osgoods', had been like a home to her. It looked the same. Why did she find that a comfort? Because if it was the sight of her heartbreak it had also been home to her happiest memories. She had become engaged here, she had sampled the pleasure of her first kiss in the back garden. She had ended her engagement there as well.

Despite the anguish of that memory, the sight of the house, so solid and substantial, drew a smile.

Caroline hurried by and then paused to wait for the more slowly moving child. Marguerite had rested most of the way from their last stop, but sleep in a bouncing coach was hardly restful. "Are you tired?" Caroline asked.

"Yes."

Caroline stopped and bent down so that her eyes were level with Marguerite's. "We only have a little farther to go, darling. We even have a full moon to light our way."

Marguerite nodded.

Was it a trick of the moonlight that made her face look so pale?

"You do know that we are safe now? We are in England, the revolution is behind us. I know Susan will take us in until I can find work."

Marguerite gave her a wan smile in answer. "We can count our blessings and not stop at two."

It was a game they had played for the last two years.

"Yes, we have much more now than our health and each other."

"We have not run out of money."

"We are almost at the end of our journey."

"The night is lovely. The rain has stopped."

"We each had a seat on the coach."

"The meat pies we had for dinner were lovely."

"Are you hungry, Marguerite?" The child was walking without much energy, but hunger had rarely slowed her down before.

Caroline stopped and watched as the little girl proceeded a few more steps before slowing. Her hair had not seen a plait for days, her dress had once been blue. She had left her homeland and never once complained.

Caroline counted this child her single dearest blessing. This funny, impossible, impetuous *enfant* was everything to her, even if Caroline was no more than her governess. There was nothing that she would not do to keep her safe. The last two years had indeed been a test of that.

The two of them would continue to be their own cobbled sort of family, until Caroline could find relatives to whom she could entrust Marguerite.

The girl was of noble birth with the blood of kings in her veins. She deserved the life she had been born to even if her parents were gone, lost to the revolution. Caroline was determined to return her to family. Even though it would break her heart to send Marguerite away.

As the child turned to question her, Caroline noticed that she was holding one arm close to her chest. "Why, you are hurt. Why do you try to hide it?"

Marguerite tried to straighten her arm, but the pain was such that she wavered as though she would faint. With a small gasp of dismay, Caroline swept the little girl up into her arms.

She would have to see him. She would have to call on Reynaud Osgood. Steeling herself for the unwanted meeting, she turned back toward the familiar house they had only just passed.

"But, Miss Morton, do we have enough money for a doctor?"

"Of course we have enough money." The absurd question brought tears to Caroline's eyes. She paused to control the upset that gave an edge to her voice. "That was no reason to try and hide your injury. We are home now and soon we will be as comfortable as a kitten nestled against its mama cat."

"C'est bon, Miss Morton."

Caroline did not correct the French, had not even heard it as such, as she stopped before the front door. With a deep breath she summoned courage, energy, composure.

The house had an air of shabby gentility that conveyed reassurance rather than neglect. The shutters needed paint, but there was a new very elegant brass knocker on the front door. Light filtered out between the drawn drapes on the first floor and down the stairs to the fan light over the door. The ground floor was dark. Did it still serve as the surgery?

Caroline nodded when Marguerite raised her good arm to the knocker. The commanding thunk on the door drew a satisfied smile. Marguerite let it fall one more time and then looked up.

"Is anyone home?"

Torn between maternal concern and personal vanity, Caroline did not know which to wish for and then marveled at her selfishness. "I am sure someone will answer the door in a moment."

When Reynaud Osgood did open the door, he was still shrugging into his coat. The spill of light from the hallway lit him from the back but she could see that his hair was mussed. He must still have that habit of running his hand through it.

As her eyes adjusted to the light, she realized that five years had hardly touched him. His eyes were still fine and brown, his eyebrows more beautifully shaped than a man deserved. His jaw bore the faint stubble of a day's growth of beard and he was smiling.

The smile was her undoing. One would think that he would be irritated at the interruption of his evening. But his smile spoke otherwise. It reached his eyes and there both invitation and interest lingered.

If she had recognized home before in the familiar streets and buildings, she felt its welcome now.

Caroline forgot the gulf of bitterness that had separated

them, forgot the vanity and the guilt that had made her draw her hood closer around her face, and forgot the fact that he might be married.

His smile was so familiar, so endearing that, for the first time in ages, she felt buoyed. She was not alone anymore. Here was someone who would help her, share the burden, ease her heart.

"Reynie?" She breathed his name and leaned a little closer, almost begging for his touch.

His smile of invitation never progressed to recognition. He looked at her as if she were a stranger. Reynaud Osgood had been a friend from childhood, her fiancé for two years, and now did not know who she was.

Useless tears gathered again and this time they fell with a will of their own.

He nodded, still unaware of who she was, and looked away from her embarrassment. The tears seemed to be all the explanation he needed. "The child is hurt." He made it a statement and held the door open for them. "Come in."

They stepped into the hallway and he opened the nearest door. His words drifted back to them from the depths of the darkened room. "Let me light the candles so that you can find your way."

"Miss Morton?"

Marguerite whispered, and Caroline looked down at her. The child's expression held absolute terror.

"Am I going to die?"

It was the best cure possible for her tears. "No, never, *chouchou.* The worst that has happened is that you have broken your arm."

"Bien. That I can bear." The little girl hesitated. "Then, please, why are you crying?"

"I think I must be very, very tired."

Marguerite nodded sagely. "It has been a very long journey and not always a comfortable one."

Before Caroline could agree, Reynaud Osgood came back to the door. He pretended not to notice their déshabille.

It was Marguerite who spoke first. "I fell out of the coach and into the mud."

Osgood smiled at her. "Yes, I can see that. I will wager you that the mud has saved you from serious injury." His interest was all for the injured. He barely glanced at Caroline.

"Put her here, if you please." He watched as Caroline lowered Marguerite to the top of a table in the middle of the room.

Still watching his charge, he nodded absently to a chair near the window. As Caroline moved to the seat she caught a glimpse of herself in a glass and instantly understood Reynie's lack of recognition. The hood hid most of her face and what he could see was streaked with mud. Her eyes were so deeply shadowed that her skin appeared more gray than white. She pushed the hood off, smoothed her hair and sank into the chair.

"It was wise of you to come right away." Reynie was speaking to Marguerite. "These injuries rarely improve with time. It will hurt when I move it, but it is the only way for me to determine the extent of the damage."

Caroline watched Marguerite's slow nod. She could not see the child's face, but knew her eyes would be wide and her expression very brave.

Reynie placed a bucket next to her on the table. "Use this if you feel unwell."

It was a miserable few moments. Caroline's arm thrummed in sympathetic pain and Marguerite did indeed use the bucket, but there were no moans or tears from either of them.

Reynie's only comments were a series of "hmmms," each with a slightly different cadence or lilt. Caroline found the sounds more comforting than annoying, even if the meaning was as foreign to her as Italian would have been.

Reynie straightened and patted his patient's head. "You were a very brave soldier, little one. I know it hurt."

"Is it broken?" Marguerite asked the question with an eagerness that made Caroline smile through her worry.

"No. It is not. It is only a strain. It is painful, in some ways more painful than a break but it will heal faster." He spent the next few minutes preparing a cold water bath and urging her to place her arm in it. "This will ease the pain and then we will bind it close to you. You must pass the night here. Rest is the best restorative. I have a room prepared for such. Your mother can stay with you."

Marguerite turned and looked at Caroline with a huge grin. *"Maman?"* It was a word they had used for protection and convenience while still in France but since they had landed in England, Caroline had insisted on Miss Morton.

As though he sensed a joke, Reynie looked from the little girl to Caroline and his own expression changed from tolerant amusement to shock.

"Caroline?" He whispered the name as though he suspected she might be a ghost. Then he took a step toward her. "Caroline Morton?"

Two

She looked terrible. Reynie kept his expression neutral, hoping the shock did not show. It was more than the mud-spattered cloak and threadbare dress. Her eyes were sunken, and if he was not mistaken, the flush on her cheeks was due to ill health rather than embarrassment. She needed medical attention as much as the child.

"What are you doing here?" He looked from the child to her. "This child cannot be yours. She must have at least eight years."

"Ten. She is small for her age." Caroline corrected him automatically. "I am her governess."

A governess? What governess would look as she did?

"Was the coach in an accident? There has been no message."

"No, no, it was only as Marguerite said. She fell from the door."

He nodded, a jerky, uncertain gesture. That hardly explained why Caroline looked as she did. Her haggard expression, the circles under her eyes were more than hours old.

"Where have you been? What has happened? Why are you here now?"

"Why am I here, Mr. Osgood?" She paused as though she had to think about her answer. With a deep sigh, she shook her head. "I have come home."

But where have you been? She was so clearly not the same person who had left him. The Caroline he knew would never appear with dirty, threadbare clothes, unkempt hair. He did not ask again, not wholly sure he wanted to know the answer.

"I am sorry if it will make you uncomfortable, Mr. Osgood."

Mr. Osgood? He stiffened at the formality of her words. He had called her Caroline and she was still so formal?

"It is quite simple, really. We had no place else to go."

No place else to go? And given the state she was in, how desperate must she have been to return home, to let the people of her childhood see her this way?

"I have been in France these last years, most of the time in Paris and Amiens, but lately on the coast near Calais. No one here in Yorkshire can begin to know . . ." She pressed her lips together. "I owe you no explanation."

"In France? All this time? In the midst of the revolution?"

"Yes, in the midst of it."

Her face was closed to him. No emotion showed. From that alone he knew the changes went beyond the way she looked. Before he had always found the answers in her eyes, the way they sparkled with laughter or tears. Now they were empty and hard.

Yet she had cried for the child.

He turned back to Marguerite, away from Caroline's bruised eyes, and lifted his patient's arm from the water.

Marguerite looked at him in some surprise. "It hardly hurts at all."

"It will, I am sorry to say. The cold has numbed it just enough that we can bind it against you without too much pain."

He tended to her medical needs and then watched as Caroline used the water to clean off as much of the mud as possible and remove the child's clothes. She folded them as though they were of the finest cloth and set them on the dresser nearby. She eased Marguerite into a borrowed nightgown and then insisted on carrying her into the bed in the adjoining room.

He watched all this as he mechanically tidied the items he had used to treat the child. Caroline and Marguerite murmured to each other in French, the child trying for bravery, Caroline as gentle as she would be with a newborn. There was such a bond of affection between them that he was hard-pressed to believe that she was not Caroline's child.

He knew as well as anyone that it was not possible. Caroline's virtue was, or at least had been, unassailable. He had wondered more than once how their lives would have been different if he had given in to his carnal urges, if they had made love. With that tension gone and that commitment between them, Caroline would never have run away.

Now she looked no better than the women who stood on the corners and begged for attention. He could hardly contain the rage that swept through him at the thought that she had given away what should have been his.

He held on to the anger for just a moment and then commanded himself to think of her only as someone who needed his expertise. No matter what her station now, she deserved care as surely as did the child she had brought to him.

He drew Caroline from the room. She came with some reluctance and not only because she was hesitant to leave her charge.

"Now it is your turn," he said.

"Me?" She drew up in a perfect parody of a haughty governess. "I am perfectly healthy except for some fatigue."

"When was the last time you ate?"

The fact that she had to think about it was all the answer he needed.

"When was the last time you had some fruit or greens?"

She shook her head, refusing to answer.

"And when was the last time you actually slept in a bed, alone?"

She turned away from him abruptly, but he could see the tears that question drew.

"We have been traveling for months, Mr. Osgood. We had to wait in Calais for weeks before we were able to find someone to transport us. We had to save our money for the cost of the trip. We ate, we both did."

But not enough, Caroline. There was a story here, but now was no time to press for explanations. She looked on the edge of collapse.

"Come sit here." He did not mean to sound so angry. Looking away from her drawn face, he cleared the table of the bowl and wiped the wet spots. "Sit here and let me examine you." He still sounded stern but at least the anger was under control.

She stiffened. "No! I will not." The words were shouted, but she pressed her lips together and when she spoke again it was in a carefully moderated tone. "There is nothing wrong with me that some sleep will not cure. And, yes, perhaps, some meat and cheese as well."

"You are thin to the point of starvation, you show any number of symptoms that indicate jaundice or scurvy and you are so vain that you will not allow the simplest of examinations." He was the one shouting now. "Some things never change. You deserve your misery. You have earned it all for yourself."

"And all you care about is medicine—"

He did not wait for her to finish the sentence. "Medicine is the one thing I can give you." No sooner had he spoken than he wanted to snatch the revealing words back out of the air.

"Still? Even after five years, medicine is the only thing

you can give? It was all you were ever willing to give of yourself."

"I am a man of science." Oh, that sounded so pretentious.

"Yes, I know. You always were first a man of science. No true sensibility must ever be allowed to overcome your thorough observation."

Her bitterness was as impassioned now as it had been five years ago. She had only started her rant, but the voice from the doorway silenced her and drew both their attentions.

"Stop this shouting. Stop it at once." His mother moved into the room, her stick before her. She stopped and leaned on the cane with both hands. "I could hear every word and the two of you are behaving no better than children."

She tried to straighten and lifted her cane to point at Caroline. "I knew it must be you. Who other than Caroline Morton could provoke my son to shout? I can hardly believe that you finally had sense enough to come home."

Mrs. Osgood stepped farther into the room, and came between them, shaking her head as she did. "You should both be ashamed of yourselves. There is a sick child in the other room."

Reynie watched as color stained Caroline's too-white cheeks. She made to move toward the sickroom, but his mother raised her cane and Caroline stopped on the command.

"You, Caroline Morton, look like a street vendor. Go to the bathing room and, Reynie, you go sit with the child. Caroline, after you have bathed away all that filth and thrown away those clothes you will come upstairs and sleep in the room next to mine. Reynie, go up and bring down one of my nightdresses and a covering. Then give this woman the privacy she needs."

In no time it was as she commanded. Reynie found himself sitting by the child's bed, watching her rhythmic breathing.

It took a while for the water to heat, but soon enough he could hear Minnie. The kitchen maid's high-pitched voice accompanied the sounds of the first of the water being poured into the bath.

"Mr. Osgood thinks that what he calls the 'water cure' is as important as any of his other treatments. He makes anyone he thinks is too dirty take a bath before he examines 'em. I think he learned it in France when he went there."

"He went to France?"

He heard Caroline's surprise. Or was it curiosity?

" 'Bout five year ago now. He would be always having letters from some French doctor after his first trip. I think he would have gone again but they have some kind of war there now and you'd be a fool to travel."

"He came to France?" She spoke in a sort of dreamy voice and he could imagine her head lolling back on the rim of the tub.

He heard Caroline mumble something, but had no trouble hearing Minnie's piercing voice as she replied, "No, ma'am, Mrs. Osgood says I am to stay with you to make sure you do not fall asleep and drown."

Reynie smiled. His mother was half doctor herself. How many years had it taken him to grasp a lesson that had been hers with motherhood? She had not read Hippocrates or Paré, but still knew that curing disease was as much about caring for the patient as it was about diagnosing the illness. How many surgeons were willing to say that their mothers were as fine a mentor as any man who had trained them?

He settled back in the winged chair, pulling the blanket around his waist and angling the candle so that it did not shine in the child's eyes. He could read. *De Sedibus* was as entertaining as it was informative. But his mind was elsewhere. He could admit that to himself, if no one else. Even the well-written descriptions of Morgagni's studies would not hold his attention tonight.

He heard Caroline's voice but not the words and when the door to the bathing chamber creaked open, he stood up. With a glance at the sleeping child, he went out into the surgery.

"Minnie, you can leave the bathwater until morning, but would you please go up and make some warm milk with bread and butter for Miss Morton?"

"Yes, sir." With a quick glance at Caroline's face, she hurried up the stairs.

His mother's gown and robe were voluminous on her. Caroline had cinched it tight around her absurdly small waist. Her hair, curled from the damp, made a halo around her face. Despite the deep shadows under her eyes and her poor coloring, he thought she looked quite beautiful. Not like the Caroline Morton who had run away. This was a woman of character, even a little mystery.

She pulled the robe tightly around her throat as though it were an adequate defense of her virtue, whatever virtue she had left. Her cheeks, pink from the bath, reddened.

"I am a surgeon, Caroline. And you are my patient. There is no reason to be self-conscious."

"I will not be examined."

"Yes, yes, you already made that clear." He shook his head as he spoke. Her stubbornness had always annoyed him. It was perversely reassuring that at least this had not changed. He raised two fingers to the bridge of his nose as if that would ease the tension and then tried to summon a smile. "Caroline, I want to help you."

She seemed to soften a little. Her hand did not clutch at the robe so tightly. She lowered her chin a bit, not so imperious now.

"I will do anything in my power as a surgeon to restore your health."

She lowered her hands and folded them neatly in front of her. She straightened her body, her softened eyes were cold again. "As you say, you are a surgeon, Mr. Osgood, and I am an intelligent woman. We both know what is wrong with me. I do not need an examination, only some decent food and rest. I thank your mother for her hospitality tonight. When Marguerite can travel we are going to Landreau Hall." With a curt nod, she walked, barefoot, he noted, toward the door.

"Caroline, I made two trips to Paris." Did it sound too much like a confession? It was. A confession of his weakness, of his need for her and of his love.

Genuine surprise was replaced by a smile, the first he had seen. In that moment she was the Caroline Morton he knew and missed. "The maid said that you came to Paris. Did you really? To look for me?"

How odd that five years of hardening his heart should evaporate at her first smile. And how foolish. She had run away with no explanation, with an unfinished argument his last memory. He ignored his relief and longing. His heart ached with the burden of it, but he had years of practice at hiding his feelings and he had learned to school his expression as well.

"I had been following the work of François Bichat and I was able to arrange a meeting with him. We did have some amazing conversations. He has taken Morgagni's work one step further and we discussed the book he is preparing."

That admission cooled her pleasure. "Oh, I see. Your science took you abroad."

"I did look for you." He tried to make it sound like a practical series of inquiries, unwilling to admit the frenzy of activity, the sleepless nights, his aching heart. "Knowing your mother was French I thought it entirely possible that you had gone there from London. And when I confronted Susan Landry she admitted it, but would give me no more detail than that. I never found a trace of you in Paris."

"You must have searched in all the wrong places." She spoke with a casual dismissal of his weeks of misery. "Before

I left London I had already been hired as governess to a count's family. It was all done through a London agency."

"If you were indeed that child's governess, then where are her parents?" he asked as though it were a challenge that she could not possibly meet.

"They are dead, Reynie." She hissed the answer at him. "And you are an insensitive lout for even mentioning it within her hearing."

With that final insult she left him. The way she swept from the room, as though his mother's nightgown were a court dress, showed him that she had learned something in France. Five years ago, she would have thrown her bonnet on the ground and stomped from the room.

Those bursts of temper had been for him alone. To the rest of the world her volatility showed itself in cheerful good humor, a quest for adventure, an inclination for silly jokes.

He had tried to analyze her tantrums and decided that her feelings needed some outlet. The kisses they had shared had been more fuel than release.

He had allowed himself to be reassured by the bursts of temper, told himself they were a sign that her feelings were truly involved. Could that still be so? Or had he been completely wrong before?

He went back into the bedchamber and sank into the armchair. Picking up the volume on the table at hand, he settled it on his lap but did not open it.

He was about to close his eyes and relive the past when he glanced at the child. Her eyes were wide open and she was studying him as though he were some unknown species.

"Dr. Osgood?" Her voice was almost a whisper.

"I am Mr. Osgood, my dear. I am a surgeon, not a physician."

She nodded without taking her eyes from his face. "Miss Morton is never angry with anyone."

She looked away for a moment and he could not contain his smile.

"Not even with you, Marguerite?"

The child looked back at him. "If I am honest, then I must admit she has been angry with me, but she never once raised her voice. Her disappointed look was enough to make me feel tears. When I was little she would always then make me laugh, but I new better than to do whatever it was again. For she is, after all, as a mama to me."

"But not your true mama?"

"Oh no, sir. My *maman* had very black hair and she was *trés petite.* Miss Morton is very tall, is she not?"

She nodded as if answering her own question, then closed her eyes. It looked as though she were doing her best to avoid some less than happy memory. If he pressed her on this then he would, indeed, be the insensitive lout that Caroline named him.

He waited to see if she would fall asleep. She shifted once and the pain woke her again. He decided he could give her a trace of laudanum if the discomfort grew too unbearable.

"But, Mr. Osgood, I have never seen her angry with a man before. She is always able to make them smile and do exactly what she wants."

"Ah yes, I remember that myself. When we were little she would use that smile on me and I was more than willing to catch all the butterflies she wanted."

"In Calais, she made the man who stole our food give it back. She could always get the best price for the things we found to sell." Marguerite looked at him and he watched her eyes narrow as she searched for an explanation and then shook her head.

"Sir, if she could charm you before, how is it that you are the only person she shouts at now?"

She did not wait for an answer, which was as well since any answer he would have given would be no more than a guess.

"I hope it is not because she is angry with me. She was so relieved to finally be here, to be less than a mile from her friend, Miss Landry. We have talked of it for such a long time. I am so sorry that I spoiled it."

The tears came in a quiet stream, trickling down her cheeks and onto her neck. He reached for a cloth and wiped them away.

"You have not ruined anything, Marguerite. Miss Morton needs treatment herself and would never have come except for your accident."

Marguerite nodded with some skepticism.

"She has been too long without the right food, or enough rest. Illness can take hold much too quickly when the body is so weakened."

"You mean that my strained arm is a blessing in disguise?"

He recognized one of Caroline's favorite sayings and smiled, "Yes, my dear, it is."

"I suppose it could be." She studied his face for a moment. "You have been longing to see Miss Morton?" She asked with the sly smile of a ten-year-old who has guessed a secret.

He leaned closer to her and nodded. "I did not know how much until I saw her tonight."

Confusion replaced her triumph. "Then why were you yelling at each other?"

"Because we were yelling at each other when she left five years ago. It is an unfinished argument."

"And that is why you wished to see her again, to finish your argument?"

"Oh, no and oh, yes at the same time."

The child made a small sound of annoyance. "I speak English very well, Mr. Osgood, but still I do not understand how you can mean yes and no at the same time."

"When you are my age you will understand perfectly."

"But, Mr. Osgood, that is so far away that I will have forgotten the question by then."

Which is just as well, he thought.

"If you wish to argue with Miss Morton then when we are with Miss Landry you must come visit us and go for a walk. That is what Maman and Papa did when they wished to argue."

"I am afraid it will not be that easy. I suspect that after tonight it will take nothing less than another broken arm to bring Miss Morton anywhere near me."

Marguerite gave him a long, considering look and then yawned, a huge yawn, that cracked her jaw and made her blush. "I am sorry!"

"No, no, child, I am sorry. Here I am, talking with you as though you were an adult and we were in a taproom when you are exhausted and should be asleep."

She sighed and settled into the covers with such prompt obedience that he felt guilty. With her eyes closed she added, "But if we were in a taproom there would be smoke and pickpockets and neither one of us would be in a comfortable chair."

He watched sleep claim her. Her body relaxed, and a small smile settled on her lips.

"Dream sweetly," he whispered and picked up Morgagni. He opened to the page he had last marked. As he began to read the autopsy of ". . . a woman of twenty-nine so long on the streets that there could be no doubt of her profession . . ." he wondered exactly how much time Caroline and Marguerite had spent in a taproom and exactly what they had been doing there.

Three

"What a joy to finally have you with me." Susan Landry kept her arm around Caroline's shoulder as she dabbed at the tears in her eyes.

If her meeting with Reynie had not been what Caroline had anticipated, Susan's greeting was everything that she had longed for.

"But where is Mr. Osgood? I was sure he would insist on bringing you himself." Susan looked down the lane as though she expected Reynie to be coming along any moment.

"He was called away. Mrs. Osgood told me that some of the young men who came to town for the fight thought it a perfect excuse for one of their own. And then, she said, he was called to Mrs. Beltran's lying-in."

"So he was too busy to bring you to me?" She asked the question again as though not happy with Caroline's first answer.

"That is as it always is with surgeons. You know that. He has been very kind to us. Just as one would expect from a longtime neighbor."

"I see," was all that Susan said, but with a mischievous smile that made her skepticism all too evident. To Caroline's intense relief Susan did not pursue the subject. Instead she nodded to the unusually silent child who clung to Caroline's hand.

"So this is Marguerite."

Marguerite made a creditable curtsy. The gesture was not at all necessary, but Caroline knew well Marguerite's inclination toward the theatrical. Susan was charmed.

"Such beautiful black hair, Marguerite, and what a wonderful brace that is."

Marguerite grinned down at the fabric that supported her injured arm. "It is a shawl that Mrs. Osgood offered me as a loan."

"And the red and blue are perfect colors for you. It alone will convince everyone that your injury was caused by some grand gesture."

"Like rescuing a kitten?"

Susan stooped down to Marguerite's level and nodded enthusiastically. "Saving it from drowning."

The two grinned at each other, both their imaginations taking flight. Caroline shook her head in some amusement. How could she have forgotten Susan's lifelong penchant for fairy tales.

"I think perhaps we must put her to bed, Susan. Mr. Osgood did say that rest was the speediest way to recovery."

Susan nodded. "I have put you in the nursery wing so that you can be together. And I do believe that Cook has some luncheon prepared that will suit a weakened appetite."

Whether out of deference or fatigue, Marguerite did not refuse. She took Susan's hand when it was offered and Caroline followed them up the steps, barely listening as Susan encouraged Marguerite to recount how her arm came to be hurt.

At least today was starting better than yesterday had ended. Caroline had been nothing less than relieved when Mrs. Osgood had told her that Reynie had been called away. The news had eased her nerves enough to allow her to eat some of the breakfast Mrs. Osgood thought appropriate after the rigors of travel. The cheese was mild and delicious, the bread sliced thin and buttered with the sweetest creams.

Despite his mother's sincere welcome and generous hospitality, Caroline knew that it would be a challenge to treat Reynie Osgood as a neighbor.

Mrs. Osgood obviously entertained renewed hopes for Caroline's future with her son. The old lady acted as though her abrupt departure had been five days ago and not five years and no more than a girl's inclination for some adventure before she settled down.

No matter what Mrs. Osgood's fantasies, it was ridiculous to believe that she and Reynie could actually be friends. It was a lie she had built for herself to make this homecoming tenable. When she first saw him at the door last night, she had realized that despite the dramatic change in her own life, some of her feelings for him survived.

If she had realized those sensibilities still existed would she have come back? Of course she would have. For she did, indeed, have nowhere else to go.

A long "Ooooh" of pleasure from Marguerite recalled her to the present. The three of them entered the hallway as the warm spring light flowed through the door and the windows that surrounded it.

It was only then that Caroline looked about her. "It is such a lovely house, Susan."

"And exactly as you described it, Miss Morton." Marguerite swung on Miss Landry's hand and looked at the ceiling, high overhead. "There are the Titans painted in each corner."

"You described Landreau to her?" Susan looked at Caroline, but it was Marguerite who answered.

"It was one of my favorite bedtime stories."

"Marguerite, if you go up those stairs and down the first wing you will find the nursery and schoolroom. We will follow right behind you."

Delighted at the prospect of discovery, she hurried up the stairs.

Caroline and Susan followed.

"I described Landreau to her so that she would have something to take the place of her burned-out home. So that she would know we had someplace to come to."

Susan nodded, again raising the handkerchief to her eyes. "Yes, yes, I understand. Well, of course I can hardly begin to understand. The most unpleasant thing I have ever had to face is a fireplace that did not draw properly. I am touched, that's all. And pleased that it gave the child some consolation."

They had reached the landing where two wings branched to either side. They turned to the left and followed Marguerite's fast-disappearing form.

"What did Mr. Osgood say when you told him of your experiences?"

"I did not tell him anything. He could not possibly understand. Susan, all he wanted to do was examine me! I was nothing more than a scientific specimen to him. He has not changed at all."

"Of course he wanted to examine you. You do not look at all yourself. We must do something about that hideous hairdo."

Caroline raised her hand to the knot of hair at the back of her head and blessed Susan for pretending that her awful coloring and dull looks were due to nothing more than a poor hairstyle.

"He is a very busy man, Caroline. His practice is increasing all the time. Even women who have only used the midwife are turning to him for their lying-in. He is everything that is kind and thoughtful."

"Reynie?"

"Yes, he was always that way in childhood. Why is it surprising that he should be that way as a surgeon?"

"Because somewhere in his training he lost it. He cared only about understanding the cause of the illness and curing it with bleeding or some restorative."

"He still studies more science than any surgeon I know." Susan nodded in agreement. "My father says that he has the learning of a physician without the title and prefers his care to any man in York."

Susan stopped their progress and looked at her friend. "But he does more than examine people, Caroline. He listens. He will sit forever, enduring my stepmama's complaints and then he asks questions that make her think she has given him the key to her cure."

"Are you saying that he tries to understand their sensibilities as well as their symptoms?"

"Yes, exactly, and it is the very reason he is in such demand."

"This does not sound like the man I knew five years ago."

"Surely you saw that in his treatment of Marguerite last night."

Caroline reflected a moment and then had the grace to blush. "You are right, he was all that was kind and attentive. I was tired." Caroline shrugged her shoulders slightly. "And I was angry." She looked at Susan with real indignation. "The truth is he did not recognize me! For a full twenty minutes he had no idea who I was."

"He did not recognize you?" Susan all but squeaked in dismay. They were at the door to the nursery, but Susan paused to look closely at her again. "We must change that excuse for a coiffeur."

They went into the children's day room and Caroline was struck by how different it looked when viewed as governess rather than student. It was an efficient composite of rooms well away from the more adult entertainments and would keep them in great comfort.

Susan waited while they ate the food that had been left for them and soon Marguerite was settled into bed. Caroline and Susan found chairs by the small fire in the cozy sitting room, with cups of tea at hand.

"But, Susan, how could you give up a Season in London on the chance, the veriest chance, that I might be coming?"

"My dear, I was presented at Court five years ago when you came to London with me, and if I did not take during those first few Seasons, why would you think this one would be any different? Indeed, I could hardly enjoy myself for worry. Your last letter was so . . ." she paused and then went on with apology in her voice. "Your last letter sounded so desperate, Caroline, that I was hard-pressed not to fly to Dover and wait for you there."

"I am amazed that it even reached you, or that your answer was waiting for me at the Anchor in Dover. But, I will tell you that your letter gave us a goal, a prize to strive for. You have been our savior more than once."

Susan shook her head. "Perhaps this time, but I will never be convinced that I did the right thing five years ago. When you agreed to accompany me to London I should have known something was amiss. I should have known and insisted you tell me. Instead I was so pleased to have you for a companion, even for a little while, and so excited about my Season that I never noticed that something was terribly wrong. Why else would you have left me and gone to France instead of coming home to Mr. Osgood?"

Caroline drew a deep breath and then closed her eyes. "I could not bring myself to tell you, to tell anyone, that Reynie did not love me."

"But that's nonsense. You have been as one since you were children, at least until you were too old to play together. He has always had eyes only for you."

"You should write fairy tales, Susan, really you should. Reynie may have loved me, but he loved science more."

Susan bit her lip.

"See you cannot deny it."

"He was enthralled with it, Caroline. He had discovered

something that made his view of the world change and expand."

"I thought our love would do that."

Susan looked away from her and nodded, conceding the point.

"His studies were more important to him than I was. I pressed him on it and he told me it would be at least two years before we could marry. It was then that I realized that I could not stay here a day longer."

"So you came with me to London and then went on to France."

"Yes."

"You always were impulsive."

A long silence fell. Caroline decided Susan's silence came from her unwillingness to find any further fault with her. What a dear and loyal friend she was.

"My dear, I am not impulsive anymore. I now give each decision the most careful consideration." She wanted to confide, she longed to. But how could anyone who knew little more than the peace and tranquility of Thirsk understand war and its appalling demands.

"I think I will miss the impulses, Caroline. But perhaps now that you are back they will peek out again." Susan reached over and patted her friend's hand. "You know that you are welcome here for as long as you wish to stay."

"Your generosity is legion, Susan, but I will find a post. I must. Surely my experience in France, even without a reference, will be support enough."

"It will be as you wish. But before you do anything else, we will find you some clothes and I will have my maid bring her scissors down. You will see, a new hairdo will be the first giant step toward restoring your confidence. Then you can read the papers or arrange to go to one of the agencies."

"Thank you, Susan. You almost convince me it is as easy

as some new clothes and stylish hair. Perhaps it is. The *ton* has always set such store in appearance. It could be all it will take to convince them that I am an experienced lady's maid."

"A lady's maid? But why? You are a successful governess."

"And find that I am not at all suited to the position."

"But Marguerite obviously loves you."

"Yes, and that is precisely the problem. I find that I am not able to maintain the proper demeanor as a governess. No, I am not suited to it at all. Lady's maid is the perfect position for me."

Caroline could see that Susan was not convinced, but was too well-bred to argue.

"There is one more important matter, Susan. More important than clothes or hair or even my employment."

"More important than fashion?"

Caroline nodded and would not return Susan's smile. She waited until the smile faded and she had Susan's complete attention. "I must find Marguerite's relatives. Her parents are gone, but she must have family that will want to know that she has survived. You understand that she is of the aristocracy and even though they no longer have any standing in France, they are respected here and in other parts of Europe."

Susan nodded slowly. "Will you advertise? Travel to London?"

"I already have. My father had some friends from his Oxford days who are based in London. I called on them while we were in town and they have already begun the search. When she is safe with family and no longer needs me, then I will move on."

"But the two of you are so close—"

Before Susan could complete the thought, they both heard a noise from the bedroom, a whimper that became a cry that rose to a scream.

Caroline rushed into the room. Sunshine leaked around the edges of the drawn curtains. There was enough light for her to see Marguerite tossing and turning, tangling herself in the sheets. When she sat in the chair near the bed and reached for the child, Caroline could feel the sweat that left Marguerite's hair damp.

"Shh, shh, *mon amie.*" She wanted to lift Marguerite into her arms, but was afraid the movement would hurt her more. Instead she stroked the child's head, alarmed at the sweat that had dampened her hair.

She came awake slowly, which was unusual and an additional worry. Marguerite looked up at her with wide, alarmed eyes.

"It was a dreadful nightmare, Miss Morton."

"I am so sorry, *chouchou.* Can you tell me about it?"

Marguerite shook her head. "I have no wish to remember it." She looked away and just when Caroline was about to allow her to forget, the child spoke.

"I was surrounded by strangers who all wanted to hold me and hug me. They spoke a language I could not understand and their hugs turned to pinches and they made me parade in front of a different committee every day. And I could not find you anywhere." She looked back at her and Caroline saw a stubborn light in her eye, when she had expected tears. "And, Miss Morton, you were the only person I wanted to be with."

They both sat in silence. Marguerite closed her eyes again. Caroline watched, her heart filled with worry and guilt.

"Perhaps I should not have told you about the search for your relatives."

But it appeared that Marguerite was already asleep again, as she did not answer.

Caroline left her side long enough to explain to Susan. While she sat with the child, Susan went down to the next wing, to her room, to see if there might be some gowns that could be altered to fit Caroline. Even as she sat there, the child began to move restlessly. It sounded as though she was sobbing and Caroline heard her beg for "Miss Morton."

Caroline moved to wake her when she heard someone in the outer room. She stood up, unnerved by Marguerite's distress, uncertain whether waking her up would be the wisest thing to do. Hoping for some wisdom from Susan, she hurried to the door and found Reynie Osgood setting his hat on the table.

His familiar smile gave way to immediate concern.

"What is it, Caroline?"

He came forward and took her hands. She did not even pause to wonder if he did that with all his patients, but held on, as though his knowledge would pass to her through the pressure of his fingertips.

"Marguerite. She is having nightmares. Almost as soon as she falls asleep."

He released her and hurried to the door. Caroline followed him and they both saw nothing more than a quietly resting child.

He came back into the sitting room but left the door ajar. "She sleeps."

"Now she is, but truly, she is having nightmares. I counted two this morning since breakfast."

He pursed his lips and narrowed his eyes, but said nothing.

"Surely, you have a more practiced medical opinion than that."

"Yes, my dear, I do, but will not commit myself until I speak with the child." He glanced at the door. "We will wait to see if she awakes without a nightmare."

Caroline nodded.

"And that will give us the opportunity of a few words in privacy."

* * *

Without answering, Caroline turned her back to him and Reynie knew exactly how difficult a conversation this was going to be. He had rehearsed his words five times on the road here from Beltran's farm, but despite the practice he felt tongue-tied, unprepared. Her reluctance shook his certainty.

So he started with the familiar. "You look much better this morning."

She turned back to him, but still did not invite him to sit. Her own posture was waiting, defensive.

He picked up his hat for no reason other than to give himself something to do while he organized his thoughts. "If one good night's sleep and some decent food could help this much then perhaps you are not as ill as I feared."

She nodded.

He watched her for a moment. Let her think it was the man of medicine at work. She might look healthier, but she still looked downtrodden, impoverished in more ways than one. When had she last smiled? With whom? Was it him, or was it her experiences that made her so brittle now?

"I do want to help you, Caroline. I offered last night and I think you must have misunderstood. This is not only about medicine and your health." He paused and cleared his throat, banishing the desperation from his voice. "I can only imagine what the last few years have cost you. I want you to know that if you feel the need to speak of it, I will listen. I will understand."

It was her turn to stare. He could read the longing to confide as clearly as if she spoke it, but only for a moment. She turned from him with a sharp movement, but not so fast that he did not see her expression pass from wishful to something that was filled with heartache, or was it hopelessness?

"Please be assured that listening is as important as any suture or bandage I provide." He held his own aching emotions in check, hoping his practical explanation would make her confession easier.

"Mr. Osgood"—if her longing to speak had bridged the gap that kept them apart, then her use of his name and her careful pronunciation of it, put the distance between them again—"there have been hardships. War is appalling and make no mistake the revolution is as much a war as it is a political upheaval. It forces impossible choices on adults and children alike. But I went to France as a governess and still hold that position despite the change in Marguerite's circumstances."

"There is no need for you to lie, Caroline." He wanted to help her but could not until she gave him the truth. "You were a governess? You come back here with a child as dirty and thin as you are, with no baggage and you expect me to believe that you are caring for the child of a count?"

She stood with her arms folded across her chest, her lips pressed tightly together.

"And what training did you have as a governess? Apart from learning French at your mother's knee, what accomplishments would prompt a count to hire you to care for his daughter?"

She looked away from him, raising her chin, staring at the far wall as though she were letting him talk for his own sake. As though she did not care for a single word he said. He wanted to shake the truth out of her, but kept his hands clenched at his sides.

"I came to Paris, I looked for you. I asked agencies and searched shops."

"And now because you could not find me, you think that I am lying?" She looked at him with accusing eyes. "You think I was kept, in secret, by some man in one of those pleasure pavilions that surround Paris?"

His expression must have betrayed him, for yes, this was his worst fear: that he had driven her away and into someone else's arms.

She laughed, a breath of sound that was filled with

ridicule. As if making a concession, she took one small step toward him. "I assure you that Marguerite's heritage is of the sword. Her family have served the King for generations. At the last they danced attendance at Versailles and spent very little time speaking of their children much less their employees."

He nodded, relieved that she was finally talking to him.

"Marguerite and I stayed at their *hôtel* in Paris. Monsieur le Comte employed me because he wanted his daughter to learn English, to be able to speak it as well as French. As for the rest, I knew enough to teach her to read, write, and do numbers. We learned the globe together and her mother had begun to teach her the basics of the pianoforte."

"It could be true." Reynie was almost convinced, but then she turned to pace the room and the too-large skirt of his mother's dress swept the floor. He saw the way she moved, that natural grace that time had not yet changed. Those Frenchmen would have noticed. They would have found her irresistible.

"It is true, damn you!" Her anger boiled over and she paused to gather some self-control. "My days in Paris were filled with Marguerite and her needs. In the last year or so I have had to make difficult choices, but I was a governess always. Marguerite has always been my main concern. My reason for everything."

"I can understand that."

"How can you? You have never loved like that. You made your choice. You are a man of science."

She made it an insult, when it had been his only consolation.

Four

From the other room, the sound of crying grew to sobbing. For the first time in his life Reynie was relieved by a child's distress. There was more here than he could understand right now. Call him a coward, but he was grateful for an escape.

They both hurried into the room. Marguerite had stopped crying and was awake.

"Could you leave us please, Caroline?"

She hesitated and he stepped closer to her, speaking in a voice for her ears only.

"Marguerite is old enough to express herself clearly and I will be better able to give her a reliable diagnosis if we speak in confidence."

"But what could she say to you, that she could not say to me?"

"I cannot imagine a single thing, my dear, but then we are not ten years old."

Caroline stopped wringing her hands. "You are exactly right. You must speak to her in private. I have treated her as an adult too much these two years. She is still, after all, only a child." She drew a deep breath, walked over to the bed, and pressed a kiss to the child's forehead. "I will be in the next room, *ma belle.*"

Reynie watched her walk from the room, then moved to

the window and threw the curtains open. Rain clouds had darkened the spring sky, but still the light was startling.

When he turned around, Marguerite had her eyes squinted shut against the burst of daylight. He moved closer to the bed, blocking the light, so that when she opened her eyes they did not continue to water.

"If your sleep is not restful, Marguerite, then we will talk awhile."

She looked at him with an expression close to terror. "I cannot sleep. I have the most terrible dreams. That they are taking Miss Morton from me."

He sat down in the small chair by the bed, wondering if it was meant for a fully grown man. He turned his attention to the child, noting the hollow eyes and the sheen of wet on her forehead.

"How did you know to come so soon, Mr. Osgood? I should think that nightmares would have to last for a number of days or be very violent for you to be called."

"Hmmm." He looked away from her and scanned the room. It was filled with child-sized furniture, including a toilet stand on which sat a pitcher and bowl. It was perfectly tidy, except for some wet spots on the floor, drips between the stand and the bed. He looked again closely at Marguerite, who was watching him with equal interest.

"I was on my way home from Mrs. Beltran, who had another healthy baby boy, and thought that I would stop in and see how your arm is mending. The nightmares that Miss Morton reported were a complete surprise."

"Then perhaps it is too soon for you to know what is causing them."

He laughed. "Oh, my little soldier, it is hardly surprising that you should have nightmares."

She looked pleased with that and he shook his head.

"But my question to you is whether you have had them before?"

She considered her answer for so long that Reynie felt compelled to add, "Perhaps I should simply ask Miss Morton after all."

"There is no need." She shook her head with exaggerated agitation. "No, I have never had nightmares before."

"I see." He rubbed his chin with his hand. "But now that you are settled they haunt you?"

Marguerite nodded cautiously.

"And they are serious enough to make you sweat?"

He stood up and then wiped her forehead with his handkerchief.

She nodded, eyes wide and guileless.

"Hmmm." He spent a few moments inspecting her arm, soon satisfied that it was mending as it should. As for the nightmares, he had so little experience of this type of illness and he was unsure how to proceed. Oh, he could recall the basic cause as well as the suggested treatment but why should she have nightmares now when there was no longer cause for worry?

"You know that there is no war here? No Committee of Public Safety can reach you."

"Yes, I know that." She spoke with purely adult exasperation. "But safety means very little to me, if I must leave Miss Morton. I think I would run away and come back to her if she sent me from her."

Aha, he thought and tried to disguise his interest in these last words. Here was the heart of her problem. She feared losing the one person left who meant anything at all to her. He could understand that with no effort at all.

"Have you told Miss Morton how strongly you feel?"

Marguerite nodded. "But she says that she has a responsibility to find my family."

"And you do not want the same thing. To be reunited with an aunt or uncle?"

"No. I think she will find they are all dead too." She

said this with a matter-of-fact detachment he found unnerving.

"Perhaps not," was all he could manage.

"And even if they are alive it would not matter. She is all the *maman* I need now. We can contrive to make a living. I know we can. We did before."

The child had learned her stubborn certainty from a woman who defined the word. He wiped her brow one more time.

"Rest now, Marguerite." He stood up. "You do not need to sleep if you are afraid of dreams." He walked to the nursery shelf and took down a yellow-haired doll that looked well loved. He brought it to her.

"Here, let Missy entertain you while I speak with Miss Morton."

Marguerite took the doll and settled her in the crook of her bandaged arm.

"I will send Miss Morton to you, shortly. Perhaps she can read to you. Do you have a favorite fairy tale?"

Marguerite nodded. "'The White Cat' or 'Goldenlocks.'"

"I will make both a part of the recommended suggestions for recovery."

Leaving her smiling, he went into the sitting room and his other, much less reasonable, patient.

Both of the women were in the sitting room surrounded by masses of fabric that made the room look like a draper's shop. Caroline immediately abandoned the clothes and turned to him.

"How is she?" Caroline asked.

"Already recovering." He gave her his full attention. "Buchan says that nightmares are caused by a nervous affliction and arise chiefly from indigestion."

"The nervous part is nonsense," Caroline scoffed. "Unless her natural curiosity could be called nerves. Indeed, I have never known a child less prone to worry." She paused and considered a moment. "Now I can agree that indigestion from rich food is entirely a possibility. She did eat an amazing number of griddle cakes this morning."

"My mother has always thought food the surest way to good health. I wish it were always that simple. Buchan speaks of any number of treatments, but I think it is best to keep her diet very bland."

"Less food?" Caroline asked on a note of incredulity.

"No, not less, as I suspect that hunger may be as realistic a cause of her dreams as an imbalance of humors. Just a bland diet, fewer griddle cakes, and more bread and milk. It will be better for her arm as well."

Caroline nodded.

"And it would also help to distract her from what upsets her. She wants you to read her 'The White Cat' and 'Goldenlocks.'"

Now Caroline exchanged glances with her friend.

"'Goldenlocks.'" Susan Landry grimaced. "I hate that fairy tale. And it's Marguerite's favorite?"

Caroline nodded, "It has been her favorite for years now. When she was younger she preferred 'Little Red Riding Hood,' but then she switched." Caroline turned to Reynie. "'Goldenlocks' is about a man who is set a number of impossible tasks before he can receive his heart's desire. In this case, the princess he loves."

Reynie wondered if the man's name was Reynaud, but pushed that thought to the back of his mind. "Whatever will distract her from her upset."

He reached for his hat, but was diverted with a question.

"What do you think, Mr. Osgood?" Susan Landry held up what he now recognized as a light blue dinner dress.

"I think that in less than an hour you have managed to turn this sitting room into a shop that would rival anything in York."

"Hardly, sir. These gowns are months old, but I thought

with only a few adjustments they would suit Caroline perfectly."

"This is hardly an area that I know much about." Escape was paramount in his mind, but he had not quite yet completed all his business.

Caroline was standing near a mirror that some footman must have brought into the room, as it had not been there before. Her expression was uncertain and now a blush of embarrassment replaced that.

"Susan, I cannot take all these."

"Of course you can. I'll never wear any of them again. I have no idea what possessed me to order that plum-colored day dress. It does not suit me at all. I cannot tell if it is the style or the color that is wrong. You will be doing me a favor by taking it. In fact, I suspect that it will not suit you at all either."

Caroline turned to Reynie. Her embarrassment had faded, replaced by a rueful smile.

Reynie smiled back at Caroline. "Miss Landry's generosity is something else that has not changed, Caroline. And there is no convincing her of its excess." His smile became a grin, pleased beyond all reason that they could share this little understanding. Perhaps he could build on this small step.

Caroline nodded and would have turned from him. He cleared his throat and waited until she turned back.

"I am loath to distract you, but there is, ahem, one more thing."

Caroline put the dress down as if relinquishing all frivolity and turned to him with new concern.

"Marguerite will be healthy again, soon, Caroline, I am sure of it."

Some of the tension passed from her.

"But If I could understand her background perhaps I would understand what ails her." He set his hat down again and spoke directly to Caroline after a nod at her friend. "Could you please tell us both a little of your experience."

"Oh no, I cannot imagine that would help at all." Caroline looked appalled at the very idea.

She looked at Susan for support but her friend was nodding.

"If Mr. Osgood says that it will help Marguerite then I think you must tell us." She began clearing gowns from the sofa so they could sit. "It is as I told you this morning, he draws some of his best cures from his patient's explanations."

Bless you, Susan Landry, even if you do make me sound like a magician. Better that than a charlatan.

"But I am not his patient."

"Caroline," Susan spoke without hesitation. "You know her mind better than anyone else in Thirsk, in all of England even if there are a dozen relatives in London." She patted the seat next to her. "Dearest, I know this will be difficult, but it is for Marguerite."

Reynie kept silent. Caroline would accept Susan's persuasion and most likely reject his, which was exactly why he had included her in the suggestion.

"Very well." Caroline drew a deep sigh, but belied the distress that it revealed with a set expression.

He watched her face, her eyes, and tried to read their expression, as she searched her memory for where to begin.

Tell me everything, he thought. *Were you happy? Did you miss me? Were your five years as half lived as mine?*

She did not take a seat, but stood before them in front of the empty fireplace. Since she did not sit, Reynie chose not to sit as well, and took a place behind the sofa.

With a vague nod, Caroline composed herself.

"After the fall of the Bastille, Monsieur le Comte sent word that we would return to his chateau in Amiens. Marguerite was delighted."

"She must have been terrified." Susan Landry was sitting on the edge of her seat, her handkerchief in hand. *So this is all new to her as well.*

"Oh no, Susan. Marguerite had very little idea of the riots in the city. It was that she so loved the country. And Monsieur le Comte insisted that we would be safer there."

She looked up at the ceiling and then back at her audience, dry-eyed but in pain.

"He was right. We were there for two years and it was easy enough to pretend that the chaos would never reach us. But when the King was executed everything changed."

When Susan raised her hand to her neck and shuddered, Caroline merely nodded.

"There were riots again, as there had been during *Le Grand Peur* after the fall of the Bastille. But Amiens had been spared then and Monsieur le Comte was certain that reason would prevail. Besides, Madame was increasing and he was worried about her health."

"So you stayed?" Susan asked this with a breathless amazement, as though this were the one crucial bad decision.

"Yes." Caroline nodded. "And not three days later a band of rabble descended on the chateau with torches and their own homemade weapons."

Caroline closed her eyes and shook her head. "Marguerite was not the only one afraid. We all were. Her father tried for calm, assured us that he could reason with the mob, but he took the precaution of finding us a hiding place. He made us promise to stay there."

Caroline was telling the story with so little emotion, as though she had long ago come to terms with this horror. Susan was already dabbing at her eyes.

"We did as he wished, until we thought we were alone and feared the fire more than the brigands. Her parents were gone, the chateau was afire. We never saw them taken away. We simply never saw them again."

She stopped and shook her head, obviously still finding that difficult to accept.

"It was the reason I decided to stay at the chateau. I hoped that her parents would return or send someone for us. But no one came." She paused a moment. He watched her as she edited the story for her audience and wished that they were alone.

"I never told Marguerite they were gone forever, but when we began our trip to Calais she understood that there was little hope left."

She spoke with a calm voice, as though recounting an ordinary life and not one that had gone awry.

How did you survive? Why did you not write? He kept silent with effort. It was her story to tell.

"We waited in Calais until we could find transport. There was an Englishman on a yacht and I thought he would help us. But in the end that proved a vain hope."

"But why? He was English. Surely he would help a fellow countrywoman?"

Susan's naiveté made Reynie wince.

"Oh, Susan, the price he was asking was too high."

"He was going to make you pay?" She was aghast.

Reynie could imagine what the payment was and his imagination turned his stomach.

Caroline shrugged off further explanation of the perfidy of the mysterious "English lord." "In the end a fisherman gave us passage. I suspect he was more usually a smuggler. But he agreed to take us and we landed at Dover."

"Then you made the journey here by coach." It was the first question he asked and the gentlest.

"That was the easy part. There are only four passengers allowed on a mail coach." She explained this to Susan, whose only familiarity with a mail coach was as one seen in passing. "The other passengers were very entertaining."

It was a trip that would have sent most women to bed for a week. Her claim that the coach trip was "the easy part" told him more about her previous months' struggles than any other part of her very guarded story.

He moved forward. "Thank you, Caroline. That helps a great deal." It was a lie. It was such a simple account, told with little detail and even less emotion that it gave him little insight into Marguerite's worries. But he knew enough not to press. To be grateful for this first step to understanding.

Susan was not as restrained as he was. She jumped up from the sofa and wrapped Caroline in a hug more maternal than ladylike. "It is behind you, dearest. You can forget all about it now and think only of happy times."

"Miss Landry?"

They all turned to the open door, where one of the kitchen maids stood, hopping from one foot to the other.

"Gracie dropped the skewers what was roasting the chicken for dinner, Cook is beating her something awful, and the housekeeper has gone to market day."

Susan dropped the dress she had just picked up and flew to the door. "Really, we must do something about Cook's temper." She paused at the door a moment. "Will you wait, Mr. Osgood? I do hope that a surgeon will not be required, but I would hate to have you leave and then call you back."

"Do you want me to come with you now?" He moved toward the door.

"No. No. I should like to try to keep this to ourselves." She hurried after the maid, leaving Reynie alone with Caroline.

Reynie turned back to find her busily collecting the clothes strewn about. Her face was a white counterpoint to the colorful clutch of fabric now gathered up in her arms.

She avoided his eye, but could not ignore his presence. She skirted the room, moving around where he stood even though there were three garments draped on the chair closest to him. He picked them up, amazed at how light they were. Summer gowns, surely.

He knew she longed to escape. He was equally determined not to allow it. He walked closer to her and would have handed her the dresses, but her arms were full.

"Miss Landry is the most loyal of friends, is she not, Caroline? If her generosity is an embarrassment then it is one that I hope you will bear with charity."

"You make it sound as though I am the one doing her the favor. You should have been a diplomat."

"There is much of diplomacy in medicine, something I have discovered with experience. She is so pleased to have you home." He shook his head. "We are all pleased to have you back again." He grimaced at the triteness of it. He nodded at the clothes in their arms. "And this is how she celebrates."

Caroline disappeared through a door to what must have been her bedroom. He stayed where he was, determined to wait for her return. She came back a few minutes later with a look of exasperation. He made no apology for not taking her hint to leave and smiled as she carefully took the garments from him.

"Caroline?" He was not about to let her escape again now that there was no excuse for her to return from her bedroom. "I must apologize."

Five

Oh, why must he say her name in precisely that way? Her heart softened despite her determination to keep it firm. He looked so intent, as though he were holding back a torrent of words.

"I apologize for misjudging you." He bowed to her, the gesture as much an apology as his words. Surely she could be as gracious, but he was watching her with such intensity that she could barely think of what to say, much less speak. And while she struggled for a response he mistook her silence for disdain.

"I should have given you time to explain the last five years before rushing to a conclusion that embarrassed both of us."

"Thank you." She wanted to be generous, to accept his apology, but there was something about the way he stood guarded, but eager at the same time, that made her afraid he would want more than she could give. "You once knew me better than any other man in the world. But our lives are very different now. I can, I do accept your apology but nothing can be as it was."

He did no more than run his hand through his hair in answer, but it conveyed his frustration. "Five years ago, I knew you so well that you had only to enter a room for me to know your mood." He stepped closer to her. "I still do. You did not tell us everything. Tell me the rest."

"I told you as Marguerite would have. I told you what she knew, what she experienced, so that you could treat her."

"I want you to trust me enough to give me all the details."

"You do not need my experience to treat the child."

"I need them to understand you."

She raised her hand to stop him and he took it in his. Could he feel the panic?

"Save me from my imagination, Caroline. I have already created one nightmare for you when the one you lived was quite bad enough."

"Did you think I was nothing more than a genteel slut? That because you did not want me, I would give myself to the first man who did not have your remarkable self-control? Is that what you thought?"

"No, never." He shook his head, then looked down. "Yes, yes, it was my worst fear."

"And you thought you knew me better than any other man?" She wanted to be angry, but was only disappointed. "You knew me so well you thought I was capable of that?"

"No, no. I never thought that you were a loose woman. Never! But for me you have always been so desirable."

His words came in a soft whisper that was seductive, even if it did sound like a confession wrung out by torture.

He turned from her. "I am hard-pressed to believe any other man could not view you in the same way." He stood with his back to her as though confessing to the empty room in front of him. "I used to lie awake at night terrified that some man might mistake your openness and joy for flirtation. God knows you made it almost impossible for me to deny myself." He turned back to face her again. "I am honest even if it does disgust you."

Disgust? No, never, she thought. Amazement held her dumb. She stood silent, marveling at his frankness. Willing now to try a little of her own.

"You never told me." She spoke the words with true dismay, anger even. "You acted as though what I wanted was more than a woman could expect, that self-control was more admirable than unrestrained affection."

"One of us had to be reasonable, Caroline, or at least I thought so then. I was older than you. Your parents might have been gone, but they had trusted me with you from our youngest years. But it was agony. You were as irresistible as a magnet. It was all I could do not to make you mine, not to take what you were so eager to give me."

Her face lit with an amazed surprise. With two steps, she narrowed the distance between. She was close enough for him to take in his arms. "I can hardly credit this. You are saying that your growing coldness, your disinterest, was all a sham, a way to protect me from myself?"

He nodded.

"I cannot believe it. Your work was everything to you."

"It was important to me. It still is. I needed to establish myself before marriage was a possibility."

"And all along I thought that science was taking you from me, turning you into someone to whom books were more important than people."

She looked away from him and then back despite the tears in her eyes. "If you are telling me the truth, if you truly were only hiding your feelings from me, then running away is the most foolish thing I ever did."

He reached for her, but she held up her hands to hold him off. "It is too late, Reynie. I am not the woman who left. I am not the woman you loved. There is no joy in my life, only responsibility to an orphan child. She commands what little feeling I have left to give."

She started to turn from him, but he stopped her. His restraint had worn thin. It gave way to passion. She could see it in his eyes, in the set of his chin, the flaring of his nostrils as he turned her to face him fully.

"You have nothing left to give?"

"Nothing."

"I do not believe it and I can prove you are wrong." He pulled her to him, whispering, "I have waited five years for this."

With a movement he could never have learned in a sickroom, Reynie pressed her to him and took her mouth with his, in the middle of the nursery dayroom where anyone would feel free to walk in.

That was the last coherent thought she had. He became the whole focus of her being. His mouth as it branded her, consumed her, and filled her whole self with a wanting that she had only ever imagined, if she had allowed herself that. His mouth held her and she gave in to its tasting, tempting demand and opened herself to him; not just her lips but her whole body warmed to his, pressed to him, invited.

They ended the kiss by some unspoken intimately shared agreemcnt.

He looked at her with kind eyes but without a smile. "That tells us everything, does it not? An everything that we both already knew. It might have been five years, but it is still not over."

She tried to ease from his arms. "It is attraction, pure physical attraction. Lust." She used the coarsest word she could think of. "You do not know the Caroline Morton who has come back. The body is familiar, the lips may taste the same, but you do not know what five years has made me."

He let her go and she edged away from him.

"I will wait until you tell me, Caroline. I can be patient. You deserve at least that much penance from me. Even before you left for France your joy was wounded. I took it from you as surely as the war in France did. I want to be the one who gives it to you again."

She hardly knew how to answer him. Hardly knew this man whom she had known forever. Where had this compassion come from? Where in his books had he discovered this sympathy? Had he changed as much as she had?

"You cannot understand, can you, Reynie? You have changed for the better." She had moved a step closer to him, but now she backed away again. "You have changed for the better, but I have not."

Then they both heard the sound of heel-clad feet clicking along the marble-floored hallway. Caroline whirled away from him, hurrying to the bedroom and Marguerite.

The little girl lay in the bed, cuddling the doll, and looked up at her governess with marked irritation. "I told him to take you to the garden, Miss Morton. No one would disturb you there."

Caroline ignored this too-adult advice and went to the window to close the drapes halfway. Her hands were shaking as she reached for the cord. With some concentration she steadied them as if closing the curtains smoothly would attest to her self-control. She stood in the narrow length of window that remained and stared, unseeing, at the garden, rain-drenched, the color of the myriad flowers dimmed by the mist.

She could still see his eyes, feel his hands on her arms. *Feel,* she thought. How long since she had allowed herself to feel anything? Had it shown in her face, in her eyes? When he had pulled her into his arms had he seen how much she wanted his touch? She drew in a deep breath, sighed out her anxiety, and turned to Marguerite, who was talking quietly to her doll.

Caroline walked over to the chair nearest the bed and sat down. This kind of love was so much easier to understand, to give. Marguerite smiled at her and placed the doll in her lap. It was so much easier to accept as well.

In a few moments they were deeply into the adventures of Avenant, his dog Frisky, and the demanding Goldenlocks. By the time Avenant had met the third of her challenges and been crowned King to her Queen, Caroline was calm, the familiar routine restoring her usual composure. She stood up and walked to the bookshelf, intent on finding something new to read.

At the same moment, Susan came into the room, bearing a tray.

"My maid waits for you in your room, Caroline. I will stay with Marguerite awhile."

Without waiting for an answer, Susan settled the tray on the table and herself in the nearest chair.

Ignoring Caroline, Susan leaned toward Marguerite. "I have a fairy tale I made all my own, Marguerite. Once upon a time there was a magic mushroom that upon eating would bless you with all you longed for, but in looking for it there was always the danger that you could eat a poison mushroom instead of the magic one."

Marguerite brightened at the thought of a new tale and Caroline slipped from the room.

The dayroom was as it had been before the fashion parade. Even the mirror had been removed. Reynie was gone and all their untidy emotions had evaporated as well.

How long before she could banish them from her heart? His presence still spoke to her senses in a way no other man's ever had.

How was she to make her body accept what her mind knew? She had left home still a girl but had come back a woman, hardened by war. How could anyone here, in the quiet goodness of Yorkshire, accept her choices when she herself was overwhelmed by them?

She would build a new life for herself, but it would be as far away from the old one as she could make it. As far away from the memories of what she had been and could have been.

Caroline heard humming and followed the sound of it into

her room, where Susan's maid was carefully arranging the clothes so they would be at hand for the necessary alterations.

Reynie had said she must accept the burden of Susan's generosity. The thought made her laugh, just a little. Hardly a burden. She picked up one of the dresses and began to shake out the wrinkles. "Miss Landry tells me that you have brought your scissors with you."

Six

The days passed in a haze of simple joys: sleeping in comfort, sitting by the fire. And the absence of fear. On Caroline's silent list of blessings this was the one for which she was most grateful. There was, however, entirely too much time to think.

She had reached some useful conclusions. She had learned enough about life in the last five years to distinguish between attraction and love. That had been the problem before. Her natural woman's curiosity had been enthralled by the feelings. Reynie, too, had confessed much the same. He had found her as "irresistible as a magnet." Flattering, but hardly the basis for a sound marriage.

She knew now that the youthful Reynaud and the ingenue Caroline would have made each other miserable, both lacking in the understanding and comfort that made for a successful union.

She supposed the knowledge was a blessing, but how long would it be before she could end the fantasy, before she could accept that he was only a man and not a person who could be the other half of herself?

She resumed lessons with Marguerite, surprised at how easy it was to slip back into the old routine. What a relief it was to banish the memories, of Reynie and of France, with numbers and reading.

Marguerite welcomed the activity, but seemed to tire easily. Caroline would sit in the quiet room and watch the child as she slept. Tears would fill Caroline's eyes, sobs so near that she dared not leave the nursery lest she break down in front of Susan or the servants.

Now Caroline was the one having nightmares.

"I asked her what France was like."

Reynie nodded as Susan continued.

"It was after tea one evening. Marguerite had been complaining of a stomachache for most of the day and it had been a long fractious hour before the dear thing fell asleep."

"Did Caroline try the peppermint tea I recommended for the nightmares?"

"Yes, I do believe that she thought of it."

So that was not the reason for this summons.

"But the child is still complaining."

Hmmm, then perhaps it is. He stood up.

"But please wait, Mr. Osgood, just a moment more."

Reynie sat down. His dinner would be cold but then he was used to that.

"When I asked Caroline about France she told me that she saw very little of Marguerite's parents, that life was very simple." Susan recounted this in a hurried way as though it was only a path to what was truly important.

"Then I said, 'It must have been very different after the revolution.'" She paused and bit her lip. "I am very worried about her, Mr. Osgood. When I made that statement Caroline nodded very calmly and said, 'Yes it was.' That was all she would say, not another word. And I was silent for a whole minute, hoping she would feel compelled to speak."

He should have known it was worry that had the usually sensible Susan Landry babbling like her stepmama.

"My dear, she is keeping her own counsel. That is not a medical condition, but a choice she has made."

"Yes, but, sir, you know Caroline was never like that before. She used to tell me everything."

She stood up and began to wring her hands. "Indeed, Mr. Osgood, I was the one she wrote to when she was so desperate for a place to stay. Now she is here. But it is as though she left part of herself in France. When she smiles it is for effect, when before a smile was the most natural thing in the world for her." She paused for a long moment, turned from him a little, and then spoke in a rush. "I was hoping she might talk to you."

"Miss Landry, if this is the heart of the matter, the solution on which you rest your hopes, I must apologize even before I try." He put his hat on the table near the door and gave her his full attention. How could he explain to this dear soul that Caroline hardly considered him a friend anymore? Instead of trying, he settled for a simple statement. "She will not confide in me."

"But you listen with such kind regard, as though you do understand and always have the exact right answer and besides, it was not my idea to summon you today. Caroline suggested it. She trusts you, Mr. Osgood." She said that as though it were the key.

"Ah, yes, I will grant you that. She does trust Reynaud Osgood, the surgeon." He stopped himself there. It was much too intimate a thing to explain to her that Caroline knew him beyond his scientific world and books. She might trust him in all things medical, but Caroline did not trust him as a man. He picked up his hat and turned to the door.

"I will go and speak with Marguerite and then see if I can encourage Caroline to unburden herself."

"Oh, thank you, Mr. Osgood, that is what I was hoping you would say."

He gave her a small bow. If he always seemed to have the right answer, it was because he was so good at telling people exactly what they wanted to hear. Whether it was the truth or not. It was his own kind of placebo and did often cure the problem. Even now, she looked relieved.

"In the meantime, perhaps you should have some of the same peppermint tea that Marguerite is sipping." He said it with a smile and she laughed.

"It is only that I love Caroline so dearly and she seems so unhappy."

He nodded. "Yes, I know, my dear." *And I have a feeling that I am the root of it.* Or was that merely wishful thinking on his part? How awful, to wish he was the cause of someone's heartache. Awful, yes, but if it were true then at least he would have some idea as to the cure.

There was no one in the schoolroom, and he walked through the door into the dayroom to find that empty as well. He could hear voices from the nursery and realized that Caroline was sitting with Marguerite in the half darkness. He put his hat on the table and walked toward the door. Marguerite's voice drifted out to him.

"But then you see, Miss Morton, it will be so much better here, for we can advertise and both find employment and need not worry at being discovered."

Did Caroline hear the anxiety hidden in the urgency of the child's words?

"No, we will not both find employment. I will find your family and you will go to live with them. That is as it should be."

Did Marguerite hear the heartache beneath the hardening of Caroline's voice?

"No, it is not, Miss Morton. I am meant to be with you, as your daughter. Forever."

Reynie smiled. If she did hear the heartache, the little girl had her own solution. She might prove as stubborn as Caroline could be.

"Life is not a fairy tale, *chouchou.*" This Caroline said on a sigh and he wondered when she had learned that bit of wisdom for the first time. When her parents died? When they had first argued?

"Our life is, Miss Morton. For have we not overcome all the trials and tribulations set before us? Now we must triumph. It is the only way that the story can end as it should."

There was a very long silence and Reynie knew exactly what Caroline was loath to say. *Not all stories end with "happily ever after."*

Before Caroline could ruin the child's daydream, Reynie leaned in at the door. "Excuse me."

Caroline all but jumped from the chair near the bed, whirling around with such tension in her body that he thought she might attack him. Instead, she drew a deep breath and held herself very still for a moment.

"Hello, Mr. Osgood!"

Marguerite's greeting was all enthusiasm and welcome, which added a little to his diagnosis. She hardly seemed to be suffering at the moment. Pausing long enough to promise the child his full attention, he followed Caroline into the dayroom.

"Are you quite well, Caroline?"

"Yes, it is only that you surprised me. It has been a very long while since I was comfortable sitting with my back to the door. I did not expect you so soon, that is all."

The only other person he had seen move in that precise way, with that explanation, was one of the veterans of the Colonial wars. He filed that small insight and turned his mind to Marguerite.

"Miss Landry reports that it is the stomachache?"

Caroline nodded, her hands now folded, her face composed and concerned. No one had ever looked less like a war veteran.

"Right after eating. And she is already eating quite simple meals. I thought it was perhaps a digestive problem but it does persist."

"Perhaps you will go out for a walk while I examine her." He wanted some privacy with Marguerite and had just witnessed how effectively voices could carry through these rooms. "I will call the nursery maid and come speak with you when I am finished here. It is a perfect evening for the rose garden."

They both looked toward the long windows that filled this room with the light that still slanted through the sky. It was several hours from dark at this time of the year.

"I prefer to wait here." Caroline turned from him and began to gather up the maps on the table.

"Only because I suggest otherwise."

She had the good grace to smile at his sarcasm. "All right. I have not been from these rooms since morning. A walk will be lovely."

"Thank you. Your smile is one of life's sweeter pleasures." He gave her a courtly bow and then deliberately redeemed his flirtation by adding, "Such prompt agreement all but convinces me that you are the one unwell."

Her smile disappeared, replaced by the look of a trapped animal.

He turned away, pretending not to have noticed. The words had been meant as a tease and not an accusation. He *would* make an effort to talk to her. Susan Landry was right. Something was amiss. In the old days she would have laughed at him or tossed back her own riposte.

"Caroline, perhaps you could ask Katherine to come up as you go out the door." She had already turned from him, halfway to one of the four doors that led from the dayroom. She nodded without turning around and he wondered if she was crying. Later, he would urge her to talk, if not to him, then to someone.

He found Marguerite in an animated, whispered discussion with the doll nestled in the crook of her arm. Here was one person who had meaningful conversations even when she was alone.

"Marguerite, I do believe that you are spending entirely too much time in bed. Is that doll holding you prisoner or are you trying to avoid the schoolroom?"

He settled in the chair and she handed him the doll.

"Oh no, Mr. Osgood, you can see it is I who am taking care of her. I am teaching her French."

He took the doll and sat it on his lap so that Marguerite could talk to him, or the doll, whichever she preferred.

"And I study every day just as Miss Morton wishes."

"Hmmm. Very good." He got up, putting the doll on the chair in his place, and wandered over to the shelves, idly perusing the titles. "Tell me what hurts, would you please."

"My stomach."

He listened to another three or four vague complaints and then turned from the shelf and nodded. "I do not know many fairy tales. But my nieces are very fond of 'Sleeping Beauty.' Do you know that one?"

"Oh, yes."

"You do? Very good. Because I am thinking that you are trying to compete with Beauty herself."

Marguerite smiled, pleased by the compliment then considered the comparison. "But I am wide awake."

"Yes, you are." He came back and sat in the chair, once again propping the doll on his lap. "You are indeed as bright-eyed as anyone can be in a room with curtains drawn all day. But you are competing with Beauty to see if you can stay abed longer than she did. And it was one hundred years, was it not?"

Marguerite nodded.

"I suspect you believe that the more ill you become the less likely it is that Miss Morton will send you away."

She would not answer him at first, but stared at the doll instead. He let her consider confession versus further deception. When she looked at him he knew which she had chosen.

"I never thought of sleep as an illness."

"No, of course, you would not. You are much too clever for that." He handed the doll back to her and she settled it under the covers next to her. "It would be very boring and you would have had to endure terrible hunger."

"And I have had quite enough of hunger, but not nearly enough of lying in a comfortable bed."

"So you decided on a series of illnesses."

She nodded cautiously.

"Far more clever than a sleeping beauty, Marguerite. First there were nightmares, now a stomachache. What was it to be next?"

"Ear ache."

"Oh very good." Her guilty look evaporated and she smiled at his approval. It was an impish smile and gave him a hint of what it must be like to deal daily with this immature but fertile mind. "The extreme pain of an ear ache is known to cause epileptic fits. That could be quite dramatic."

"But, sir, you are wrong to think I did it to ensure that I will be with Miss Morton though that is what I want more than anything in the world."

"What other reason is there?"

"I wanted you to have an excuse to come, to see Miss Morton, to declare your feelings, to propose to her and make her happy again. And then, yes, perhaps you two would invite me to be your daughter."

"Are you certain that your name is not Machiavelli?"

She shook her head, "No, sir, it is not and you see it has worked. You have come whenever we have sent for you."

"If not Machiavelli then Quixote, the eternal optimist, for I have hardly impressed Miss Morton and do not see how you can think that I will make her happy." And was he insane to be having this discussion with a ten-year-old who saw herself as a matchmaker?

"Oh but you will, you have. You were her dearest childhood friend, Mr. Osgood. Even dearer than Miss Landry. She has told me all about you and your childhood together."

"Caroline has told you?"

"At night in France"—Marguerite nodded—"after the fire, when we had nothing to read, Miss Morton would tell me of a boy and girl who used to have all sorts of quiet adventures. For, you see, quiet adventures were very appealing to us then."

"And what were these stories?" He was curious, but convinced himself that his question verged on medical necessity as it would help him in dealing with his other less cooperative patient.

"She told me about the time you raced into a barn during a storm and found some kittens that had just been born. About the time that you both climbed a tree to find the bird's nest and the mother bird attacked you. About the time you followed the cart carrying fruit to market and collected the pieces that fell off and then gave them back to the farmer. And how he gave you each a piece of the best fruit in thanks."

He let her rattle on, too moved to stop the recital of very familiar tales.

"And when I met you and you told me about catching butterflies for her, I knew, I just knew that the stories were real and you two were the friends that she spoke of. They are all true, are they not?"

"I must be. As for all the stories being true, I do not recall the one about the broken gate and the wandering sheep. But I suppose that it could be I have forgotten one or two. Did she tell you about the time we were invited to Landreau Hall for a party and had to stay overnight because it rained so hard the roads were flooded?"

Marguerite shook her head.

"So there, you see, there are some stories that Miss Morton has forgotten and I remember."

Five years, five long, endless years of separation. His had been filled with the familiar, but empty of the companionship that would have made his life complete. And hers? Now he knew that hers had been at least as lonely as his had.

Seven

He found her in the shadiest part of the rose garden, this after he had looked for her on every bench of a sunny aspect. This alone told him that something was wrong. Caroline Morton loved the sunshine, breathed it in as surely as she breathed in air. Now she sat in darkened rooms and had claimed the shadiest part of the garden. Or had she chosen it because it was the only one with a protected back.

"Would you like to walk?"

She shook her head and he made to sit next to her. She pulled her skirt closer and he sat with some small space between them.

"Are you warm enough?"

She nodded.

From a charming chatterbox of a child to someone who made a statue look garrulous. His ears might need a rest, but his mind would not allow it.

"Marguerite's complaint will be short-lived. I asked the nursery maid to arrange for a tisane of chamomile and give her as much as she would take. I think you will see a marked improvement within two days, or even less."

"Oh good. She has always been so happy, so healthy. I was afraid that bringing her here may have been a mistake, though I have no idea what else I could have done."

"No, Caroline, it was the wisest thing for you to do. Have

you heard from London? Both Miss Landry and Marguerite have told me of your efforts to find some family."

"One letter came, but only to advise me that their search was continuing. It could be that her parents escaped to Russia or Austria. It could take months to reach them."

"Hmmmm. That would make things difficult." Sending a letter to a possible battlefield was a less-than-certain communication.

"Oh heaven, yes. Every day that we are together makes it harder for me to send her away."

She had completely misunderstood his reference, but even more important, had shared a bit of her heart. Now she looked away from him as though she were sorry she had made that confession.

"I can understand how you are dreading that day."

"No, you cannot." She turned back to him. "You have no idea what it will be like." She stood up, but he stayed seated. He had promised both of them that he would wait for her to volunteer her story. He was not going to chase her around the garden. But though she stood up, she did not hurry away.

"You are right, Caroline." He spoke quietly. "I cannot begin to understand. Will you tell me?"

"It will be like ripping out a part of my heart and letting what is left bleed forever."

Now he did stand up and stepped closer to her. "Physically impossible, my dear, but quite an effective picture." He made light of her pain quite deliberately. If she gave in to the heartache now he would know no more than he had before.

When she still did not turn to face him, he circled in front of her and lowered his head so that he could almost see her eyes. She was as still as a frightened doe. But that was only on the outside. The surface calm was at odds with the chaos in her heart. He was sure of that.

"Tell me then, Caroline, when being together is what both of you want, why would you send her away?"

"Because she is not mine to keep."

She spoke so softly that he had to step even closer to hear. He could smell roses and wondered if it was the flowers around them or her perfume.

"She is not yours to keep because she is the daughter of nobility?"

"Yes, she deserves what they can give her."

"The guillotine?"

She looked at him, anger in her eyes. "No, never. She was born to privilege and prestige."

He took her arm and was pleased that she did not stiffen, but let him lead her along the angled paths that crisscrossed the garden. The scent was heady and romantic. At the moment he was feeling anything but.

"Forgive me for reducing this to a political discussion, Caroline, but have not the French shown that times have changed? They have abolished the monarchy and proclaimed a republic. Marguerite may be the child of the aristocracy, but by their new laws she is no longer its heir."

Caroline paused and looked at him. "Do you think that that there will never be a king in France again?"

"I have no idea what is coming, but I suspect that for now Marguerite will be safer here than anywhere else. Especially if there is family eager to reclaim money and property, too eager to consider all that could go wrong before the chaos ends."

He resumed their slow pacing, now over a small footbridge that led from the garden to a square ornamental pond, its edges lined with boxwood.

"Here she has love and can be given an education that will prepare her to support herself or care for a family. Surely that is of far more value than what they can give her. It is the very road you have been on for the last few years and I must think that it is meant to be."

"No, I saved her from the revolution, but now it is someone else's place to raise her to a young woman."

They were silent a long while until they were at the edge of the home wood. They could see deer not far off. A doe and not one, but two fawns. There was an old wooden bench nearby and he paused, wondering if sitting would encourage more conversation or not. He let go of her arm, but held on to one hand and raised it between them.

"What better model of goodness and honor can she have than her dear Miss Morton?"

If they had been moving toward some sort of delicate understanding, it ended with that sentence.

Her face paled; she pulled her hand from his and put it to her mouth as though she were about to be ill.

"What is it, Caroline?"

She swallowed as she lowered her hand. "You could not have said any one thing more certain to have me send her away."

He blocked her way on the path and would not give her escape.

"Tell me."

She turned from him and made the corner they were in her hiding place and remained silent.

"I will know, Caroline." He told her as gently as he could so she would know that, if he left, this would only be a reprieve. "Perhaps not today. I can see you are tired and pushed to the limit of your sensibilities."

She nodded.

"But whether it will comfort you or not, I want to say this now since it went unsaid years ago and that to my great regret. You are as important to me now as you ever were. I will do everything in my power not to lose you again."

He stood a moment longer, disappointed that she did not respond, even with a gesture. He turned away, his feet crunching lightly on the stone at their feet.

It was a gasp of breath that slowed him. Tears were the last thing he expected, but he saw her shoulders shake with the effort to contain them. The occasional gasp for air was the only sound she made.

He reached for those shaking shoulders and began to turn her so that he could see her face.

"No, no, no." She repeated the words in a hopeless cadence. "If you are kind to me I shall die of the pain. Just leave me. Please, just leave me." This last was gasped between ragged breaths.

"I will not leave, Caroline. I will wait until you can talk." He did not mean to sound didactic, but in truth, she frightened him.

"Caroline, trust me." He whispered the words, praying that she would not refuse him this greatest gift.

She gave up the fight and abandoned herself to him, burrowing her face into his shoulder as if she could hide there until the grief passed.

Tears were nothing new to him, but these were as painful to watch as any he had ever endured before.

Finally she pushed against his chest and looked at him, her expression filled with confusion and rage.

"How can it be? How can it be that one minute everything seems so perfect and then a mere moment later you know it is not?"

"Are you talking about our kiss?"

"It is one example. When you kiss me the world is perfect. But the moment you stop everything shifts and I know it's a lie."

"If I kiss you again will you be a little more convinced that the world can be perfect?"

He could tell by her expression she saw no humor in the invitation.

"No, Reynie, because I know it for the lie it is. My time in France proved that beyond all bearing. One moment life was pleasant and I thought I could finally be content with the choices I made. And in less than a minute it all changed."

He led her to the old worn bench and hoped it would hold them. She kept on talking. "How could her parents abandon her that way? They are dead. Surely that is the only explanation. That alone is pain enough. If you could have seen the hope drain from her face with each passing day. If you could have seen the way she began to cling to me in their place." She drew a long, shuddering breath. "And me to her."

He ran a soothing hand over her back, counting the bones that he could feel through the thin fabric but giving her his total attention.

"Why did you not write for help?"

She looked at him, clear-eyed now. "Reynie, there was no paper." She spoke as though she were trying to explain something he could not be expected to grasp. In simple sentences, with the governess's edge to her voice. "The fire took everything. There was only ash and ruin. We slept in the stable while we waited for Marguerite's parents to come back."

How long did it take for that hope to change to despair?

Her eyes filled again, but she brushed these tears away with an impatient hand. "And when I found paper we had no money and there was no one to frank the letter for us. And even if there was I feared that it would call attention to Marguerite."

"Oh, my dear. I am so sorry." It was all he could say, humbled by her pain and her fortitude.

"God help me, I made a game of going through the ruins and finding items we could sell for food. Marguerite was very good at discovering things that we could turn to our use. I would take the larger items to the nearest good-sized town and sell them. Even that was dangerous. I was always afraid someone would question me as to how I came to own whatever it was."

She drew a deep sigh and he wondered if she would be

able to finish the story. He wished he had a little brandy with him or perhaps some wine, but she continued without the stimulant.

"Finally the day came when I was returning to the ruin empty-handed. No one wanted the rags that we had found and there was so little money. I stole some bread and fruit. I took it off the peddler's cart. I did leave the rags for him, but it was hardly a fair trade."

She paused and searched his face. Did she think she would see anything less than compassion?

"After that it was easier. To steal. To take what we needed to survive. Money became everything to me. To have enough to pay for our passage, to have enough to bribe the guards if we did not have the right papers. I would steal even when I did have money. And I look so innocent and so ladylike that I was never once caught. But it was all a lie. I was no better than the men who hung at the crossroads; the only difference was that I was never caught."

"You did what you had to do in order to survive."

She shrugged off the rationale but then said, "Yes. I did."

She looked at him again and he did nothing more than nod.

"And then I found out Marguerite was stealing too." Her expression switched from regret to anger. "And you think I am good and honorable and the best possible influence on a child."

He could see she was close to hysterical.

"My noble influence taught her to steal." She put her head in her hands and rocked back and forth on the bench. "Oh God, it was a hideous thing to teach your charge."

She sat that way for a long moment, flinching when he began to stroke her hair. He moved his hand away and waited.

"It was then that I knew I had lost all right to be her governess, that I must find family who would teach her right from wrong, undo the evil I'd done."

He shook his head at her rigid morality, her inability to see the difference between the needs of the moment that made compromise essential. He did not say a word. This was hardly the moment for philosophical discussion.

"I knew that I had to leave France, to bring her to England." She sat up straight, put her hands in her lap, and looked him in the eye. "In the end I was willing to sell myself if it meant we could leave there. Come back to England."

Now he did feel sick. This was worse than his worst imaginings.

"There was an Englishman in Calais. I mentioned him before."

Reynie nodded. "Yes, I remember. The one with the yacht."

"I met him . . ." she began and then stopped herself. "Oh, the details hardly matter. He invited me for supper on his yacht one evening and I knew what else the invitation included. And still I went, knowing that I could bargain for passage home. But when I reached the quay, the yacht was gone. There was no note, no explanation. I was not even worth that courtesy. I walked back to our horrible hovel of a room and I cried." She paused and shook her head. "To this moment I do not know if I cried because I was relieved or disappointed."

Both, he thought.

"I tried to stop the tears, but could not. I was so tired and so afraid we would never be able to escape. I thought I was being quiet, but Marguerite must have heard. She came to me, crawled up into my lap and she was the one who comforted me that night."

Caroline looked at him with defiance. "Reynie, I would have sold myself for her." She looked at him in challenge. "I would have killed for her."

"Of course you would have. You think to shock me? You cannot. Of course you would have done whatever you thought necessary."

"I am that debased a person?" She sighed and all her passion escaped with the long breath. "I am so tired of living with this, of knowing that the war reduced me to someone without honor, that I was not capable of more noble action."

"You think it the war that drove you to those desperate acts?" He wanted to laugh, his own kind of hysterical relief. "It was not the war, darling Caroline. It was hardly fear for yourself. Do you not see that it was the child that changed you."

"Marguerite?" She looked uncertain.

"Of course. You did what you had to do for Marguerite. To save her. To bring her to safety. To give her a chance at a life that was more than fear and loss." He took her hands now, longing to touch her with more than words. "Caroline, you did it because you love her. She is the child of your heart. In every way yours but by birth. *Of course* you risked everything for her. I would expect nothing less."

He smiled. She did not return the smile but her death grip on his fingers eased a bit.

"You make it sound so worthy, so right." She spoke with a reluctant wonder.

"Because it is." He laughed now, relieved, so mightily relieved that she was willing to believe this. "You did what you had to do to save her. There is nothing but glory in that. There is nothing but honor." He raised her hand and kissed it in salute.

She tried to pull her hand from his, but he would not allow it. "You are only saying this because—"

"Yes, exactly. I am saying it because I love you and because, as you recently said, I know you better than anyone else in the world. I know your capacity for giving, for living and for loving."

She drew another deep breath and straightened a little, her hand curled around his and she leaned against him.

As he kissed her head, Reynie noticed that her hair

smelled of rose water. He was content to sit with her for all of a minute.

"There is one other thing that I dare hope."

When she nodded and eased back to look at him, he took courage. "I dare to hope that your noble, generous, loyal heart is so large that you will find room in it not only for that most charmed of children but also for this most fortunate of men."

She did not speak, but he had his answer the moment that her lips touched his.

Eight

It took time. Rebuilding anything worthwhile takes time and patience. The loyal friend had all the patience in the world. The long-denied lover was far less tolerant.

Susan Landry gave them all the privacy they needed and even Reynie's patients seemed to have decided to take the summer off. The days were filled with sunshine and picnics. The normal routine of life finally convinced Caroline that the past could be put to rest and a future considered.

They were standing on the bridge across the Codbeck, having walked from Thirsk to Sowerby village. Both were loath to end a day that had brought such welcome news and they watched as Marguerite tossed pebbles from the bank some distance ahead of them.

"She does not seem upset at all." Caroline was studying her charge with intensity.

Reynie nodded, pleased to see that she was throwing stones with her once-injured arm, throwing them with considerable force. "Not only is she not upset, she is thrilled. You know that all she ever wanted was to stay with you."

Caroline drew in a deep breath of relief and sympathy. Reynie patted her arm.

"One bachelor uncle fighting with the Austrians."

Caroline nodded. "Is it selfish of me to be so pleased that he cannot manage a child and a war at the same time?"

Reynie laughed. "Since it is the answer to all our prayers

I can only agree with his wisdom, and the insight he had in having his lawyer draw up the papers needed to put her into your care."

Marguerite looked up and waved. They both waved back.

"I do believe that she is as happy and healthy as a child can be." Reynie took Caroline's arm and tucked it into his. "Once I would have said that it is my greatest pleasure, but now I find that my greatest pleasure is standing beside me."

Caroline smiled even as she shook her head at the endearment. "You are a wonder. Now that I am recovered from my own selfish misery, I can see that if I am not the same person, you are not either."

He waited, hoping this was a compliment.

"You are more kind. You were always a thoughtful man, now you are a caring one. You see those you care for as people not as science."

"As people *and* science." A compliment was always welcome, but there was more to it than that. "I am still a man of science, Caroline. I will always see them as worthy of study, but now I see them as worthy of caring as well."

"But that makes all the difference, does it not?"

Marguerite ran past the bridge, waving a stick as though she were urging a horse on. Caroline let go of Reynie's arm and turned to watch the child. Satisfied that she was only searching for more stones, she gave Reynie her full attention.

"How did this caring for people happen? Why?"

"When you left me." He took her arm and they began to walk after Marguerite, who was scampering farther and farther afield. "After all that racing around trying to find you, my trips to Paris, I settled here at home and tried to go on, tried to accept that you did not want me." He shook his head. It was a time he would rather not relive. "But I saw you everywhere. In every person I was called to help. I saw you."

"Everywhere? Oh, I do understand, for it was the same with me."

Reynie looked at her and was comforted by her expression filled with understanding.

"I began to listen to them as I had never truly listened to you. I soon discovered that they needed to talk as much as they needed any physic I could provide. And yes, I did approach it as an experiment, with careful study, and it worked. It proved itself."

"Did you keep notes?" She asked this with a smile and he was delighted once again to see the joy coming back into her life.

"Yes, I did and only longed for someone to help me keep better order of them. I thought I would write a book and it would be as well regarded as Morgagni's on the cause of disease. I was going to title it 'A Study of the Influence of Other Factors on the Cure of Disease.' I still have those notes somewhere."

"So your scientific study was blended with this new insight?"

"Yes, and other reading I did confirmed it. I finally grasped that the medical man's primary obligation is to his patient, that it is not the disease that must be eliminated but the patient that must be cured."

"It seems like both mean the same thing."

"It might to you, my dear, to any woman with the wisdom all women call their own, but to this man of science there is a very clear difference between the two."

He leaned forward and touched his lips to hers. She smiled beneath the kiss and he knew it was balm for her soul as well as his.

"If you had not left, Caroline, I might never have realized that. I would have poured all the caring I was capable of into your heart and into our life together and my science would have been incomplete."

"It was a blessing?" she asked with a note of incredulity in her voice and he could only nod.

"If it was, my dear, it was a blessing in as complete a disguise as either of us could imagine."

Caroline walked briskly down the street, holding Marguerite's hand and barely listening to her chatter.

"It will snow, will it not, Miss Morton?"

She was Mrs. Osgood now, but did not correct the child. After three weeks of trying, Caroline had decided that Miss Morton was as much an endearment as a name and had given up.

"Yes, it will snow. You can feel it in the air."

Would Reynie be home for dinner or should she try to put it back? He was called away from home on a constant basis, but long before their wedding she knew this would be a part of their life and a small price to pay for the happiness now theirs.

"Will it snow soon, before dinner?"

Caroline looked up at the sky. "It will snow when it will, *chouchou,* and no amount of asking will make it snow sooner."

With some relief Caroline noted that Marguerite accepted that as the final word. But she was only silent for a moment. They had almost reached the front door when she asked, "Do you think Mrs. Osgood will have made some of those cream cakes?"

"We can only hope." How lucky she was that Reynie's mother had been so willing to relinquish the management of the household and how lucky for all of them that she still enjoyed baking.

"I have never seen snow, have I?" Marguerite looked anxiously at the sky. "It will not wait until dark will it?"

The child had seen snow. But Caroline would never once

remind her of those days. It was enough that the nightmares and complaints had ended. She would do nothing to bring them on again.

"If it begins to snow after you have gone to bed, I promise to wake you up so you can see."

"And go out?"

"No, not until the morning."

Caroline was sure the child would have argued, but at the same moment they both noticed Reynie walking toward them. With a whoop Marguerite ran to him. Reynie braced himself and caught the flying bundle and swung her up into his arms.

From where Caroline stood, they made the perfect picture. The two she loved more than any in the world. Safe and part of her life.

She waited for them at the door, smiling a welcome that overflowed with joy. Reynie did not set Marguerite down as he leaned closer for a small kiss. It was the barest meeting of lips, but reminded her of how much closer they could be and would be as the snow fell tonight.

Reynie let his smallest love reach for the knocker and the practiced rap that would announced their presence. With a smile of deepest satisfaction, Marguerite turned to Caroline.

"It is perfect, is it not, Miss Morton? Mr. Osgood? Snow and cream cakes and all of us around the fire."

She did not wait for an answer but raised her face to the sky to welcome the first of the snowflakes that were drifting earthward. "Indeed, Miss Morton, I do think that we shall all live happily ever after."

Rescuing Captain Rocher

Julia Parks

For Frances, Patty, and Dwayne

"Please, Papa, I would much rather sail with you than go to all those stuffy balls!"

"I will not hear of it, *ma chérie.* It is past time for you to make your bow to Society, and so you shall."

"Would you force me to wed where my heart is not engaged?"

The beleaguered Captain Rocher gave a quiet laugh and kissed his daughter's cheek. "No, no, *ma petite,* but how can you say your heart will not become engaged once you are presented? There is certainly more chance of it than on board the *Marie Claire.*"

"But, Papa, I love the *Marie Claire,* and I love taking care of you."

"And so you shall, but in our little house on Curzon Street, not on board the ship. Come, come, you do not want to disappoint your grandfather."

"No, I suppose not, but I had hoped, after spending six long years at school, away from you and the *Marie Claire,* that I might get to sail once more before . . ." She fell silent. Once her father gave her that look, she knew arguing was fruitless.

"That's a good girl," he said, bowing his head against hers, their dark curls mingling. Stopping, he looked up at the sign and nodded. "This is the one Lady Best told me about. Let us see what they have to offer."

They entered the dressmaker's shop and stood for a moment, allowing their eyes to adjust to the gloom. Along one wall, piled almost to the ceiling, were lengths of cloth—every color of the rainbow.

Marie brightened and said, "You'll let me get something other than white gowns, will you not, Papa? After six years at Mrs. Brown's Academy with nothing but white gowns to wear every evening, I cannot wait to wear something bright and beautiful."

"You may have any color your heart desires, *chérie.* And all the trimmings, too!" he said, grinning when she threw her arms around his neck and stood on tiptoe to kiss his cheek.

Perhaps, thought the handsome captain, getting to know his daughter again would not prove as difficult as he had thought. He allowed himself to gaze at her while she stroked soft velvets and silks. She was every bit as beautiful as his Claire had been. Remembering how wild and fierce his late wife had been when dealing with her own father, Bastien devoutly hoped Marie would prove more amenable. He was out of his depth in London Society, and he would need all the help he could get if his daughter was to have a successful Season. The last thing he wanted was to have his little Marie run away with some roguish French sea captain.

"Good morning, sir. So sorry to have kept you waiting. How may I be of service?" asked the gray-haired woman, her words shaking him from his reverie.

"You are Madame Bouvier, the owner?" asked the tall, handsome gentleman, a slight accent flavoring his English.

"Yes, of course," said the shop owner.

"Eh bien, madame, nous voudrions . . ."

"I'm sorry, sir, I . . . I only go by the French name because it adds a touch of class to my establishment." Leaning closer to the French gentleman, she winked and said, "I'm from Ireland, really, but these Londoners wouldn't give my shop a second look if I called it Mrs. O'Donnell's."

"I see. Yes, very well. Madam, my daughter is in need of a wardrobe suitable to her age and station."

"But not white," said Marie, peeking around her father's broad shoulders with an impish grin for the frumpy couturier.

"No, not white," he said, giving her shoulder a squeeze.

"I see, sir. We can certainly manage that. What occasions?"

"Occasions? Balls, the theater . . ."

"Alfresco pique-niques and rides in the park," said Marie, mimicking a perfect French accent.

"Of course, Miss, uh . . ."

"Miss Rocher. And I am Captain Rocher. Here is our address where we are staying," he said, handing her a card. "Now, I really must go, Marie. Remember, Madam is the expert. Follow her advice. I will return in two hours to fetch you."

"Merci, Papa," said Marie, standing on tiptoe to kiss both of his cheeks.

"I leave my daughter in your capable hands, madam."

"You may rely on me," said the seamstress, her eyes glistening in anticipation of the large order.

When the door had closed behind her father, Miss Marie Rocher reached for the brightest length of pink silk she had ever seen. Stroking it, she closed her eyes, envisioning herself swathed in the heavenly cloth.

"I must have a ball gown out of this, madam," she said.

"If that is what you wish, Miss Rocher," said the dressmaker, glancing at the name and modest address on the card in her hand. "Most young ladies prefer the simple sprigged muslins, miss."

"But I am not one of those young ladies," Marie said emphatically, "and I choose this one. Oh, and this yellow. Do you not think it suits my coloring?" Taking the length of yellow satin to one of the many mirrors that dotted the room, Marie held it up to her face and smiled, pleased with the effect against her blue eyes and dark hair.

"Very becoming," said Mrs. O'Donnell. "And I have a splendid grass green that will be perfect for a carriage dress." Looking over Marie's shoulder, the dressmaker added, "We will keep the lines simple. Young ladies do not need very much ornamentation."

"Oh, but I want ruffles and ribbons and lace, madam. I have been wearing nothing but plain white tents for years. I want to stand out, to attract. Oh," breathed Marie, crossing the room to touch a red velvet gown with a deep *décolletage* edged in white fur. Around the bottom, the gown boasted four tiers of ruffles, each trimmed with the white fur. "This is lovely. Is it already sold?"

"Yes, miss. I'm afraid so—to a Miss Colette Duvall, the latest singer from the Continent at the Opera."

"Oh, what a shame. Perhaps you could make up something similar for me. Perhaps in a blue carriage dress."

"Perhaps, miss," said the dressmaker. "First, we must take your measurements."

The little bell over the door tinkled as another customer entered the shop.

"Allow me to turn you over to our senior seamstress for measuring and then we will discuss the details of your wardrobe."

With a final stroke of the red velvet, Marie followed the dressmaker through heavy curtains to the back of the shop, where she was handed over to an elderly woman with a tape measure.

As Mrs. O'Donnell swept through the curtains to the front of the shop, Marie heard her gush, "Lady Westhaven, how delightful to see you again. I hope you have the lace we talked about?"

"Turn around, please, miss," said the seamstress.

* * *

It was the middle of February, but the small garden on Curzon Street was dappled with afternoon sunlight—a sure invitation to enjoy the unseasonably warm day. Lady Westhaven had taken her needles and threads to the garden. She closed her eyes and breathed deeply, envisioning the flowers of spring.

"Enjoying the afternoon sun, Mother?"

"Matthew, what are you doing home? How wonderful to see you, but . . ." she said, pleasure in her voice. Then, sagging back on the hard stone garden bench and lifting one hand to her forehead, she moaned, "Oh, no, Matthew. Not again."

"I can explain, Mother," said the youth, striding closer and delivering a disarming grin before kissing her cheek.

Her eyes blazing, Lady Westhaven sat forward and glared at her wayward son. "What was it this time, young man?"

He had the grace to look abashed as he moved the trail of lace his mother was making and sat down by her side. "A bit of gambling trouble. Nothing, really—more of a misunderstanding."

"Oh, Matthew. Did you learn nothing from your father's mistakes?" she asked, dropping her needles and gripping his hands fiercely.

"Father was never as lucky as I am," said the young man, pushing away from his mother and rising to frown down at her. He was blond like she was, with those same bright blue eyes, but he was all legs and arms, towering over her.

"Oh, yes, I can see how very lucky you are. That is why you have been sent home from school yet again. Matthew, what am I to do with you?"

"It's only until next term, Mother. You just wait and see.

I'll help you fix things around the house. I'll help old Wheezer and Mrs. Helpless."

Carefully, Lady Westhaven wound the row of intricate lace around her needles and set it aside. Rising, she stood on tiptoe and held his face. Her head was only chin-high next to him, and she grimaced. He must have grown another inch since Christmas.

"They are Mr. Wiser and Mrs. Helper to you, young man, and I daresay you will make their work ten times worse, but there is nothing for it. I cannot turn you out of the house."

"That's the spirit, Mother. I knew I could count on you," he said, patting the top of her head.

"I suppose you have a letter from your headmaster—or whatever you call him."

"Yes," he replied, pulling a crumpled envelope from his pocket.

"This has been opened," she said.

"It's all there," he grumbled.

In seconds, Lady Westhaven had perused the letter and had the facts. Her son, Lord Westhaven, had been running a gambling hell from his room. He had been too successful, it seemed, and a few of the boys had complained. Though he had not been found guilty of cheating, he had been sent down for the remainder of the term.

"I'm sorry, Mother," he said quietly when the letter fluttered to the ground.

"Matthew, I . . . oh, go to your room," she snapped before turning her back on him and striding away.

Passing the ancient gardener without a word, Anne hurried along the pebble pathway that led to the far wall. There, she turned and continued, pacing round and round the perimeter of the small garden, muttering to herself, until her energy and anger were spent.

She loved her son, but having him home complicated

things. If he was home, she would have to feed him, too, and her food bill would soar. And clothes! Matthew would insist that he be clothed in a manner that befitted a peer of the realm.

What hurt the most, however, was all that money she had so carefully hoarded to send him to school for yet another term. All that money—up in smoke.

"Drat you, Matthew!" she exclaimed, glancing upward and shaking her fist at his window. "I ought to send you out as an apprentice and be done with you!"

On the other side of the stone wall, Marie swept a deep curtsy and danced across the terrace, calling. "Papa, how do I look?"

Turning away from the stone wall where his neighbor's words had caught his interest, Bastien's eyes widened in surprise. His daughter continued across the lawn to curtsy in front of him, her ample curves defined too well by the bright rose-colored silk. While he had been sailing the world, his little girl had grown into a young lady.

Smiling, Bastien swept her a courtly bow and kissed her hand, saying softly, "You look beautiful, *chérie.* I know your mother is smiling down from heaven on you."

"Thank you, Papa," she said, dimpling up at him. Taking his arm, she led him back to the terrace, all the while chattering happily. "I think Mrs. O'Donnell did a wonderful job with this gown. She sent several more, but not the entire order, of course.

"I told her I wanted this gown for tonight to wear to my first party. Do you think we might practice playing silver loo again this afternoon? I do so want to win."

"Winning is not nearly as important as the impression you make, *ma petite.* Tonight you will meet numerous influential ladies who will spread the word that the charming granddaughter of the Marquis of Belwich is in town for the Season and must be added to every guest list."

"Oh, Papa, do you think I will be able . . ."

"Do not fret, *chérie.* You will win them over without even trying. How could they not be impressed? You have everything these English ladies value—breeding, beauty, charm, and fortune. Tonight, all you must do, my sweet, is enjoy yourself."

"Thank you, Papa," said Marie, standing on tiptoe and kissing his cheek before twirling away from him and disappearing into the house.

Captain Bastien Rocher's smile faded, and his tanned brow creased in a frown. Suddenly, he felt rather old and staid. Having a grown-up daughter, he supposed, was taking its toll. He knew Marie would be a great success during her Season; her mother had been, too, until she had fallen in love with him—the son of a French émigré, struggling to make his way in the world.

Claire. He had been thinking of her more than usual of late. Not surprising. Marie had her eyes and her small nose and perfect mouth. Twelve long years Claire had been gone. His business had kept him busy, but every once in a while, he still recalled her soft touch and gentle voice.

Shaking off his reverie, Bastien descended the stone steps and strolled along the path of pebbles toward the low garden wall. Cocking his dark head to one side, he listened for his neighbor's intriguing feminine voice beyond the shrubbery. Silence greeted him. With a Gallic shrug of his shoulders, Bastien returned to the house.

Whatever problem had caused his neighbor to shake her fist at the heavens, it was no affair of his.

The card party they had been invited to was in the most fashionable square in London—Grosvenor. Many of the carriages pulling up to the front door had crests on their doors, attesting to the fact that only the crème de la crème of Society had been invited to Lady Best's for the evening. Though Captain Rocher's carriage did not boast a crest, it was new and shining, just like its younger occupant, Miss Marie Rocher, granddaughter of the wealthy Marquis of Belwich.

"I am so nervous, Papa," Marie confided to her father as the carriage pulled up to the door and their footman, equally resplendent in his new livery, threw open the door.

The elegant French captain hopped out first and turned to take his daughter's hand. Bowing his head to hers, he whispered, "They are just people, *chérie*. You are, after all, the granddaughter of an English marquis and the great-granddaughter of a French *duc*. You have nothing to worry about."

She put on a brave smile and took his arm to mount the steps to the house and her destiny. Their first obstacle was a receiving line, a silvery serpent consisting of gray heads, and feathered headdresses bobbing up and down, back and forth.

Fixing that polite smile on her face, Marie hid her dismay as she was introduced to her hostess and her sisters. Glancing beyond the line to the drawing room, she could not see a single person under the age of sixty in attendance.

Ah, she thought, red hair. She would not be the only young person present. Marie's hopes were dashed, however, as the lady turned, revealing a face fully lined by life.

"Charming, dear Captain Rocher. Quite charming," cackled her hostess, and Marie dipped into another curtsy. "Allow me to present you to my brother, Lord Hepplewhite."

Raising her voice, their hostess said distinctly, "Hepplewhite, this is Captain Rocher and his daughter Marie. You remember. I told you about her. She's Belwich's granddaughter."

"Yes, yes. I remember. Delighted to meet you, Captain. And your daughter. Well, aren't you a lovely thing," declared the old roué, stroking his moustache as he stared down Marie's *décolletage*.

She turned scarlet and proceeded down the line, where she

met countless other ancients, all related in some manner to Lady Best or her late husband. When Marie and her father had finally run the gamut of the receiving line, they stepped into the drawing room, which was filled with small tables and chairs. Many were already occupied by guests, intent on their cards, and they hesitated.

The smell of spirits and peppermint warned Marie of Lord Hepplewhite's approach before he took her arm.

"Here now, why don't you come with me, Miss Rocher? Miss Feaster and her beau, retired Admiral Grant, need partners for whist. Captain, why don't you join that table over there?"

"Bonne chance, my dear," said her handsome father, giving her a little nudge.

As she and her escort threaded their way through the tables and chairs, Marie searched in vain for someone closer to her own age. She had dreamed of meeting a handsome young man. Now, she would have settled for another young lady—anyone closer to her own age. But there was no one. Instead, she noticed that the majority of the guests were closer in age to her grandfather. Even her father, who was almost forty years old, must feel out of place.

When the introductions had been made and play had begun, Marie found it hard to concentrate as the admiral subjected her to a minute scrutiny. Screwing up her courage, Marie met his gaze and smiled.

"Just looking to see some resemblance to old Belwich, m' dear. Can't say that I see any at all," he added, his eyes coming to rest on her bosom.

Marie blushed and stammered, trying to think of some suitable rejoinder to his most unsuitable inspection. Surprisingly, Mr. Hepplewhite came to her rescue, though his response made her blush deepen.

"You won't find a resemblance to Belwich there," he said, pointing at Marie's heaving breasts. "But I'm like you,

I don't see much resemblance between Miss Rocher and her grandfather."

"Well, stands to reason, doesn't it. She's a girl, not an old man," said Miss Letitia Feaster, a spinster of some sixty years.

"I have been told that I have my mother's eyes," said Marie.

"Hmph, could be. Don't really remember your mother. Look like your father though," said Miss Feaster, dismissing the subject that had so captivated the males at her table. "Are we going to play cards or not?"

"Prettier, of course," supplied Lord Hepplewhite, once again twisting his moustache.

"Ha, ha. Prettier than her father. You hear that, Letitia?" The admiral raised his voice several levels and repeated the entire conversation for his partner, who glared at him impatiently.

Marie fixed her expression with a smile, and resigned herself to an evening of polite boredom.

On the ride home, Captain Rocher complimented his daughter on her manners and her patience. "I know this evening was not the sort you were expecting. I had hoped Lady Best would invite other young people. Still, the ladies present have the power to do much more for your bow into Society than young people could, and several of them confided to me that they will certainly send you invitations."

"They were all very nice, Papa, but I did feel a little out of place."

"You should write to some of your friends from school and find out when they are coming to town. Surely they will be arriving soon to have their own wardrobes made up."

"The last time we spoke before Christmas, when the term ended, they weren't certain when they would come to town. I only have an address for one of them anyway. Catherine was going straight to Wales to visit her grandmother and will not be going home before coming to London in April. But I will write to Anthea. I hope she will be coming sometime in March."

In his daughter's voice Bastien could hear the longing and loneliness. He wanted to pull her onto his lap and kiss away her fears, but that was no longer possible, he thought, studying her grown-up visage in the dim carriage lights. It had been years since he had longed for his wife to be by his side, but for Marie's sake, he wished he could provide her with a feminine hand to reassure her and guide her through the Season to come.

The carriage stopped outside their modest town home, and Bastien threw open the door without waiting for the footman. Their butler, who had served on the *Marie Claire* for years, opened the front door, and the candlelight spilled down the steps.

"What's this? Get up, you lazy cur," said the footman, nudging an inert mass with his foot. The mass groaned and moved, flopping back and draping his rumpled body across the front steps.

"Stay in the carriage, Marie, until we get rid of this person," said her father, shutting the carriage door on her.

"Two of you carry this man into the square and dump him there," said Pidgeon, their butler.

"Wait a minute," said Bastien, who squatted down and grabbed the man's lapels to shake him. Surprised by the whiteness of the cravat and the softness of the coat, he shook the man, who again groaned. "Drunk and nothing more than a boy," muttered Bastien.

"Captain, let Tom and . . ."

"No, Pidgeon, this is not a mere drunk. Do any of you recognize the boy?"

"Might be the young fellow from next door," said the footman, Tom.

Giving the boy another rough shake, Bastien asked, "What is your name, boy?"

"Hm? Matthew. Lord . . . Westhav . . ."

"He has passed out again, but I think you are right, Tom. I think this is our neighbor. We can hardly leave him on the doorstep, Pidgeon. What's more, I would not wish to disturb his household so late. Take him inside and put him on the sofa in the library."

While Bastien turned his attention on his daughter, the footman and the butler grabbed the youth under his arms and pulled him to one side. His eyes flew open as Marie passed by, lingering to stare at him, her blue eyes wide with curiosity. Grinning stupidly, the young man's bleary gaze traveled from her feet to her face.

"An angel," he rasped before passing out once again.

With a giggle, Marie allowed her father to whisk her inside.

Soft and supple. And fragrant, like roses. Young Lord Westhaven opened one bleary eye. Frowning, he scrambled to an upright position before a searing pain made him clutch his head.

"Ohhh," he groaned.

"What's wrong?" asked Marie, putting her hand on his shoulder. "Should I get my father?"

"No," he managed. Finally, he lowered his hands, squinting at her. "Who are you?"

"I'm Marie Rocher," she said, extending her hand. When he made no move to take it, she took his hand and gave it a firm shake. "And you are Lord Westhaven?"

"Yes, Matthew, to my friends. When anyone calls me Lord Westhaven, I still look around for my father. He's been dead for years." Not wishing to have the conversation degenerate into the maudlin, Matthew asked, "Where am I?"

"My house. I live next door to you, although I did not realize it until our footman, Tom, told us last night. I thought the Lady Westhaven lived there by herself. I didn't know you were there."

Matthew's attention was diverted by the whitest expanse of feminine skin he had ever seen. He looked up to find her blue eyes resting on his, waiting patiently for him to reply.

Matthew smiled at her. "I was sent home from school yesterday. I never dreamed we had such a beautiful new neighbor."

"How sweet," said Marie, smiling down at him. "How old are you?"

"I will be seventeen at the end of the month."

"I will be nineteen in the spring," she said, smiling again.

"I still don't know what I'm doing here," said Matthew, his eyes falling to her low *décolletage* once again.

"Being extremely rude," said a deep voice from the doorway. The young people sprang to their feet, and Matthew clutched his head again, swaying dangerously. Marie grabbed his arm to steady him.

"You startled us, Papa," she protested.

"A good thing," muttered Bastien. Forcing a smile to his lips for his daughter's sake, he added, "Why don't you let me and young Lord Westhaven have a word or two in private?"

Marie dropped his arm and glided toward her father. "You will not scold poor Matthew, will you? He is not feeling at all the thing."

"Do not fret, *chérie*, I shall be the perfect host."

He accepted the kiss she bestowed on his cheek, but his eyes fell to the same expanse of skin he had caught his guest staring at. Why hadn't he noticed before how very revealing her gown was? It was a simple morning gown. Surely it was supposed to cover more of her than it did. The gown she had worn the night before had also been quite revealing. He knew that fashion demanded it of the ladies of the *ton,* but surely young ladies did not wear gowns with such terribly low *décolletages.*

Shaking off this worry, Bastien turned to the task at hand.

"Now, young man. Allow me to introduce myself. I am Captain Bastien Rocher. You have met my daughter Marie, of course. I understand you are just arrived from school."

Under the stern gaze of the French captain, the boy stood at attention as best he could.

"Uh, yes, sir. I am Lord Westhaven. My mother lives next door. I must apologize for landing on your doorstep last night. Not planned, of course, but there you have it," he said, beginning to shift from one foot to the other.

"Precisely. Now what are we to do with you?"

"I beg your pardon, sir, but there is nothing to be done. I thank you for your hospitality, and I will now take my leave of you." His show of bravado was ruined as he took a few steps, turned a ghastly white, and grabbed the back of the sofa.

Bastien reached for the boy's arm and led him to the fireplace, propping him up on the mantel and stepping back to study him. "Do you intend to present yourself to your mother looking like that? I would think your absence has caused her enough anguish."

"No, I mean, I do look a little tired," said the youth, sagging as he studied his image in the glass over the mantel.

"You will frighten her to death if you go home looking like that. Sit down, Lord Westhaven, and I will have my man fix you a restorative."

"It's very good of you, sir," said Matthew, sagging gratefully onto the soft sofa once again.

"Nonsense, I do recall what it was like to be your age."

With this, Bastien left the room, giving Pidgeon instructions to clean up their visitor and set him to rights before sending him home. Bastien straightened his own cravat and headed next door to meet the woman behind the voice in the garden, which had intrigued him so the day before.

"My lady, there is a Captain Rocher to see you."

"I am not acquainted with the gentleman. Tell him I am not at home, Wiser."

"I hesitate to do that, my lady. He does not appear to be the sort of gentleman to take no for an answer."

"A gentleman?"

"Undoubtedly, my lady. I would not trouble you with a tradesperson."

"No, of course not, Wiser. Very well, send him in."

Lady Westhaven smoothed her gown, wishing she had not chosen this day to wear her oldest, most threadbare garment. Ah well, she reflected, against the threadbare furnishings her gown would look positively resplendent.

"Captain Bastien Rocher, my lady," said the butler, stepping to one side to allow her guest to enter.

The captain's broad shoulders seemed to block out all the light from the hall as he entered the room. He crossed to her immediately, bowing before her, followed by a crisp nod.

"Good morning, Lady Westhaven. I am Captain Rocher. I have taken the house next door for the Season." When she didn't respond, Bastien added, "My daughter Marie is making her bow into Society."

"I am pleased to make your acquaintance, Captain. Please be seated."

The captain perched on the edge of the delicate chair beside the sofa, making it seem small and spindly. The impression of broad shoulders was expanded to long, muscular legs, and strong hands. It had been years since her little house had received such a very virile specimen of manhood. Anne realized she was holding her breath and expelled it in short puffs so her visitor would not guess the effect he had on her.

Her voice showed no sign of her thoughts as she said politely, "Did you need some assistance? I'm afraid I do not get about in Society myself. I am a widow."

"My sympathies, my lady. I, too, have lost a spouse. But I did not come today to speak about myself. I am here because of your son, Lord Westhaven."

"My son? What has he . . ." she began, tensing once again. With a brittle smile, Anne controlled her emotions and commented, "I cannot imagine . . ."

"If you will allow me to explain. I know you must be worried about him, and I have already chastised him for the anguish he has caused by remaining out all night . . ."

"I beg your pardon, Captain Rocher, but my son is upstairs asleep, even as we speak. Now, if you will excuse me."

Anne rose, and then wished she had not. The handsome captain towered over her. Still, she held her ground.

"If Lord Westhaven is upstairs asleep, madam, then I have an impostor in my library. My footman seemed quite certain, when we found the young man asleep on our doorstep last night, that he was our newest neighbor. But if you insist . . ."

"One moment, Captain." Anne swept past him and into the hall, speaking to the ancient butler for a moment before turning to face her visitor once more. Her expression told the tale, and she grimaced when the captain nodded smugly.

"I will send Wiser over immediately to fetch him home. He . . . he is not harmed, is he?"

"No, merely a little tattered. Like most young men, they think they have harder heads than they do, and suddenly the drink catches them up."

"I do apologize, Captain Rocher. I assure you this will not happen again."

"There is no need to apologize, my lady. In the course of

my work, I have had many encounters with young men. If I might give you a word of advice. It does not do to coddle them. Give him some sort of task to do. Have him muck out the stables."

"I do not keep horses, Captain."

"I do. Feel free to send him over."

"I am sure your stables could use a cleaning, Captain Rocher, but I do not think a peer of the realm should be the one to clean them. Thank you, however, for your advice. Now, if you will excuse me?"

With this, Anne swept out of the room and up the stairs, keeping her shoulders straight and her spine stiff until she reached Matthew's room. When he came home, she would give him a good talking-to.

Anne lifted the lace one last time before pronouncing it satisfactory to take to the dressmaker. Smiling, she wrapped the brown paper around it and tied it with a string. Mrs. O'Donnell's customer would be well pleased. What was more to the point, thought Anne, she would be able to give Mrs. Helper, who served as cook and housekeeper, more money to purchase food for their table. Matthew had been home only one day, and already Mrs. Helper was complaining that the week's worth of bread was gone, and the apples she had set aside to make a tart had been consumed.

"I will be back shortly, Wiser. If my son should rise before I return, do please remind him that I wish to speak to him before he goes out again."

"Very good, my lady. I do wish you would let me fetch a hackney cab."

"A hackney? Now, why should I spend our hard-earned money on that? There is nothing wrong with my walking."

"Will you take Tilly with you?" asked the old man.

"No, I will be fine. I am only going to the dressmaker's, Wiser, and I am a mature lady. No one ever bothers me."

With this, Anne secured the tie on her bonnet and headed out the door. She kept her eyes straight ahead and on the pavement, especially when she entered the busier streets. But soon she was inside Mrs. O'Donnell's shop.

Looking around to make certain there were no customers, Lady Westhaven greeted the dressmaker with a familiar, "Good morning, Mrs. O'Donnell. How are you today?"

"I am fine, my lady. Thank you for asking. Have you brought the lace?"

"Yes, and I must say, it is quite exquisite. I think your customer will be pleased. What is she going to put it on?"

"It is for an underskirt, but the lace will peek out from beneath the hem, so your work will not be completely obscured."

"Oh, good. I do like to think that my lace will be noticed. It will make for new customers for both of us."

Just then, the shop bell rang, and both ladies turned to watch the dark-haired beauty enter the shop with her maid.

"Miss Rocher, good morning."

"Good morning, Mrs. O'Donnell. I have come for my fittings."

"Excellent. Let me fetch Mrs. James to help you. If you will excuse me, Lady Westhaven."

"Lady Westhaven?" said Marie, coming forward and curtsying before the lady. "You must be Matthew's mother."

Anne blinked twice at the brightness of the girl's gown. If she had caught the girl's name correctly, this must be the daughter of the arrogant Captain Rocher, but she was dressed like a lightskirt. Anne's opinion of the captain fell even lower.

"Yes," she said regally, gazing up at the willowy girl with wide blue eyes. "I am Lord Westhaven's mother. And you must be our neighbor, Captain Rocher's daughter."

"Yes, I am Marie Rocher. I am delighted to make your acquaintance. You also use Mrs. O'Donnell's services?"

"No, I mean, yes. Of course. That is why I am here. Did Mrs. O'Donnell make your gown?"

"Yes, she did. She managed to have several made up very quickly, but the majority of my gowns will be delivered in a few weeks. It was a very large order because I am to make my presentation into Society this spring."

"Indeed. Your mother is bringing you out?"

"No, I . . . my mother died when I was six years old."

"Oh, I am sorry, dear. But who is sponsoring you?"

"My father, I suppose."

"But, my dear girl, do you not have some female relative to take you under her wing, to act as chaperon?"

"No, my grandfather did not think it necessary. And my father, whom I believe you have met, is my only living relative other than Grandpapa—the Marquis of Belwich."

"The marquis . . . I see. Miss Rocher, if I might make a suggestion?"

"Certainly, my lady," said the girl.

"Perhaps you might consider changing . . ."

"Please step this way, Miss Rocher," said the dressmaker.

"Yes?" asked the girl.

"No, nothing. Run along to your fitting."

Marie nodded to Anne and followed Mrs. O'Donnell from the room. Moments later, the dressmaker returned to pay Anne for the lace she had made.

Lowering her voice, Anne said, "Perhaps I should warn you, Mrs. O'Donnell, that Miss Rocher is quite well-connected."

"My lady, you know that I serve everyone equally."

"No, please do not take offense. I merely wondered if you realized it. Miss Rocher's gown is quite . . . unusual, don't you think?"

Lowering her own voice, the dressmaker said, "It is precisely what she wanted. I tried to tell her that young ladies do not wear violent colors—nor do they wear gowns that are, well, cut for someone of more mature years. She would have none of it. I just assumed she and her father were, shall we say, of the trade class. I mean, he introduced himself as captain, so . . ."

"I fear you are mistaken. Her father may be a mere captain, but her grandfather is a marquis. Miss Rocher will be making her bow into the highest circle of Society."

The dressmaker covered her face with her hands and wailed, "I will be ruined if she goes about looking the veritable tart!"

"You must delay her order until I have spoken to her father. The man has no one to guide him. I will try to reason with him. The girl seems very nice, and I would like to help her."

"Oh, thank you, my lady. Thank you so much!"

"Think nothing of it. I believe I will wait here until Miss Rocher is finished. Perhaps we can walk home together."

As it turned out, Anne was invited to share Marie's carriage. Sinking against the blue velvet squabs, she closed her eyes. How long it had been since she had ridden in such a fine carriage . . . or any carriage at all, for that matter. Nearly destitute after the death of her spendthrift husband, she was accustomed to walking wherever she needed to go.

"I hope you will not mind if I sometimes ask your advice, my lady. It is just that I have no one else to turn to."

"I will be delighted. You must feel free to come over anytime, my dear. Having only a son, I would relish having a girl around."

"Thank you. And I will speak to Papa about finding a suitable chaperon for the Season. Can one hire a chaperon?"

"I suppose it is done on occasion, but it is usually some poor relation, if a girl has no close female relatives. But if your father is in town and is willing to escort you everywhere, at least there can be no question of impropriety."

"Oh, that's good."

"Then your father will be staying with you? I mean, he is not planning to sail off someplace."

"No, Papa has enough people capable of sailing his ships. They can well do without him for the Season."

"So he has a fleet of ships?"

"Yes, he sails all over the world. Well, he does not. When he sent me to school, he restricted his personal ship to short voyages so that he could come and visit me often. He spent a great deal of time sailing back and forth to Spain or Portugal with supplies for our troops."

"But he is French," said Anne.

"Yes, but my grandfather left France when the old king was imprisoned, escaping with very little except his family. Papa was only a boy at the time. And then, when he grew up, he married my mother, so his ties to England are at least as strong as his ties with France. He has very little patience with his countrymen who came here and did nothing but, as Papa calls it, rest on their laurels. As he said, he could use his title and call himself the Duc de Beaulieu, but that would not put food on the table. So he earned money, bought his first boat, and never looked back."

"I see. You know, my dear, it is fine to tell me this tale. I am not, after all, a Society hostess. I think it would be better, however, if you were not quite so frank about your father's business with others."

"Really? Why?"

"The story is perhaps a little too, uh, democratic for some of the *ton*'s high sticklers. As you know, Society has its rules."

"I know that. I have a friend whose older sister was almost ruined during her first Season. She finally went home and wed the local squire. Anthea said it was quite a scandal."

"These things happen," said Anne, smiling at Marie's wide-eyed horror. She would do well, if she could only be persuaded to change her mode of dress to a more conventional style. With her dark hair and bright blue eyes, she could wear the plainest sprig muslin, and still, she would stand out.

Anne smoothed her own blond hair. Except to put her hair up in the tight chignon she always wore, she had not studied her own appearance in years. She wondered suddenly, how much or how little she resembled the blue-eyed belle one of her suitors had once labeled her.

Nonsense, she thought, folding her hands in her lap. She was a mature lady of five-and-thirty. The only thing that should matter to her was that she should be neat and presentable. What did she really care about fashion!

The carriage stopped in front of her house, and the footman threw open the door to help her descend.

Marie followed, asking, "Is Matthew at home?"

"I believe he is, my dear, but I imagine that he is still sleeping."

"Oh, then I shan't disturb him."

"Thank you for bringing me home, Miss Rocher. Do you think I might have a word with your father?"

"Of course!" said the girl, linking arms with her newfound mentor and leading the way.

The next fifteen minutes was spent in polite conversation between Anne, the captain, and Marie—who did not appear to notice the tension in the air.

Finally, the captain rose and said formally, "If you will excuse me, Lady Westhaven?"

"Actually, Captain Rocher, I was hoping to have a word with you in private. Marie, you will excuse us, will you not?"

"Yes, I need to write to my friends," she said, rising and leaving them alone in the neat drawing room.

"What did you wish to say to me, my lady?" said the captain, staring down at her from his great height.

"Will you not be seated first?" When he was seated again, she continued. "It is about your daughter's wardrobe."

"What about it? I think she looks very fetching."

"Fetching? Perhaps, sir, but I cannot help but wonder what sort of person she will fetch, wearing such an unsuitable garment."

"Unsuitable . . . madam, I will have you know . . ."

"Please do not be defensive. Surely, as her father, you must realize her . . . chest is too . . . exposed."

His nostrils flared, and his dark eyes blazed with blue lights as he leaned forward, glaring at her own *décolletage.* "Marie is no more . . . exposed . . . than you are, my lady." His tone made her title sound like a curse.

Anne leapt to her feet, a tactic that served to put the arrogant captain's gaze on the same level as her heaving bosom. Turning scarlet as he continued to stare, she said, "Your daughter is sweet and beautiful, a delightful young lady, but no one will give her a chance if you allow her to go about dressed like common Haymarket-ware . . ."

Leaping to his feet, the captain pointed at the door. "Get out, madam. Get out of my house!"

Anne's blue eyes filled with tears—a weakness she had when her anger got the best of her. With a stamp of her foot, she said, "Why, you . . . you stupid man!"

Two weeks passed, and the heads of the neighboring households refused to budge. Marie and Matthew spent hours together, chatting, playing games, and bickering like brother and sister. Though Bastien refused to associate with his attractive neighbor, he did not forbid Marie from doing so. Her conversation became charged with, "Lady Anne says . . ." When he chided her for using her given name, Marie explained that while she was Lady Westhaven because her late husband had been a baron Westhaven, she was Lady Anne in her own right since her father had been an earl.

After this lecture on English titles, Bastien vowed to ignore any and all references to the lady next door.

Bouncing into his study at the end of February, Marie asked, "Papa, it is such a fine day. Do you think we might go for a drive in the park?"

Bastien's face transformed as he looked up from his desk and rested his dark eyes on his beautiful daughter. "An excellent idea, *chérie*. I will order the carriage while you fetch your cloak and bonnet."

Marie hurried out the door, and Bastien ordered the carriage before returning his attention to his company books. Unlike most members of his class, Bastien had chosen to make his own way in the world instead of living in the past. His fleet of ships had a reputation for solidity and punctuality around the world, and though he was temporarily retired, he still kept a close watch on his business.

Closing the ledger, Bastien stretched. The work would be there when he returned. It was February, after all, and one could not afford to waste an afternoon of fine weather at this time of year.

Since Lady Best's card party, Bastien had escorted Marie to several entertainments. Though his father-in-law was too sick to come to town, he had written to all his old cronies, and the invitations were trickling in. Marie had even made the acquaintance of several young people, though she seemed to prefer their neighbor, the sophomoric Matthew.

The door to his study opened, and Pidgeon appeared. "Lord Westhaven has arrived, Captain. I left him waiting in the hall. Should I show him in?"

"No, not today. Marie and I are going for a drive. Tell him I am not . . ."

Pidgeon moved to one side as his young mistress tapped

his shoulder and said brightly, "Look who has come to call, Papa. It's Matthew. I have invited him to join us on our drive."

Bastien looked from his smiling daughter to her new friend and acquiesced. Matthew was two years younger than Marie, and since their first encounter, he seemed to view her more as a sister than . . . Lady Westhaven's words came back to haunt him again. He could still hear them when he looked at Marie and noticed how much of her chest was peering back at him. Haymarket-ware. No, Lady Westhaven was wrong. No one could mistake his sweet, innocent Marie for a bit of fluff.

"Yet another excellent idea, my dear. How are you today, Matthew?"

"I am fine, sir," said the young man.

"No more adventures?"

Matthew turned red and stammered, "No, sir. Not in the past week."

"Good. Perhaps you have learned a valuable lesson."

"Papa, pray do not lecture poor Matthew," said Marie, taking the young man's arm and practically dragging him out the door.

Bastien shook his head and rose, following the chattering duo more slowly. As he passed the butler, he said, "Were we ever that young, Pidgeon?"

"There have been too many years and too many voyages to remember that far back, Captain, but it is good to see Miss Marie so happy." The butler watched fondly as Marie reached up to straighten Matthew's cravat. "She has turned into quite the young lady."

"Aye, that is what worries me," muttered Bastien, stepping more lively when his daughter called to him to hurry up before they lost the sun.

* * *

Bastien took the rear-facing seat in the open carriage, allowing Marie and Matthew to sit opposite him so he could study them both. Matthew was dressed in a fashionable coat of dove gray, his cravat simply tied. He was a handsome youth, with blond hair and blue eyes, like his mother—not that he had noticed such intimate details about the Lady Anne.

Marie wore another new gown, a simple gold color that accentuated her clear complexion and dark coloring. Instead of a cloak, she had donned a cream-colored spencer trimmed with gold braid. It was very becoming, but once again, the cut seemed too daring in her father's eyes.

"Lord Westhaven!"

Bastien turned on the seat to study two young men on horseback. They wore the clothes of dandies, their neckcloths so high they could not turn their heads more than an inch or two. Consequently, they guided their mounts from side to side to keep Matthew in their line of vision, dismissing Bastien's presence as they would a servant.

"How fortuitous that we should meet, Westhaven." The stranger lifted his hat to Marie, his gaze lingering on her longer than necessary. "Yes, quite fortuitous, and not just because you have such a pretty bit of baggage with you."

Bastien cocked his head at Matthew, whose cravat seemed to be choking him. But the boy rose to the challenge, saying, "That's enough, Montgomery, Kilgore. You'll excuse us if we don't stop," said Matthew, nodding to the driver to continue, but the men would not take the hint.

One of them rode to the front of the carriage and blocked the way. Bastien leaned forward, giving the man beside the carriage a hard look.

The man flinched before nodding to Bastien. "Beg pardon, sir." Returning his attention to Matthew, he added, "Didn't know you and your companion had company, Westhaven. We will talk later. Tonight at nine? You know the place."

Tipping their hats to Marie, the two men cantered away, and Bastien signaled to their driver to continue.

Matthew gave Marie a tight smile and laughed. "A couple of old family friends."

"Matthew, are you in some sort of trouble?" asked Marie.

"What? Of course not," he said, patting her hand.

"But those men . . ."

"Marie, one doesn't ask a gentleman to explain his choice of friends," said Bastien. "If Matthew is in need, I am sure he knows he can count on us."

"But I'm not, of course," said the youth. Changing the subject, he asked lightly, "Do you ride, Marie?"

"No, I have not had the opportunity to learn."

"Perhaps your father would allow me to teach you," he said, looking at the captain. "I do not have my own horse, but I am accounted quite good."

"Perhaps," said Bastien, wondering how he could warn the unapproachable Lady Westhaven that her son might be in trouble.

What Matthew really needed was to return to school, but since that was out of the question, he should probably be sent to the country until the next term began. Judging from Lady Westhaven's home and her own garments, the likelihood of her having a country estate to which to send the boy was doubtful.

He forced himself to smile at his charges. Matthew was as tall as he was, but he was gangly like a newborn colt. Marie, of course, was beautiful and graceful—every inch a lady, except that she was still his little girl. Really, they were little more than children.

"Do we have any suitable horses?" Marie was asking.

Bastien shook his head. "I have my own mount, and there is another hack the groom sometimes rides. What if you and I go to Tattersall's, Matthew, and select a couple of likely mounts?"

"That would be wonderful, sir! My father took me there once when I was a little boy, but we were selling our horses, not buying."

"Very well, next week we will go, and we will take along our groom. He has a better eye for horseflesh than I do."

"You shouldn't be so modest, sir," said the boy.

"Not modest. Just truthful. It is not often a sea captain needs a horse. Actually, I may let you ride my gelding. He is a little fresh for me. When we get back to the house, you can put him through his paces." *And give me an opportunity to judge for myself if you are such an experienced horseman as you say,* thought Bastien.

"Really, Captain? Splendid!" exclaimed Matthew, practically bouncing for joy.

"You will be careful, Matthew," said Marie.

"Oh, there is nothing to it. I promise you, I really am accounted quite good with horses, you know."

"Yes, and when he has proven himself to me, and we have purchased a suitably gentle mare for you, Marie, then Matthew will teach you to ride."

"Thank you, Papa! Oh, that means I must have a riding habit. Blue, I think! And a black horse. It must be a black one, Papa!"

Matthew rolled his eyes and said, "Girls. All they think about is clothes."

"That reminds me, Papa. We should be getting home if I am to have enough time to dress for tonight's musicale."

Bastien grinned and winked at the boy. "You heard her, Parker. Time to pick up those ribbons and take us home. We have to get ready for tonight."

At this, Matthew grimaced, and Bastien's thoughts returned to the two young men on horseback. They were too old to be friends of a boy. There had to be some other reason for their interest in him.

One way or another, he would have to find out what

Matthew was up to. Then he would have to discover a way to save the boy without him knowing and without his prickly mother kicking up too much of a fuss.

Children, he thought, shaking his head.

Bloodied and beaten, Matthew collapsed on the ground, willing his attackers to leave him.

"Shoot him."

"Naw, I ain't going t' waste it on him. Besides, they didn't say nothing about killin' the cove."

"But 'e's seen our faces."

"Not so's he'll be able to tell anybody. Not for a while, I'll see to that." The man picked Matthew up by the lapels and shook him.

"Eleven o'clock and . . . 'ere now, who's that!"

"It's the charley, Boyd. Come on!"

With a final kick to his ribs, Matthew's attackers ran down the dark, smelly street, their footsteps mingling with the clacker the watchman used to summon aid.

"Help," groaned Matthew, using all his strength to raise up on one elbow.

He was rewarded by a gruff, "'Ere now, man—why, you're only a boy. Can you stand, lad?"

"I . . . I don't kn . . ."

Unable to speak, Matthew relaxed as his rescuer grabbed him and hefted him over his shoulder. The next thing Matthew saw was a gas streetlight when the burly watchman laid him down on the pavement again.

"You're awake again, eh? We're safe here. Don't know what a fine young gentleman like you was doin' in that hellhole, but you very nearly snuffed it, from the looks o' you."

Matthew moaned as he gingerly probed his swollen eye and bleeding lip. Trying to raise himself on one arm, he groaned and fell back.

"Seem to have broken my arm," he mumbled before swooning once again.

Seconds later, he was roused by someone slapping his cheek.

"Where do you live, boy?"

"Curzon, number . . . 12," he said before returning to blissful oblivion.

Pidgeon opened the door but stood on the threshold, effectively blocking the way.

"Here now, let me pass. I've got your young gentleman," said the watchman, who had been joined by a friend. "He's a long-legged thing. It's taken two of us to get him home."

"There must be some mistake. We don't have . . ." Pidgeon lifted the head of their burden and grunted. "Bring him this way, please."

"He's likely got a broken arm," said the watchman.

Turning, Pidgeon called the footman forward, saying, "Tom, go and find a surgeon for young Matthew."

"Right away, Mr. Pidgeon. Should I go next door first and . . ."

Pidgeon silenced the footman with a glance. "Just do as I say, Tom. The captain will decide that when he gets home. Very well, gentlemen, please follow me," he said, leading the way up the stairs to the small, spare bedroom.

When the watchmen had deposited their load on the narrow bed, Pidgeon pulled out several coins and paid the men before escorting them back to the front door and closing it behind them.

The housekeeper, a gentle soul named Mrs. Reese, appeared at his elbow. "What has happened, Mr. Pidgeon?"

"It seems Lord Westhaven has gotten himself into a bit of a scrape. I have sent for the doctor and settled Master Matthew in the spare room upstairs."

"Should we not send for his mother?" she asked, wringing her hands.

"No, Mrs. Reese. His condition would only upset her. After we have set him to rights, we'll send for her. The morning will be soon enough."

"And the master and mistress?"

"I shall wait up as late as necessary to explain the situation to them when they return. Perhaps you would be so good as to heat some water for the doctor."

"Right away, Mr. Pidgeon."

"How is he?" asked Lady Westhaven, gripping Marie's hand for comfort and looking anxiously from the surgeon to Bastien as they emerged from the sickroom. "May I see him?"

"Of course, but he is probably asleep by now. You mustn't worry, Lady Westhaven. The boy will recover. He should rest for several days, but the arm is merely wrenched, not broken."

"What a relief," said Anne. "Is it safe to move him home?"

"Not tonight. In a day or two, my lady. He has so many cuts and abrasions, he would do well to remain still and give them a chance to begin healing."

"We will be happy to have him, my lady," said Bastien, smiling down at the petite matron.

"Splendid," said the surgeon, pulling on his coat. "I will call again this afternoon. I have given him a dose of laudanum. When he wakes, if he is too uncomfortable, he may have another dose. Mr. Pidgeon knows the proper amount. Good evening, Lady Westhaven, Captain Rocher, miss. I will see myself out."

Pidgeon appeared, carrying a basin of bloody water and tattered clothes. Anne gasped and Bastien took her arm to steady her.

"Marie, why don't you go to bed? You must be exhausted. I'll take Matthew's mother in to see him."

"Yes, Papa."

Bastien led Anne into the dimly lit room and stood back while she hurried to her son's bedside. His swollen and bruised face made her cringe, but she took Matthew's hand and held it, leaning over to kiss his cheek. His eyes fluttered, but remained closed.

"He is so quiet," she whispered.

"In my experience, laudanum will have that effect. We should let him rest," said Bastien, touching her shoulder.

Anne shook off his hand and said, "No, I will sit with him."

"If you will pardon my saying so, my lady, a boy his age would probably prefer to be attended by a male. I will stay with him."

"No, I couldn't ask . . ."

"And you did not," he replied, lifting her hand for a chaste kiss.

It hit her like a bolt of lightning that she was, for all intents and purposes, alone in a bedroom with the handsome captain, and wearing only her nightrail and wrapper. She detached her hand from his and took a step back, happy that the gloom would hide her blush.

The captain must have sensed her embarrassment, for he turned away and walked to the door. "If you will wait here, my lady, I will have a bed made up for you next door. That way you will be close enough to check on Matthew whenever you wish. I will send Tom next door to tell your servants, and to let them know that their young master is going to recover."

"That is very considerate of you, Captain."

Bastien grinned. "I am not always inconsiderate," he replied, leaving her alone to recover from her surprise.

Anne's emotions had been in an uproar since Wiser had

roused her from a sound sleep and told her about Matthew. She had thrown on her wrapper and shoved her feet into slippers before running next door. There, she had been forced to wait with Marie while the doctor examined her son—her little boy.

Now that she knew the danger was past, she felt ready to collapse from exhaustion. She was past making decisions, and allowing the captain to take over felt sinfully lazy—and good, so very, very good.

Anne sat down on the chair beside the bed, resting her elbow on the soft wool counterpane.

"Matthew," she whispered. "What am I to do with you? You are too much like your father—too rash, too foolish." She smoothed a lock of hair from his brow. "When your father died, I thought the desperation was finally at an end. All those nights, wondering how they would end. Would he come home singing and jubilant because his purse was full? Or would he come home angry and dejected, ready to come to cuffs with anyone and everyone? If only you had been a girl, my only worry would have been having enough money to present you."

Anne felt a gentle hand on her shoulder and blushed again. She rose, looking up at the captain's dark, kind eyes.

"We should talk in the morning, my lady. I think it is time we both swallow our pride and become allies."

Anne frowned, her exhaustion fueling her confusion. "I don't know what you mean."

"I think you do," he said, nodding toward the still figure in the bed. "And, though I was too stubborn to admit it before, I now realize I could use some help with my Marie. But it is too late tonight to speak of such things. Let me show you to your bed."

He took her arm and led her next door. The bedroom was full of massive furniture and a cheery fire. The covers on the bed were turned back, warm and inviting. It was his room, his bed.

"Where will you sleep?" she asked breathlessly, peering up at his smiling face.

"Do not trouble yourself, my lady. I can sleep anywhere. Rest well." With this, he kissed her hand and left her, quietly closing the door behind him.

It was foolish of her, staying in his house and taking his bed. But she didn't wish to be too far from Matthew, and this captain, whom she had taken in instant dislike, had taken her feelings into consideration. He had read her mind and hit upon the best solution to her problems. She couldn't recall anyone taking such good care of her since she had wed Westhaven at the age of seventeen.

Climbing into the big bed and pulling the covers up to her chin, Anne sighed. She could grow used to this delicious feeling of security very easily. Inhaling, she could smell the scent he wore, and as she drifted off to sleep, her comfort and his thoughtfulness were irrevocably entwined.

"Good morning, Captain," said Anne, slipping inside Matthew's room. "How is he this morning?"

"Improved, I think. His arm hurts, and he asked for some more laudanum around dawn, so he is still sleeping. I trust you slept well."

"Yes, thank you. The bed was very comfortable," she said, managing not to blush. "I am going home to change, but I wanted to check on Matthew first."

"I will escort you home," he said, rising from the chair and stretching.

Anne's mouth went dry as she watched. He was so very tall and muscular. His black hair was too long to be fashionable, but it was shiny and neat. He ran a hand through it, smiling at her.

Realizing she had been caught staring, Anne stammered, "I hope you did not sleep in that little chair all night, Captain."

"No, I had the cot," he said, pointing to a short, hard bed in the corner. "It is not as uncomfortable as it looks."

"Hmm, but it hardly fits you. Your feet were probably hanging off the end," she said, her blue eyes twinkling.

Laughing, he said, "More than my feet, but as I said last night, I can sleep anywhere. Years on the sea have taught me. You sleep when and where you can, for you never know when your next chance will come."

Taking her arm, he led her out of the room and down the stairs to the front door. Looking down, he inspected her, pulling her cloak more tightly around her and smoothing her long, blond hair. Frowning at the lacy cap she wore, he removed it and reached for the bonnet Marie had left on the hall table.

"Really, Captain, it is not necessary."

"Yes, it is. With your hair down like that, you could pass for my . . . daughter. The wind is howling, and while I do not expect anyone to be about, there are always the neighbors looking out of their windows. We would not wish to become the topic of gossip."

"No, of course not," said Anne, marveling once again at his thoughtfulness.

Opening the door, he poked his head outside and studied the street for a moment before leading her down the steps and along the pavement to her own front door.

Stepping inside, he surprised both Anne and her butler by bowing and kissing her hand again. "I hope you will do me the honor of joining me for breakfast when you have had time to refresh yourself, my lady."

"Why, yes, thank you."

With a nod, he was gone, leaving the old butler to stare expectantly at his mistress.

With a wrinkle of her nose, Anne said, "He is French, you know."

"I am delighted that you consented to breakfast with me, my lady," said Bastien, smiling down at her after seating her at the small, intimate dining table. Taking his seat at the head of the table, he added, "For two reasons. One, I hope we may come to an agreement to help each other."

"And the second?"

He leaned forward and with a conspiratorial smile, said, "Secondly, I hate to eat alone, and what better companion for a man than a beautiful woman?"

His neighbor sat back in her chair, putting as much space between them as she could without leaving her seat.

"Captain Rocher, I am not some green girl who will fall for a handsome face and an interesting accent. I prefer rational conversation over meaningless flattery."

"I see. Then I am sorry, my lady."

"What do you mean?"

Bastien straightened and looked down his aquiline nose at his prickly guest. "I mean that I thought it was the business of gentlemen and ladies to observe the social niceties. If I insulted you with my conversation, then I must apologize."

"No, I . . . I apologize, Captain. You have been nothing but thoughtful and kind. As my excuse, I can only say that I fear it has been too many years since I mingled in Polite Society. I lead a very quiet life."

"But you do know Society, do you not?" he asked.

"Yes. That is, at one time I was accustomed to going about in Society, but that was years ago."

"Why did you abandon it?" he asked, then wished he had not done so as her eyes became shuttered. He reached across the polished mahogany and patted her hand. "Please forgive me. I had no right to ask. I only do so for I have a great favor to ask of you."

"What could I possibly do for you, Captain Rocher?"

"I want you to tutor my daughter, to guide her through her first Season." She was already shaking her head, and he captured her hand, saying softly, "I know it is terribly forward of me to trade on the friendship our children have forged, but I am the father of a motherless girl, and I would do anything to make my Marie a success—to make her happy."

Blue eyes searched dark eyes for a moment. Finally, Anne nodded, saying softly, "Very well, Captain. I will do it. But, Captain, I hope you are not counting on my connections to secure invitations, for I have no connections."

"No, no, my dear Lady Westhaven. Marie's grandfather has smoothed the way for her introductions to influential hostesses. No, I am more interested in your guiding her in her behavior, helping her choose which invitations to accept, engaging a dancing master, and . . ."

"And changing her mode of dress?" asked Anne.

Bastien had the grace to look penitent and nodded. "Especially changing her mode of dress. I know now that I overreacted before when you tried to tell me the truth. I simply had not realized my daughter had such appalling taste."

"Not at all. The colors she chose are wonderful with her coloring. They are not, however, what other young ladies will be wearing. And to be brutally frank, Captain, if she appears in public wearing some of her new gowns, people will have a very wrong impression of her."

"I have begun to realize it, though Marie was quick to point out the gowns of the more mature ladies we have met so far. Then it is settled?"

"Yes, I will be happy to help Marie. She is such a sweet girl. I am already quite fond of her."

"As she is of you, my lady. Whenever she comes back from visiting next door, she is full of 'Lady Anne says . . .' "

"Oh, dear, I hope I have not been too opinionated. I fear I sometimes talk about my son and his propensity for finding trouble. I did not mean to burden Marie with a mother's worries."

"Not at all. She tells me about the lovely lace you make."

"Yes, I . . . I sell it to the dressmaker."

"How enterprising of you," he said, smiling at her with approval. "But you touched on the second part of the bargain I hope to seal with you today."

"What is that?"

"I would like to take Matthew under my wing. I am fond of your son, too, and I see him choosing the wrong path. Yesterday, he went for a drive with me and Marie. We met two young men—rather rough customers, if you ask me. At the time, I thought I should warn him about the company he is keeping, the choices he makes, but I put it off. I feel guilty that he is now lying upstairs, wounded. If I had spoken to him, warned him . . ."

"Do not berate yourself, Captain. I have talked to the boy until I am blue in the face. He simply does not listen."

"But don't you see? If I had your permission to take him in hand, I think it would make a difference."

"You are not going to send him off to sea, are you?"

"No, no. I just think he should learn that carousing all night, drinking too much . . ."

"And gambling. Do not forget to warn him about the gambling. That was why he was sent down from school, and gambling was also his father's downfall. I do not want Matthew going down that same road."

"Nor do I. If you will give me free rein, my lady, I think Matthew might be made to see the errors of his ways. So, you will take Marie in hand, and I will take Matthew?"

Bastien extended his hand to seal the bargain. After only a second's hesitation, Anne took it and gave it a firm shake.

The next part of their bargain meant persuading their two children that this arrangement was for the best. Bastien knew he would have the harder task, convincing the headstrong Matthew that he would one day be thankful for Bastien's dose of discipline. Anne was equally apprehensive about Marie, but she began her campaign of winning over the girl at the most logical place—Mrs. O'Donnell's shop.

Never one to shrink from a difficult task, Anne left Bastien at the breakfast table and sought out Marie immediately. She found her sitting with Matthew.

"Good morning, Mother," said Matthew with a hangdog air.

"Good morning, dear. I am happy to see you are awake. Any pain?"

He flexed his wrenched arm and groaned.

"That's good. Not too much pain. Marie, I wonder if I could drag you away from Matthew for a while. I have asked your father if you could accompany me to Mrs. O'Donnell's."

"Oh, I would love to, my lady."

"Wonderful. It is quite chilly today, so wear something warm. Your father has sent for the coach. It should be here soon so do not dawdle."

"I will be as quick as possible, my lady," said Marie, hurrying away.

Lady Westhaven bent over and kissed her son's brow. "Have a pleasant morning, Matthew."

"Mother, aren't you going to say anything else to me?"

"No, I don't think so."

"But, Mother, aren't you going to lecture me?" he asked, sounding almost hurt by this show of neglect.

"No, I don't think I shall. It has made no difference before, so I have decided to keep my own counsel."

"Really?" he said, grinning as he sank back against the pillows.

"Yes, really," said Anne with a smile. Inside, she was seething. The cheeky, young coxcomb. With an airy, "I will leave you now, dear. Rest well."

"But, Mother . . ."

Anne squeezed his hand and turned away. With a smug smile, she left her son to wonder about her lack of maternal lamentations. The look of bewilderment on his face had been enough to give her the confidence that she had been right to hold back her emotions.

Now, if only the captain could achieve what she had been unable to do in the past six years.

Descending the steps to the front hall, Anne hesitated. There was the captain, deep in conversation with his butler. She had not allowed herself to dwell on his dark eyes and hair, the gestures that were an integral part of his speech. There was something sensual in the way his mouth moved, his lips neither too full nor too thin. Anne suddenly wished she had a fan to cool her flushed face. She cleared her throat, and both men looked up to watch her finish her descent.

He held out his hand and drew her into the drawing room. "Well?"

"Marie will be down in a few minutes to accompany me to the dressmaker's."

"Splendid," he said, his voice soft and smooth. "And, Matthew, you did not tell him of our little plan?"

"No, I decided to leave that to you." Maternal protectiveness took hold, and she lay a hand on the captain's arm, saying, "You will allow him to rest today, will you not?"

His large hand covered hers, and he smiled. "Yes, my dear. I want our Matthew to be quite healthy before I begin my little campaign."

"Good morning, Papa," said Marie. "Has Lady Westhaven told you that she is going with me to the dressmaker's?"

"Yes, and I am happy that you will have a fashionable lady along to advise you, *chérie*."

Anne glanced down at her old gown and cloak. Fashionable? Hardly. She looked into those dark eyes, and suddenly she felt she was the most fashionable, desirable woman in the world. A maidenly blush stole across her cheeks, and she turned away to regain her composure.

"Ah, here is the carriage. Listen to her ladyship, *chérie*, and learn. *Au revoir*."

"Au revoir, Papa."

"Good-bye, Captain Rocher."

"I am going to collapse," moaned Matthew, resting on his shovel.

"Nobody ever collapsed shoveling a bit of manure," said Parker, the old driver who managed the captain's small stable down the back alleyway, behind the town houses.

"That's because you have never seen a gentleman shovel manure," grumbled the youth.

"I have seen th' captain do whatever needed doing—whether it was mucking out a stall or saddling his own horse."

"Perhaps that is because he is not a true gentleman," snapped Matthew, throwing down the shovel and crossing his arms.

"That depends on your definition of a gentleman, I suppose." Bastien's deep voice held a touch of steel, and the boy stepped back.

"I didn't see you come in," he said, ducking his head.

Bastien signaled to the old man to leave them. Then he took up the shovel Matthew had dropped and set to work.

The sullen youth dug his toe into the muck and hunched his shoulders.

"How do you define that word, Matthew?"

"What word?"

"Gentleman. I would be interested in hearing your definition."

"Very well. A gentleman is someone with breeding, someone who does not clean up after horses."

"Hmm. So you are a gentleman because you are Lord Westhaven."

"Exactly."

"Then I must be doing something wrong. You are a baron, according to your title, yes?"

"That's right."

"Since I am only a captain, and I do shovel manure, I cannot aspire to being a gentleman."

"That's . . . no, I did not mean that," said Matthew.

"Oh, well, that is good to know. I have always considered myself a gentleman, you see. Not because of my breeding—though my father was a *duc,* but because I act like a gentleman. I may not have perfectly manicured hands—I mean, in a storm, I am the first one on deck, doing whatever the situation calls for. And I am not above sweeping the stable yard or worse," he added, grinning from the shovel in his hands to his protégé.

"I just do not like you telling me what to do."

"No, I suppose not, but your mother has given me permission, and so have you."

"I have not!"

"Yes, you did. You gave me permission when you gave the watch my address because you knew better than to show up on your mother's doorstep bleeding and maimed."

Bastien fixed Matthew with his steely gaze for a moment. Then he smiled and handed the shovel back to the youth. Matthew accepted it, and Bastien added softly, "Actually, that was when I knew you had the heart of a gentleman, Matthew. You were trying to save your mother's feelings. It was then that I began to view you as a man, rather than a mere boy."

The pouty expression faded, and Matthew smiled.

"Now, get this job done, and then go home and change. We are going to Tattersall's this afternoon."

"Oh, thank you, Captain!"

"No need for thanks. A gentleman keeps his word."

Anne accepted Bastien's invitation to dinner, but even as she did so, she cautioned herself to be on her guard. In the three weeks since they had struck their bargain, she had fallen into the habit of relying on the handsome captain too much. It was unwise of her. He would be gone as soon as Marie was settled. She should not allow herself to become accustomed to his presence, but it was so lovely to have someone to talk to, someone she could depend on.

"Marie and Matthew are late tonight," said Bastien, his deep voice as warm as the firelight.

"He said something about writing a letter to his friends. A first, I might add."

"So did Marie," said Bastien, handing her a glass of wine. "I begin to think they are trying to throw us together."

"Oh, no," breathed Anne.

"Do not be so distressed, my dear Lady Anne. You will hurt my pride."

"No, I did not mean . . . I meant, that it was too bad of them. It is absurd, don't you agree?"

Bastien took her hand between his and held it, staring at it as if he had never seen such an appendage.

"Not so absurd as that, my dear lady. It is not the time, perhaps, but you must admit, we work very well together."

Anne snatched her hand away. His speech came too close to her own secret thoughts, and she could not bear to have him make a game of her.

"Let us not quarrel. Here comes Marie now."

"Good evening, my lady, Papa," said the dark-haired beauty, dipping into a perfect curtsy. She wore a cream-colored gown ornamented by a simple row of tiny silk flowers at the high waist and capped sleeves. Her dark hair was swept up to the crown, captured by another row of pink roses. Her only jewelry was a strand of pearls around her neck.

"You look beautiful, *chérie*," said Bastien.

Marie took the seat beside Anne and reached over to pat this lady's hand.

"Thank you, Papa, but it is all Lady Anne's doing. She is the one who made me realize that I should wear pale colors like all the other young ladies. My bright colors were . . . how did you put it, my lady?"

"I merely pointed out that while Marie may love bright colors, if she wants the young gentlemen to notice her, and not her gowns, then she should dress accordingly."

"I could not agree more," said Bastien. Leaning close to Anne on the pretense of refilling her wineglass, he whispered in her ear, "How very clever of you."

"Where is Matthew? I sent him home with strict instructions to return as soon as he had changed," said Marie. "I think he preens more than I do."

"I am sure he will be with us shortly," said Bastien. "By the way, how are your riding lessons going?"

"It is so much fun, Papa. I never knew how wonderful it would be."

"And do you like the little mare we chose?"

"She is perfect. She looks wonderful, and Matthew says she is very well trained. I just like the fact that she does not go too fast, and that she looks so stylish."

"Ah, and you accuse Matthew of being vain."

"Me, vain? What have you been saying, Marie," asked the boy as he bounded into the room. Belatedly, he remembered to bow to the ladies, but he rounded on Marie immediately.

"Let me tell you what vain is. Miss Rocher would not leave this afternoon until the groom had found a blue blanket for her mare, one that would complement her riding habit."

"But, Matthew, a lady must always look her best in public," said his mother while giving Marie's hand a squeeze.

"I think it is dashed silly that your horse has to dress like you."

"Matthew, my boy, it is a fact of life that we gentlemen will never understand our ladies. You must simply accept that fact and keep quiet about how silly you think it is."

"Well, I . . ."

"Stop your quarreling, children, and let Pidgeon announce dinner," said Anne, nodding to the butler, who was waiting quietly in the doorway of the drawing room.

When they were seated around the small table, Bastien asked, "Guess what arrived in the post today, *chérie*."

"What?" asked Marie.

"Your first invitation to a grand ball."

"Really? When, Papa? And who?"

"Lady Best's daughter, Lady Selwyn is presenting her daughter. It is on Wednesday next."

"How delightful," said Anne. "You will finally be able to meet more young people."

"Yes, I . . . oh, what shall I wear?"

"I think the sprig muslin with the tiny blue flowers that match your eyes. I have the perfect shawl for it. It is packed away, but I will lend it to you."

"This meal is going to degenerate into a fashion discussion," grumbled Matthew, spearing a piece of roast beef and popping it into his mouth.

"But a lady's dress is the most important decision of any ball," said his mother.

Marie made a face at her friend, but her thoughts appeared taken up with some other weighty problem.

"What is wrong, my dear?" said Anne.

"I . . . I have been waiting for this for so long, and now, I am absolutely terrified."

"Nonsense," said her doting father. "You will be the most beautiful young lady at the ball. Thanks to Lady Anne, your manners are excellent, and she tells me that the dancing master was praising your grace only yesterday. You have nothing to worry about."

"Oh, you don't understand, Papa," said the girl, worrying her lower lip and frowning ferociously.

Bastien frowned back, mystified by his daughter's perverseness. Only the day before, she had been speculating when the first ball of the Season would be. Had he not done everything to ensure she would be prepared for this ball? Looking at Anne, he shook his head and sighed.

"It is understandable, Marie, to be a little nervous, but you will be the belle of the ball, I promise," said Anne.

Marie's tears became a reality and her father said, "Be reasonable, *chérie*. You know that we are right."

"Oh, Papa!" she wailed. "It does not help to know these things. I will be at this ball without any friends, any acquaintance." With this, his usually sparkling daughter leapt to her feet and fled.

"Marie, come back here this instant," called Bastien, rising to follow her.

Anne called him back with a word. "Bastien."

The shock of hearing his name on her lips took the wind out of his sails, and Bastien fell silent. His movements slow and deliberate, he turned back to the table.

"Yes, Anne?" he said, giving her an intimate smile that made her squirm.

"I was just going to tell you that I will speak to her. She will be fine."

"Mother is right," said Matthew, his mouth full of food.

"Matthew, I do not need your advice," said the captain.

"But he is right," said Anne. "Please, allow me to speak to Marie."

"I know what would make Marie feel better, Captain," said the boy, putting down his fork. The two adults looked at him in surprise, but Matthew was not discomfited.

"Marie would feel much better if you would go to the ball with her and the captain, Mother."

"What? Impossible!" exclaimed his mother, turning to Bastien for validation, but he remained strangely silent.

"Don't you see, Mother? Marie has come to depend on you for everything, and now, suddenly, she is to strike out on her own without you?"

"I think Matthew may have something there, Anne."

"Nonsense," she snapped, glaring first at her son and then the captain. "Besides, even if it were true, I cannot possibly attend this ball. First of all, I was not invited."

"I can arrange that," said Bastien.

"Secondly, I have nothing to wear. Any gown I had that would have been suitable was given away years ago."

"Why can you not have something made?" asked her son. "You are always having clothes made up for me. I think it is your turn, Mother."

Tears sprang to her eyes, robbing her of speech, so Anne shook her head vehemently.

"It is short notice, but I feel certain Mrs. O'Donnell could make up something in a week's time," said Bastien.

"She would do it for you, Mother. I mean, you're always making that lace for her."

"Matthew, there is a great deal of difference in a new coat for you and a ball gown."

"Now you are being unreasonable, Anne," said the captain.

"I am being unreasonable? You . . . I . . . oh, never mind," said Anne, rising and fleeing the dining room, too.

"Women! I will never understand them," said Bastien, shoving away from the table.

"It isn't that Mother wouldn't like to accompany you and Marie, Captain."

"Then please tell me what the problem is, Matthew, for I do not understand at all."

"It is the money. My mother probably has not had a new gown of any sort in the past six years, perhaps longer. Mostly my fault, I suppose. I guess school is rather expensive, and all she has is a small annuity from her father and what she is paid for that lace she is always making."

"The money? Why, I never meant that she should pay for the gown herself."

"Perhaps not, Captain, but you didn't say that. What's more, I am not at all certain my mother would accept such a gift from you."

"Hmm, you may be right. Well, we shall simply have to convince her," said Bastien.

Pidgeon entered with the second remove and stood looking at the empty seats for a moment before entering with the heavy tray.

"Go ahead and serve Master Matthew, Pidgeon. I have some ruffled feathers to smooth."

Bastien left the room to search for his guest. He found her back at her own house, sniffling into a lace handkerchief. He suppressed his smile when she whipped the scrap of lace behind her back and attempted to appear unaffected.

"Anne," he said, sitting beside her on the delicate sofa and taking her hand. "I have been a beast."

He had her attention now.

"I should have asked you, pleaded with you, for Marie's sake, to accompany us to this ball. You have helped her in so many ways—her dress, her manners, everything. I have done nothing, and yet, I ask her to go to this ball without you. Of course she is frightened."

"You meant well," said Anne, sniffling one last time.

"Ah, well, what does a poor father know about a daughter's feelings?"

Had he overplayed his hand? Those blue eyes—brighter than ever by her recent bout of tears—were regarding him with suspicion. A slight frown, full of fatherly confusion. Yes, that did the trick.

"So you see, I must beg you to reconsider—not only for Marie's sake, but for my sake, too. I want to make my little girl happy, and without you, she is not at all happy."

"I want Marie to be happy, too, Bastien. She is such a dear girl—the closest thing to a daughter I shall ever have."

"Then please, will you not attend the ball with us?"

"Oh, Bastien, look around you. How can I ever . . ."

"I will go to Mrs. O'Donnell's shop as soon as it opens in the morning and arrange everything. All you need to do is choose your gown."

He waited while she weighed her pride against her desires. Finally, she smiled, and Bastien breathed a sigh of relief.

"I am very grateful to you, Anne."

"Thank you, Bastien. It is kind of you to say so."

"Won't you come back and dine with us—if Matthew has left anything for us, that is."

"No, I cannot. I have no appetite."

"Very well. Then I will leave you and go tell Marie the wonderful news."

"Ask her if she would like to go with me in the morning."

"I know she will. I will have the carriage brought around at eleven o'clock." He lifted her hand to his lips, whispering, "Thank you again, *ma belle.*"

When he had gone, Anne touched her hand to her lips, closing her eyes and wondering what it would be like to kiss . . . no, she could not allow herself to have such fancies. The arrangement she had with Bastien—the captain, she amended—was more of a business affair. He was bartering his services as a father to Matthew for her services as a mother to Marie.

Business. That was all it was, and she would keep telling herself that all night, if necessary!

"I will have something dark and conservative, Mrs. O'Donnell. And inexpensive," added Anne for good measure.

Behind her, Marie signaled the dressmaker with a wink and a shake of the head.

"Of course, my lady. Whatever you say," said the seamstress, having been schooled by the handsome Captain Rocher to send all bills to him and to be certain that the Lady Westhaven ordered a complete wardrobe, suitable for her station as confidante and chaperon of his daughter.

Three hours later, Anne was still reeling from shock at the size of her order. Each time she had tried to curtail the enthusiasm of her young charge and the seamstress, she was somehow outvoted. In the end, there had been several ball gowns, carriage dresses, morning gowns, and even a satin cape lined with fur and a matching muff.

Not only did she have gowns, she had all the accoutrements to go with them because Mrs. O'Donnell, warned by the captain, had prepared well for their visit and had called in her neighbors, a talented milliner and an expert shoemaker.

When they arrived home, Anne went immediately to the captain's study to explain her extravagance.

"My dear Lady Anne," he began, pulling her into the room and seeing her seated on the soft leather sofa. "How good of you to call. I have been looking over these invitations and cannot decide which ones to accept. I hope you will help me. I am afraid I will choose the wrong ones, and make a terrible faux pas. For instance, should I accept this one? It is a masqued ball."

"Captain Rocher, I have not come to help you with invitations. That is . . . No, you should not take Marie to a masqued ball; she is far too innocent and inexperienced for such a gathering."

"You see, Anne. I knew you would know."

"Bastien, I am happy to assist you, but what I came to tell you is that somehow . . . that is . . . oh, Bastien, things went terribly awry at the dressmaker's today."

He clasped her hands and asked with as much drama as she had, "Awry? Did Mrs. O'Donnell not have any fabric suitable for you? Or was it that she could not have the gown made in time? She assured me that it would not pose a problem."

"No, no, that is not the problem. And the cloth was wonderful—all of it. But that was the problem. I do not know quite how it happened. Marie kept insisting, and Mrs. O'Donnell . . . but there, I must not blame them. I must place the blame where it belongs, squarely on my own shoulders. Oh, Bastien, I ordered so many gowns!" she said, covering her face with her hands.

Chuckling, he pulled her hands away and produced his handkerchief to dab away her tears.

"Do you mean, my dear Anne, that you ordered enough ball gowns and morning gowns, and whatever else you may require, in order to be my daughter's chaperon for the Season?"

Anne hiccoughed and nodded.

Taking her hands again, he kissed first one and then the other. Not on the back, but on the palm—an intimate gesture that took her breath away.

Still holding her hands, he said, "Then you have done just as you ought, just as I hoped."

"I will pay you back somehow," she vowed, unwilling to extract her hands.

"Yes, that is already agreed to, my dear. You will act as a mother to my poor, motherless child. And perhaps later, when this Season is over . . . but there, I do not wish to complicate things further at this point. Suffice it to say that you are doing me such an invaluable service that I would give anything to repay you. A few gowns? That is nothing."

"Oh, Bastien, you are too kind," she said, her tears coming anew. "I have never been so happy."

Then he took her into his arms, resting his chin on the top of her head, and Anne knew that her happiness was only beginning.

The ball that had caused such consternation was only the beginning of Marie's successful Season. Though her best friends had not yet arrived in London, she renewed friendships with other young ladies from school, and these led to more introductions. Quickly, Marie found herself surrounded by new friends, both male and female.

Standing at the edge of the ballroom, Bastien and Anne watched proudly.

"She is the loveliest girl in the ballroom," said Anne, smiling up at him.

He nodded, saying, "Yes, though I think we must agree that we may be slightly prejudiced on the subject. Still, her gown and her manners are perfect, and I know whom I should thank for that, my dear Anne."

"It has been a pleasure, Captain."

"Bastien, surely."

"Not in public, Captain."

"Very well, my lady. Ah, just what I have been waiting for," he said, putting his hand to his ear.

"What is that?"

"A waltz," he replied, turning and giving her a gallant bow. "Will you do me the honor?"

"Oh, I . . . I don't know. I really haven't practiced, except a time or two with Marie's dancing master."

"I am sure you will give a creditable performance," he said, taking her hand and leading her onto the ballroom floor without further discussion.

Bastien was right. Anne's natural grace allowed her to follow his lead without faltering for a second.

"It is as if you have been waltzing all your life," he said with a warm gaze. "With your grace and your beauty in that gown, you put the other ladies to shame."

Anne lifted her face; her blue eyes meeting his were alight with some emotion he had never seen there before. She shook her head, and he realized she was near tears.

Perplexed, he said softly, "Whatever have I said, my dear."

She shook her head and dropped her chin.

"I am just being silly," she whispered. "It has been so long since anyone has paid me a compliment—unless you count Mrs. O'Donnell, who compliments me on the lace I make," she added with a wry grin. The witticism erased the threat of tears, and her blue eyes began to dance.

"Oh, there was also the time that Matthew asked me why I was acting like a witch when I did not look like one."

Laughter rumbled deep in Bastien's chest. "I suppose every parent receives that sort of compliment. Once, when I had refused Marie some treat, she mumbled something under her breath about sea captains and ogres. Needless to say, she never did receive whatever treat she had begged for."

"But she is so sweet," said Anne.

"She also has her mother's temper."

"Not yours?" she teased.

"I protest! I am ever even-tempered."

"Not according to Matthew," she said with a chuckle.

"No, I feel certain our Matthew thinks I am the devil incarnate."

"A bit strong, perhaps. More like a slave driver, but please, do not let that deter you. I find him much improved since you undertook his . . . tutelage."

"I am not at all certain that he has learned his lessons, but he is too tired from all the physical labor to indulge in his less savory pastimes."

"Whatever the reason, Captain, we have made a good team."

"Tonight is only beginning," he said, sweeping her into a dizzying twirl. Looking over Anne's head, he waved at Marie, who did not yet have permission to dance the waltz and was waiting with a group of other young ladies and their swains.

"She looks so much like Claire."

"Your wife?"

"Hmm," he said, smiling down at Anne.

"Marie told me her mother died when she was only six. What happened?" she asked.

"It was my fault, I suppose. Claire wanted to go with me on one last voyage before our second child was born. I should have refused, but I never could refuse Claire. There was a terrible storm, an unseasonable storm. It was so cold, I remember thinking I would never get warm. We were so worried about Marie, who always sailed with us, but as it turns out, it was Claire who caught the fever. Then suddenly, the baby was coming. She was already so weak. She—they—did not survive."

"I am terribly sorry, Bastien," said Anne, tears springing to her eyes. "It was a boy, Marie said."

Nodding, he lifted the hand he held to his lips and kissed it. "It has been years now. I rarely think of that time, and I would not have brought it up now if you had not asked. I would much rather tell you how beautiful you look in the candlelight."

"Do you want me to cry again?" she teased, using humor to cover her tears over his sad story.

"No, Anne, I would never want that," he said, looking around them suddenly as the music came to a close. As he escorted her from the floor, he said loudly, "Sometimes, my lady, we must show the young people that we still have a dance or two left in us."

A flicker of a frown crossed her brow before she realized the reason for this remark. Their behavior on the floor, when the world had seemed to fade away, had not gone unnoticed.

Taking her cue, Anne smiled as they met their hostess. "A charming ball, Lady Selwyn. Wherever did you find such talented musicians?"

"I have my sources," said this lady. "I have not seen you for years, dear Lady Anne. Where have you been keeping yourself?"

Lady Selwyn linked arms with Anne, leading her away from Bastien to grill her for information.

"More importantly, where have you been keeping the charming captain? Trying to keep him all to yourself?"

Anne shook her head and managed a casual, "Captain Rocher? No, we are merely neighbors. I met his charming daughter and agreed to rejoin Society for dear Marie's sake. She has no one else to guide her, you know."

"Hmm, needs someone to act as her stepmama," purred Lady Selwyn. "How convenient."

Anne knew that to deny this allegation would only add fuel to the fire. Smiling, she waved toward a knot of people and said, "If you will excuse me. I must greet an old friend."

With this, Anne faded into the crowded ballroom, vowing to herself that there would be no more intimate dances with the dangerous captain—no matter how much she had enjoyed being in his arms. For Marie's sake, she and Bastien would have to remain above suspicion.

It would be a very long Season.

It was as Anne had predicted. Marie's beauty and grace set her apart from the rest and soon she was being hailed as one of the Season's diamonds of the first water. Bastien often found himself tripping over callers, both handsome young gentlemen and giggling young ladies.

Anne's vow to keep her distance from Bastien, at least when in company, proved impossible. Marie was forever sending for her to act as chaperon when she had callers. And with Bastien there, Anne could not help but be aware of him. And he, of her.

There were no more waltzes, of course, but there were gazes and conversations—enough to cause speculation among Marie's new friends and their parents.

Anne took her job seriously. If she was to allow Bastien to supply her with a new wardrobe, the least she could do was to be a good chaperon. She spent her time at the balls gathering information about the young gentlemen who paid particular attention to Marie. Then she would advise her charge accordingly. Marie was very cooperative in all this because, as Anne explained to a relieved Bastien, her heart was not yet engaged.

"How can you tell?" he asked while having breakfast together one morning after attending the theater. It was a routine they had fallen into, breaking their fast together each day to discuss the previous evening and the evening to come.

"How can I tell what?" asked Anne, handing him a cup of tea.

"How can you tell if her heart is engaged? For that matter, how can anyone tell when another person's heart is engaged?"

Anne chuckled. "There are signs, certainly, but to me, the main sign with Marie is that she has not balked when I have advised her to discourage certain gentlemen."

"But what about the others, the ones you think she should encourage?" he asked, watching her over his cup of strong black coffee.

"I had not thought of that. I suppose she might be growing fond of one of them."

"Then I ask you, if a lady is growing fond of a particular gentleman, what signs might there be?"

"I suppose a lady is more likely to laugh at his witticisms. She might smile a little more when he speaks, listen a little more closely."

"Would a lady allow him to take her hand and kiss it?" asked Bastien, taking Anne's hand and placing a light kiss on it.

"Perhaps, but I would certainly caution against allowing him that liberty," said Anne, extracting her hand. "After all, such a man is perhaps a little too practiced in his ability to attract a lady."

"Hmm, I see your point. What about him? Might he give her speaking looks?" Bastien leaned forward and gazed into her eyes, never blinking.

Anne giggled and wagged a finger under his nose. "You, sir, are incorrigible."

"That is because you, my dear Anne, fail to encourage me."

"But we were speaking of Marie, were we not?"

"If you insist," said Bastien with a sigh.

"Really, Bastien, I think Marie is sensible enough to settle on someone worthy. If she does settle on someone before the Season's end, it will be because her heart is engaged."

"Yes, I suppose so. And when she chooses, our work will be done." He sat back, frowning slightly.

"Oh!" breathed Anne, realizing for the first time what Marie's betrothal would mean to her, to them. There would be no more cozy chats, no more appreciative glances across the ballroom floor. Bastien would go back to his ships, and she would be alone again.

"Anne, I have been thinking. When Marie does . . ."

"Still talking about Marie," said Matthew, stepping into the small dining room.

"Among other things. Where are you going so early, Matthew?" asked his mother, her voice tight with emotion.

"I am going for a ride. I thought Marie might wish to join me. She has not practiced for ages."

"She is still sleeping," said his mother. "Later, she is going to pay calls with Miss Kirkpatrick and her mother."

"I wouldn't mind going for a ride," said Bastien.

Brightening at this, Matthew said, "Very well, Captain. I will go to the stables and get the horses."

"Our children are very demanding," said Bastien, climbing to his feet and smiling down at Anne. "Still, we should not complain, eh? As we were saying, they will be grown and gone before too long—even Matthew. *Au revoir, chérie.*"

Anne watched him walk out of the dining room, her heart pounding in her chest. She wanted to tear at her hair and scream, but she could not. She was Lady Anne—reasonable, forgiving, dull. Her heart could not possibly be breaking over the thought of one Captain Rocher walking out of her life, never to return. And with him would go Marie—her Marie.

Anne paced the length of the small room, but it could not hold her. Throwing her shawl over her shoulders, she left the house and went home, marching through the long hall and into the garden. Though the sun was out, it was quite cold, but Anne didn't even notice. Around and around the small garden she went, muttering under her breath. Pausing beside the cold stone bench, she looked back at the path and grinned. If anyone had been watching, she must have looked like the wild lions she had seen once at the Tower of London. At this thought, Anne dropped down on the bench and began to laugh. She became so tickled, she could hardly breathe at all. Finally, by taking short, shallow breaths, she regained her composure.

"This will never do," she announced firmly. Rising and smoothing her gown, she returned to the house.

She had too much to do to waste her time with maudlin nonsense. Marie had asked that she come over and help her choose a suitable gown for her calls. She had to finish some lace for Mrs. O'Donnell, and Mrs. Helper would need help with the menu because she had invited Bastien and Marie to dine with her and Matthew that evening.

No, wasting time on daydreams and might-have-beens was not on her schedule for the day.

March turned into April, and the Season was in full swing. While Marie continued to be a great success, she did not appear to single out any particular gentleman for her favors. Indeed, Anne worried that she might earn the reputation of being fickle if she never singled anyone out.

When Marie's schoolgirl friend Anthea Kirkpatrick was honored at her grandmother's house—a large, palatial mansion on the Thames—Anne's fears were realized. There were hundreds of guests at the alfresco breakfast. Huge striped tents had been erected with wooden floors for the ball that would take place when the sun went down.

Several of the young men, who admired Marie and her friends, began betting on which ones would be granted two dances by the dark-haired beauty. Bastien overheard their conversation and immediately sought Anne's advice.

Horrified, Anne hurried to find Marie. A word in her

ear, and Marie announced loudly that since they had decided to make game of her, she would not dance with any of them. The dozen young men, who regularly clustered around Marie and her friends, protested vehemently. Finally, Marie agreed that each of them would have two dances so that none of them would feel left out.

"I fear my daughter is a scapegrace," whispered Bastien, his lips close to Anne's ear.

"I couldn't agree more," announced Lady Selwyn, stepping around him and glaring at Anne. "I am surprised at you, Lady Anne. I would have thought, as her chaperon, that you would have trained her better than that."

Anne's eyes blazed. "You are only jealous because your daughter is not a part of Marie's entourage." And she has spots, thought Anne, but she was wise enough to keep this observation to herself.

Bastien stepped between the two ladies. Facing Lady Selwyn, he smiled and asked, "How is your dear mother? I have not seen Lady Best tonight. I do hope she is not ill."

"No, she is fine," said the sour matron.

"I am glad. You will give her my best, will you not?" he said, turning back to the fuming Anne and leading her onto the pavilion for the dance that was forming.

"A powerful hostess, Lady Selwyn," he said.

Biting her lower lip, Anne said, "Yes, and a terrible gossip, too. I am sorry, Bastien. I hope my show of temper has not harmed Marie."

"As if it could. If Lady Selwyn's spotted daughter had any sort of personality, she would be as popular as our Marie. That she is not . . . well, it is not our affair."

Her good humor restored, Anne turned her attention to the pleasure of taking his hands and dancing down the middle of the line.

* * *

Several days passed, and Anne had forgotten the incident at the alfresco breakfast when Wiser knocked on her bedroom door and said quietly, "Lady Selwyn has called, my lady. I have put her in the drawing room."

Anne grimaced and said, "Very well, Wiser. Tell her I will be with her shortly." She checked her image in the mirror and grunted. She was wearing one of her old gowns, but that couldn't be helped. It would take too long to change.

"My dear Lady Anne," said Lady Selwyn, holding out two fingers for a light shake. "How good of you to receive me. I was afraid I would not find you at home. I started to call at Captain Rocher's house instead, thinking you would probably be there."

As Anne took a seat and arranged her skirts, she smiled sweetly and said, "Why ever would you do that, Penny?"

Lady Selwyn pursed her lips and said primly, "I have not used that appellation since I married Lord Selwyn, my dear. We are not in school anymore, Lady Anne."

"Indeed not. We have long since buried any schoolgirl grudges and friendships," said Anne.

"Still, it is that old friendship that has brought me here today."

"Oh?"

"Yes, I came to . . ." The lady looked about her as if expecting to spy some eavesdropper. Lowering her voice, she said, "I have come to warn you, my dear."

"Warn me?"

"Yes, about what is being said behind your back by some members of the *ton*."

"Surely you are mistaken. I cannot imagine why anyone would bother to speak of me, Lady Selwyn," said Anne, squaring her shoulders and glaring at her visitor. "I hardly think that a poor widow would attract such attention."

"No, you wouldn't think so," breathed the dame. Then she gave that smug smile again and continued. "However, when the poor widow's name is linked so closely with such an intriguing, wealthy widower . . . well, you can see the conclusions people might draw. Not me, of course, for I know you too well."

"Of course," murmured Anne, wishing her tendency to blush would not pronounce her guilt so plainly. "Precisely what is being said?"

"Only that you and the good captain are always in company. And someone—forgive me, I cannot recall who it was—speculated on whether the captain was around before your son was born. They are both, after all, quite tall, are they not?"

Anne rose, signaling the end of the visit. "You may tell whoever is talking, my dear Lady Selwyn, that their speculations are ridiculous. Anyone who knew my husband could tell he was Matthew's father. What's more, I met Captain Rocher only recently and there is nothing between the good captain and me—nothing at all. We are neighbors."

"Certainly, my dear. *I* know that is all there is to it. But since there was no family connection, and you are bringing out his daughter. Well . . ."

Taking a deep breath to keep her temper in check, Anne said evenly, "Marie has no mother. I have no daughter. By acting as her chaperon, I was hoping to help her find her place in Society."

"An unselfish—no, a noble act, to be sure," said Lady Selwyn.

"Yes, just like your coming here to warn me," murmured Anne.

Stiffening, Lady Selwyn bade her good-bye and marched out of the drawing room.

As she heard the front door close, Anne collapsed on the sofa, calling, "Wiser, bring me a glass of sherry."

* * *

"We will have to be even more circumspect, Bastien," Anne told him after dinner that night. Marie and Matthew were in the corner, building a house of cards, but she kept her voice low. No need to alarm Marie, she thought.

"I do not see how we can behave any more properly," he replied quietly. "We do not dance at the balls. We sit together at the theater, but that is because it is a box."

"But we always arrive and leave in the same carriage," she whispered.

"So what are you suggesting? That I should walk when my carriage is already taking you and my daughter?" he demanded.

"Shh." With a glance at their children, who were bickering over where to place the next card, Anne said, "It is perfectly proper for you to escort Marie, and she is confident enough now that she does not really need me around."

"But I need you, Anne," he growled. "How do you think I am surviving all these endless balls and routs and such? It is only because afterwards, I know we will sit here together and discuss the evening—share our tales of the funny headdresses, the primping dandies. That is what has made this whole Season bearable."

"I thought it was for Marie," said Anne, smiling up at him.

How could she possibly refuse him anything? She was only postponing heartache, she knew, but she could not help herself. How could she give up a single moment of time with him? Too soon he would be gone. She would deal with her own foolish heart then.

"Oh, perhaps I will . . ."

She was interrupted by a loud groan from the corner, and Matthew said, "I told you that would topple it!"

"And I suppose your putting your sleeve on it had nothing to do with it."

"I did not!"

"Oh, do not be so childish," said Marie, rising and joining Anne on the sofa. Her nose in the air, she intoned, "Children."

"They can be a trial," said Anne, having to work at keeping her face straight. Looking past Marie, she smiled at Bastien, whose brows were drawn together in a fierce scowl.

Before Anne could tell him that she had decided to throw caution to the wind and continue their arrangement, Bastien said, "Marie, Lady Anne thinks that now you are more comfortable, we can dispense with her services as chaperon."

Anne turned to Marie to gauge her reaction. Dark blue eyes grew wide and began filling with tears.

"You do not wish to accompany me to the balls anymore?"

"No, I did not say that exactly, my dear," said Anne, patting the girl's hand. "You do not need me anymore, of course, but . . ."

"Not . . . need? Of course I need you! I . . . I wouldn't know what to think if I didn't have you to . . ." Marie pulled her hand away and stood up. "I would like to go home, Papa. I do not wish to impose any longer."

"Marie, that is not the proper way . . ."

Ignoring her father, Marie walked to the door.

Anne restrained him with a light touch. "Let me speak to her alone, Bastien."

"Marie, come back here immediately," said her father. "Matthew, come with me."

"But where are we going, sir?"

"Into the garden."

"But it's raining," said the boy, hunching his shoulders and watching the captain disappear down the hall. "Oh, all right."

"Marie, please come back and sit down," said Anne. "I should explain."

Marie shuffled her way back to the sofa and sat down, her eyes never leaving the carpets.

"I do not want you to think that I . . . that I have not enjoyed our time together."

Marie glanced up. Smiling, Anne pulled a lace-trimmed handkerchief from her pocket and wiped a tear from the girl's cheek.

"In truth, the past two months have been the best time I have ever had. Having you to dress, to talk to, to . . . mother. I cannot imagine loving a daughter more, nor can I recall ever being so happy."

"That is what I thought, too. Please, my lady, do not abandon me now. I still need you."

"Yes. I can see that you do, and truth to tell, I need you, too."

They hugged, and the world was right again. Except, thought Anne, that her own reputation would be in tatter's by Season's end. Still, what did that matter? When the Season was over, and Marie was married, and Bastien was gone, she would disappear again. The *ton* would then have no reason to shred her reputation.

"Can . . . can we come back in now?" asked Matthew from the doorway.

"Of course," said his mother. "Come in and dry out by the fire. You, too, Captain."

"Thank you, my lady, but I think Marie and I should be going. After all, we elected to stay home tonight because we needed to rest."

Marie rose and leaned over to kiss Anne's cheeks. "Good night."

"Good night, my sweet."

Matthew turned from the fire and said, "Good night, Marie. We will go riding in the morning if the rain stops."

Anne watched as Bastien led his daughter away. Lost in thought, she failed to notice that Matthew had slipped away, too. The front door closed a second time, and she was alone.

"You look dreadful," said Marie when she and Matthew were away from the head groom's watchful eyes the next morning.

"Thank you so much for the compliment," said the youth, shifting the reins into one hand and rubbing his bloodshot eyes with the other. "I did not get much sleep."

"I don't see why not. We left your house quite early."

"I went out," he mumbled.

"Matthew, I thought you had quit going to those disreputable haunts."

"I did, for a while," he said. "What else am I supposed to do with my time? You, your father, and my mother are always off at a ball or a musicale or something. A fellow cannot sit at home every night. Besides, I missed my friends."

"Friends like the ones who had you beaten senseless when you couldn't pay your debt?"

"I paid it—eventually." Matthew thought of the purse Bastien had given to him to pay off his attackers. He glanced down at his calloused hands—evidence of the work he had been doing to repay the captain.

"Look, Marie, I did not ask you to go riding so we could talk about my bad habits. I asked you because I need your help."

"Anything, Matthew—except lending you money, for I do not intend to fund your bad habits."

"No, no, nothing like that." He glanced around to be certain the park was still deserted. "Are you going to be married at the end of this Season?"

"Matthew, if you are asking if I will wait for you . . ."

"Are you dicked in the nob? Why the devil would I want that!"

"You need not be insulting, Matthew," said Marie.

"Well, of all the addlepated notions! Me marry you? Why . . . that would be like marrying my own sister!"

"Oh, Matthew, how sweet," she said, reaching out and patting his shoulder.

"Yes, well, that is what I wanted to talk to you about."

"I don't understand."

"That is because you were not listening at the door when Lady Selwyn called."

"Matthew, you should not eavesdrop."

"Devil a bit," he said. "Do you want to hear what I heard or not?"

"Oh, very well, if it will help you get to the point," said Marie, her nose completely out of joint.

"It seems our parents are at the center of some very nasty gossip." He paused to make certain he had her full attention. She let the reins drop, and he grabbed them. "Pay attention, Marie. Even a sleepy mare like Midnight will take advantage if you don't keep a firm hold. That's better. Now, back to my story. Lady Selwyn said everyone thinks that my mother and your father are . . ."

"Yes? Are what?"

"Argh, why must females be such widgeons? People are saying that they are more than friends." At her continued bewilderment, he said slowly, "Much more than friends."

"Oh." Eyes widening, Marie gasped. "Oh! But that is ridiculous. Your mother is only acting as my chaperon."

"And why, people wonder, would she do that when you are not even related? People think there is something havey-cavey about that."

"But, Matthew, it is like we were related. I mean, your mother is the only mother I have known since mine died. I . . . I love her as if she were really my mother."

"I know that. And despite your father's rather heavy-handed ways, I like him. He has certainly taken more of an interest in me than my own father ever did."

"So that is why your mother wanted to stop being my chaperon. But, Matthew, this is awful," said Marie, who had had the horrors of being ruined drilled into her only too well. "We must do something."

Matthew expelled an exasperated sigh and said, "Which is exactly why I asked you to come riding with me."

"Of course. What did you have in mind?"

"Here is my plan. I think our parents ought to be more than friends. I think they ought to be husband and wife!"

"Matthew, what a perfectly splendid idea!"

"Thank you," he said, bowing back and forth as if on stage.

"There is only one problem. I know they are friends, but I do not think they love each other."

"What does love have to do with it? I tell you, Marie, we will have to do something drastic to make them see what a perfect family we would make."

"But what can we do? They are so reasonable, so self-possessed, they will never do something so rash."

"Precisely. If we leave things in their hands, the Season will be over, you will be the one betrothed, your father will go back to sea, and before I know it, I will be back at school. So we must act fast. Next Friday night."

"Friday? But we are to go to Vauxhall that night—with Lady Best and her family, and that means Lady Selwyn. It is opening for the first time this year."

"I know, and I have been invited to go, too. That is why it is the perfect time to launch my plan. While we are at the pleasure gardens, you and I will get lost in the darkened pathways," said Matthew, giving her a knowing wink.

"Oh, Matthew, this sounds a little risky."

"Don't worry. My friend Benny Bolton will be waiting with a carriage to whisk us away. Mother will be hysterical, and your father will be forced to comfort her. Don't you see. They will realize they should be together and once their betrothal is announced, there will be no more gossip!"

"Matthew, I don't know."

"Nothing will go wrong. I promise you, Marie, by the time they find us, they will have realized how much they need each other."

Dressed in a bronze watered silk gown that set off her coloring perfectly, Anne was ready to face the evening at Vauxhall. It had not been her choice to spend an entire evening in such close proximity with her old school rival, Lady Selwyn, but the invitation had been accepted before that lady had revealed her latest machinations. Anne would have remained at home this one evening, but Matthew was going, too, having been included because of the family nature of the party.

"Mother, are you ready?" asked Matthew. "The carriage is just pulling up."

"Yes, I am ready. My, you look very handsome tonight."

"It is a new coat."

"Oh, Matthew, we cannot afford it."

"It is a present from the captain."

"How thoughtful of him. I do hope you thanked him properly."

"Certainly; I am not a child."

When they reached the carriage, Marie was already inside, but Bastien waited to help Anne ascend.

Taking her hand, he said, "You look radiant tonight, my lady."

"Thank you, sir. And you are looking very handsome yourself. Did you also purchase a new coat for the occasion?"

"Ah, so Matthew told you about that. It was nothing. He has worked so hard, you know."

Bastien climbed up and signaled to Parker to drive along.

"How long will it take to get there, Papa?"

"Not long. We will go by way of Westminster Bridge. I hope you will be warm enough with that silk shawl. I tried to get her to take something heavier. It may be the first of May, but the nights are still chilly."

"But this shawl is so pretty, Papa," said Marie with a pout. "It is Lady Anne's, you know."

"Yes, I remember when she let you borrow it. You should have returned it."

"It was a gift," said Anne, smiling at Marie and then at Bastien. "We are all looking very fine this evening. You will love the fireworks display, Matthew. It has been years since I went, but I still remember how thrilling it was."

When they arrived at the famous pleasure gardens, Matthew took Marie's arm and led her quickly down the path, putting some distance between them and their parents.

"Is everything ready?" she whispered.

"Yes. I spoke to my friends again this afternoon. They were having trouble finding a carriage big enough to hold us all, so they are asking someone else to help out."

"But I will be home before morning, right?"

"Yes, just like I told you. We'll stay just long enough to throw our parents together for the night. Shh. Here they are."

When the dancing began, Bastien rose and crossed to the back corner of the box, where Lady Selwyn had seated Anne. Anne looked up with a smile, grateful for the interruption of her tedious conversation with Lord Hepplewhite, Lady Best's rascally brother.

Sketching a shallow bow, Bastien said, "May I have the honor of this dance, Lady Anne?"

She gave an imperceptible shake of her head and glanced at Lady Selwyn, who was puffing up like a peacock.

Bastien leaned closer and added, "I don't care if I have to dance with every female in this demmed box in order to get you to say yes."

Lord Hepplewhite, who pretended to be hard of hearing, elbowed her and winked. "Go on, my dear. He seems very determined."

"Oh, very well," said Anne, rising and excusing herself as Bastien took her hand and led her through the chairs.

When they were dancing under the stars, Anne asked, "Are you really going to dance with all the other ladies in our box?"

He gave her an impudent grin and shook his head. "I don't have to now that I have you in my arms."

With this, Bastien twirled her around, moving ever closer to the edge of the dance floor. Suddenly, they were on the grass, their steps silent as the noise of the crowd faded away.

When they could no longer hear the music, Bastien stopped, looking down into her eyes. By the moonlight, he could see the curve of her lips. His head dipped, and he pressed his lips to hers.

"Bastien, we shouldn't," she breathed.

"Then don't," he murmured, kissing her again.

She held back for a moment, then mumbled, "Oh, Bastien," and gave in to her desires.

Several moments later, another couple passed by, laughing coarsely and making rude sounds.

Leaning his forehead against hers, Bastien said, "We should go back now. We will talk later."

Anne nodded and allowed him to escort her back to the box. Bastien smiled sweetly at Lady Selwyn, but he neglected to ask anyone else to dance.

Dancing under the stars was romantic, but Marie had difficulty concentrating on her partners. Matthew surprised his mother by only picking at his food, turning down the sweets completely.

"Are you feeling all right?" she whispered.

"Yes, I'm fine, Mother. I am just excited to be here. Captain, is it time to go watch the fireworks?"

"I suppose we could go now. I think that was the last dance. Yes, here come the others."

Lady Best's box was filled with her guests returning from the dance floor. Laughing and chattering about the coming treat, the young people's enthusiasm was contagious, and everyone watched in awe as the cascading waterfall was unveiled. Considered by many of Vauxhall's visitors to be the highlight of the evening, the fireworks display began, but Marie and Matthew were too busy losing themselves in the crowd.

"This way," he said, dragging her along. "Look, there's the carriage."

A huge traveling carriage loomed at the end of the dark path. Without hesitating, Matthew helped her inside.

"Get yourself inside, too," said a voice from the shadows.

"No, stupid, I'm going to ride on top," said Matthew. Turning, he added, "You're not Bolton! Hey, what's . . ."

The thud of a pistol butt silenced him, and he was quickly stuffed into the carriage at the feet of the screaming Marie. The man who had spoken jumped inside, too.

Shaking his fist in her face, he growled, "Shaddup."

"Where can they be?" cried Anne.

"I do not know, my dear, but they are no doubt together. Matthew will look after Marie, but we cannot stay here all night." He shepherded her to his carriage and saw her seated. Looking around one last time before climbing in, he shook his head. He would throttle Matthew for getting himself and Marie lost and for worrying his mother.

Sitting down by her side in the spacious carriage, he put a bracing arm around her narrow shoulders. "I would not be surprised, my dear, if we did not discover them at home when we get there."

"I pray you may be right, Bastien."

When they arrived home, the children were not there, but Pidgeon and Wiser were waiting together in Anne's front hall.

She bit her lip as Pidgeon handed a letter to Bastien.

"They've been kidnapped, Captain."

Only Bastien's strong arm around her waist prevented Anne from falling to the floor. Mrs. Helper stepped forward, waving smelling salts under her nose while the captain picked her up and carried her to the sofa. After seeing to her comfort, he turned back to his butler.

"Have you called in the Bow Street Runners?"

"No, sir. I thought you might wish to avoid the scandal."

"Quite right. We will follow the instructions in the note, and we should have them back in no time."

"You need not placate me with your brave words, Bastien," said Anne, straightening up and fixing him with a grim smile.

Pidgeon came closer and pulled something from behind his back. "This came with the note, my lady. I think it was the one Miss Marie was wearing—the one you gave her."

Her bravado slipped, and Anne clutched the blue silk, weeping unashamedly. Bastien signaled to the servants to leave them. Sitting down beside her, he took her in his arms, kissing the top of her head and murmuring reassurances.

Lifting her face to his, she put her arms around his neck and gave him tear-flavored kisses. After a moment, still encircled by the strength of his embrace, Anne took his face in her hands and whispered, "Bring them home safely, Bastien, both of them."

He nodded and kissed her once more before rising and striding to the door.

Turning, he said softly, "I love you, Anne."

Waiting in the hall, Pidgeon and Wiser leapt to attention. "Wiser, pour your mistress something strong. She is going to need it before this ordeal is over. Pidgeon, come with me."

As they started out the door, Pidgeon asked, "What are we going to do first, Captain?"

Waving the letter he still held in his fist, Bastien said, "First, we are going to load my pistols. I want you to stay behind, Pidgeon. This whole thing may be a hoax, and I want you here. Send for me if the children should return."

As Bastien headed for the door, a brace of pistols in his pockets, Pidgeon tried to reason with him one more time. "It's not safe, Captain. It could be a trap."

"Yes, but I don't have a choice. If they harm one hair . . . I have to go."

"Good luck, Captain."

"I'm telling you, you don't want to cross her father," said Matthew, still working at the ropes that bound his hands behind his back. In the corner of the dark, dirty hovel, he could hear Marie crying softly.

"Shaddup, me fine lord," said the bruiser who had dragged him from the carriage and tied him up.

"Didn't Bolton tell you this was only a farce? You know, a jest."

"Matthew, be quiet. You will only make things worse," said Marie.

"Worse? How can they get any worse. Here am I, tied up and helpless, and this ruffian is . . ."

The ruffian rose, stabbing the table with the knife he had been using to peel an apple. Matthew jumped, falling silent under the man's glare.

There was a tapping on the broken door, and it opened.

"Montgomery!" said Matthew. "So you're behind this."

"That's right, Westhaven."

"You're the man from the park," said Marie. "You're the man who had Matthew beaten, almost killed."

"She does have a memory, doesn't she?" drawled the newcomer, looking at his hair in the broken mirror on the wall.

"But how did you . . . ?" asked Matthew.

"Simple, really. Your friend Bolton owes me a great deal of money, too. He thought to repay me by telling me about your little plan. I chose to turn it to my advantage. Two hostages—two ransoms."

"But it wasn't supposed to be like that," said Matthew miserably.

"No? But you see, boy, I remembered how your friend, the captain, paid your other debt so quickly. I know he will pay well for the safe return of his only daughter. If he chooses not to pay for you, then I will have to have Dixon take care of you."

"You will never get away with it, Montgomery," said Matthew. "The captain is not the sort of man you want to cross. He's not going to give you the money and let you walk away."

"Then we will simply kill him, too."

Montgomery signaled to the big man to follow him outside.

"I am so sorry, Marie. I never thought this would happen."

"I know, Matthew. We must do something," she said.

"I'm trying to get these ropes off. I've almost got it," he said, grunting as he slipped the first loop off and struggled to free his hands. "There, now it's your turn."

He started for her, but the door opened again. The big man had his back to them, talking to someone else.

"The window, Matthew. There's no glass in it. Go! Hurry!"

"I can't leave you!"

"Go get my father! It's our only chance!"

* * *

The narrow crooked streets and the stench of unwashed bodies told Matthew where he was. He couldn't be too far from the tavern where he had received that terrible beating. Blindly, his head still pounding from the pistol Dixon had used on him, Matthew stumbled and ran as fast as he could, his only goal to save Marie and her father. Finally, he found his way out of the maze of poverty and onto a lighted street.

Pausing to get his bearings, he took a deep breath and continued on, running until he thought his lungs would burst.

Finally, he turned onto Curzon Street.

"Tom!" he called, spying the captain's footman, who was standing guard at the front door.

Within minutes, he was in his mother's parlor pouring out his tale, or most of it.

"Matthew, Bastien will sort it out. He was going to take the ransom . . ."

"He's not going to get a chance to pay the ransom, Mother. They're going to kill him, kill both of them if we don't do something!"

Anne looked at her son in horror, but she read truth there. Nodding, she turned to her butler. "Wiser, I will need my cloak, and another for Miss Rocher. And send to the stable for Parker to bring the carriage around. Pidgeon, you read the ransom note. I want you to go to Bow Street and engage as many Runners as you can to accompany you to the tavern mentioned in that note."

"Yes, my lady," said the butlers, hurrying to do her bidding.

"Matthew, you must lead me to this tavern."

"No, Mother. You cannot mean to go yourself. Let me go with Tom."

She shook her head. "Look at you, Matthew. You are worn out. Besides, we are only going so we can warn Bastien."

"Mother, I forbid it."

Anne patted his cheek. "Bless you for being so grown-up, Matthew, but now is not the time. I am going whether you like it or not."

"At least take Tom, if he is willing to go," said Matthew.

"At your service, my lady," said the footman.

"Very well. Let's go. There is no time to be lost."

Bastien knew it was a trap the minute he walked into the tavern. Every head turned—first to stare at him, and then beyond him, over his shoulders. He braced himself for the attack, feinting to the left so that the blow glanced off his shoulder.

Spinning around, he found himself face-to-face with two men—one rough character he had never seen before, and the other, Matthew's old enemy from the park.

"Montgomery!" he yelled, lunging for the scoundrel, only to collapse when the club cracked across his shoulders.

Half conscious, he felt himself being dragged from the tavern and down the street. A door opened and dim candle-light spilled onto the pavement.

"Bring him in and search his pockets," said Montgomery.

"Papa!"

He managed to turn his head and wink at her before being thrown against the wall. The rotten wood splintered from the impact, but he remained alert, every fiber of his body ready to spring.

Dixon turned him over while Montgomery tugged at his coat. Bastien brought his foot up and sent Montgomery flying. Staggering, he felt Dixon grab his throat, pulling him to his feet and slamming him against the wall.

Glancing over his shoulder at the inert body of his boss, the brute growled, "All mine now."

With this, he held the pistol to Bastien's head. The captain wriggled helplessly in the giant's iron grip.

"Dixon!" yelled Matthew, bursting into the room.

Freeing one hand, Bastien rammed his fist into his attacker's face. Dixon fell back, the shot from the gun exploding harmlessly through the ceiling.

Anne ran forward, picked up the club the man had used on Bastien, and whacked him on the head. With a groan, the giant slumped to the ground, staying there.

Matthew rushed to untie Marie while Anne threw herself into Bastien's embrace. Together, they hugged their children.

The door again crashed against the wall, and the small, dirty room was filled with shouting men wielding every sort of weapon.

Pidgeon stepped forward and snapped to attention. "Glad to see you are unharmed, Captain. Parker is outside with the carriage."

"You're a welcome sight, Pidgeon."

"Thank you, sir. So are you and Miss Marie."

Bastien turned to the four other men and said, "Thank you, gentlemen. The one over there is Montgomery. He's the one who planned it all. The other one was his henchman."

One of the Runners stepped past Montgomery and looked down at the giant. "It's Digger Dixon, my boys. We'll be glad to dispose of this one, Captain."

"Thank you. Now, it's time to go home. Matthew, take your mother's arm. Marie." He put one arm around his daughter, leaning heavily on her as they made their way to the carriage.

Exhaustion and silence reigned all the way back to Curzon Street.

"Six o'clock this evening," said Bastien. "We will meet in our drawing room before dinner to discuss what happened tonight. For now, go to bed and get some rest—everyone."

"No one answered my knock, so I let myself in," said Bastien, crossing the small drawing room in three long strides. "I hope you do not mind."

"Of course not," said Anne, moving her skirts to one side so that he could join her on the sofa. "I think everyone in the house is asleep except me."

"It is much the same at my house. I know it is only five o'clock, and I designated our meeting at six." Taking her hands in his, he added, "I simply could not bear the thought of sharing you again—not until we have settled things between us."

"Settled things?" she whispered shyly.

He nodded and lifted her chin so that he could look into her eyes. "Yes. Anne, when you told me what Lady Selwyn accused us of, I was so angry. Angry that she had upset you, that she had insinuated that you would ever be involved in anything scandalous."

"Oh, Bastien, I don't care about that anymore."

"Good, because I want you to know that that is not what made me start thinking about you and me. Perhaps it was, but it isn't why I . . ."

Anne placed her finger to his lips, saying softly, "I believe you, Bastien."

"Good. Anne, I know that you look upon Marie as a daughter. And you know Matthew and me . . ."

Bastien dropped her chin and took her into his arms.

"Anne, my sweet, beautiful Anne, do you think you could look upon me as your husband?"

Her smile was her answer, and Bastien swooped down for his reward, a gentle kiss.

Raising his head, he said, "I love you, Anne."

"And I love you, Bastien."

"Then everything is perfect," he said, holding her close and kissing her thoroughly.

After a moment, breathless and shaken, Anne said, "There is something else we must take care of before we can relax, Bastien. We must decide what to do about our children. I think there was more to this kidnapping than we know."

"I know, but we will not allow it to mar our happiness. Do you agree?"

"Agreed," said Anne. "We will discuss our wayward children later."

"Good, because I am much more interested in discussing our nuptials. I will send a messenger to Marie's grandfather and ask if he has the ear of a bishop who will grant us a special license."

"Oh, Bastien, do you think it is wise to act so precipitously?"

He grinned and proceeded to show her why haste could be a very good thing. After some time, they separated.

Leaning against the sofa, Bastien expelled a long breath. "Whew. I think we should go next door before we are discovered in this scandalous state."

"Bastien!" she protested, slapping his arm playfully.

With a straightening of clothing, they strolled next door to continue their discussion since it was almost six o'clock.

Settled on the sofa in Bastien's drawing room, they awaited their children. There was a knock on the door and Marie and Matthew entered. The duo crossed the soft carpets and stood before them, hanging their heads.

"What have you to say for yourselves?" asked Bastien.

"It was all my idea, sir," said Matthew, lifting his head to face his accuser.

"I agreed to it," said Marie.

"But things got out of hand," added Matthew.

"Very out of hand," said his mother.

"We are terribly sorry, Papa," said Marie.

"And so you should be, *chérie*. So tell me, my dear Anne, what should our daughter's punishment be?"

"Our daughter?" squeaked Marie.

"I think she should be sent to the country to visit her grandfather for a week."

"Or two," said Bastien.

"Yes, at least two weeks," agreed Anne. "And what about Matthew. What should we do to him, Bastien?"

"I think he should go with Marie. The stables are quite large on the Belwich estate. I'm sure they could use another experienced stable boy."

Matthew groaned but made no comment.

"When I write to the marquis about the bishop and the special license, I will tell him about his grandchildren's impending visit."

"Grandchildren?" said Matthew and Marie in unison.

"Yes, but you will not leave until after our wedding—hopefully within the next two or three days, if I have anything to say to it."

"Wedding?" they echoed again.

"Oh, Papa!" said Marie, throwing her arms around Bastien' s neck and then doing the same to her new mother. "Making Lady Anne my new mother is the best gift you have ever given me!"

"Come here, son," said Bastien, grasping Matthew's shoulder and giving him a quick hug.

Sitting down again, Bastien on one side of Anne and Marie on the other, they laughed at Matthew who still had not spoken.

"I think the cat has his tongue," said his mother.

"No, I just cannot believe that my plan worked! I really am a matchmaker!"

"Matchmaker or not, if I ever catch you anywhere near that tavern again," said Bastien, "You will never get the stench of the stable off your gentlemanly hands—understood?"

"Aye, aye, sir," said the incorrigible Matthew. "And speaking of that, do you think you could persuade my mother that I would benefit from some sea travel?"

Bastien shook his head and coaxed Anne to the door. "I do not think it fair, my love. You get a daughter who is soon to be leaving home. I get a son who is already trying my patience."

"It is too late to back out now, my love." Standing on tip-toe, she kissed his cheek.

Ignoring their audience and sweeping her into his arms, Bastien laughed and kissed her soundly.

"Never mind," he said. "You are definitely worth it."

ABOUT THE AUTHOR

Julia Parks resides in Texas with her husband of thirty-plus years. She has three wonderful children, a delightful son-in-law, and three beautiful grandchildren. When not writing or doing research for her novels, she teaches French at a nearby high school. Along with reading and writing, the author enjoys cross-stitch, quilting, and playing the piano. Most of all, she enjoys playing with her grandchildren. She welcomes comments from her readers and can be contacted at Kensington Publishing or by e-mail at dendonbell@netscape.net.

A Mother at Heart

Debbie Raleigh

One

No one was more surprised than Julius Sutton when he learned that he had become the distinguished sixth Earl of Rockworth.

After all, the old Earl of Rockworth was precisely the sort of cantankerous, nipfathering old tough that clung to this world with astonishing tenacity. And even if a miracle did occur and he stuck his spoon in the wall, there were three perfectly healthy male heirs to stand between Julius and the title.

Which was why, of course, Julius had elected a career in the army. With no prospects, no particular skill with the turn of a card or upon the 'Change he had been left with few options beyond the military or following his father's footsteps into the clergy. And since he would as soon lop off his feet, and his legs as well, as to follow in the footsteps of Vicar Sutton, he left the dank, cold vicarage when he was barely seventeen and set his sights upon the battlefields of Europe. A decision he never regretted despite the undoubted hardships or discomforts.

It was nearly ten years later that the messenger arrived in the mountains of Spain with the stunning news that he was to leave for England immediately. A heart attack, a hunting accident, the measles, and an unlikely duel had suddenly catapulted him into the enviable position of Earl of Rockworth . . . whether he wanted the title or not.

And, in truth, there had been more than one occasion he would have gladly chucked it all in and happily have returned to the Peninsula, he ruefully acknowledged, scrubbing his hands over the lean, handsome features that had been bronzed by his years upon the battlefields.

The estate had been in shambles when he had arrived. The previous earl had faithfully maintained his sworn refusal to spend a grout upon the house or lands up to the day he had keeled over in his chilled bedchamber. The rooms had been dark and covered with dust, the gardens in ruins, and the tenants nearly destitute.

It had taken Julius months to restore the neighboring cottages and to reinvest in the neglected fields. And even longer to begin restoration on the house. With slow, painful steps Westport was once again becoming the elegant estate that it had once been, but Julius rose every morning with the knowledge that there was still much left to do, and even more to learn if he hoped to make the estate a profitable one.

It was enough to make a poor soldier long for the simple life of marching and sleeping.

Giving a faint shake of his head at his absurd thoughts, Julius forced his concentration back to the piles of estate books that he was attempting to put in some semblance of order.

It appeared that the fifth Earl of Rockworth had been as allergic to keeping accurate accounts as he had been to spending his blunt.

It made for a tangled mess that Julius was quite certain would take the next ten years to decipher.

Struggling with the unsolvable tumble of numbers that threatened to cross his eyes, Julius was suddenly distracted as the door to his library was quietly pushed open.

"Pardon me, my lord."

Glancing up he regarded the portly butler who stood in the doorway.

Although Roberts could barely claim five feet, he possessed enough dignity for a man twice his size, which was precisely the reason Julius had chosen him from among the numerous applicants. He was well aware his humble background would allow many among society to view him as an interloper. Roberts' forbidding air of propriety was precisely what he had desired.

No one would believe the staunch servant would remain in a household that was not utterly respectable.

"Yes, Roberts?" he demanded, a faint frown marring his brow. He had already discovered that whenever his butler wore that pinched, sour expression it boded ill tidings.

"There are two ladies here to see you."

Julius gave a startled blink. "Two ladies?"

"Yes, sir."

He swallowed a bitter sigh. Over the past six months he had been plagued by an endless stream of "visitors" that had tested his dubious patience to the very limit.

"More tenants here to swear my mad uncle promised them the Rembrandt or Rubens?"

"No, sir."

"Ah, then a pair of merchants hoping the death of the previous earl entitles them to conjure a dozen separate bills he supposedly neglected to pay?"

Astonishingly the man gave a faint cough. "No, the older woman claims . . ."

His words trailed away and Julius tossed his quill aside. He would have wagered his last quid that nothing could have rattled the butler's steely nerves. Not even an invading horde of French upon the doorstep. Now an ominous unease trickled down his spine.

"Out with it, Roberts," he commanded in grim tones. "For the past six months I have been beleaguered by greedy tenants, merchants, and dirty-dish relatives that did not even acknowledge me when I was a mere soldier, all hoping to filch my newfound fortune from beneath my very nose. Nothing could shock me at this juncture."

Gathering his composure the man squared his shoulders. "The lady claims to be your mother."

An awful silence filled the study as Julius slowly rose to his feet.

"Good God."

The warm, cozy feeling that smote the heart of the most hardened criminal at the mention of his mother was decidedly absent within Julius. Instead a pang of deep betrayal raced through him.

His mother was a traitor.

After all, he had been barely five when she had flounced out of his life to join her lover upon the stages of London.

She had not given a thought to her son, or the knowledge he was left alone to bear the icy fury of his father.

In his mind she might as well be dead.

Not that he believed for a moment that it was his mother awaiting him in the foyer.

The woman may have been selfish, but she was not entirely stupid. She would have to know she would be less welcome than the plague in his house.

No, this had to be some devious scheme. A disreputable jade who had learned of his mother's disappearance and hoped to insinuate her way into his life. Or more aptly, into his fortune.

It was unfortunate for her that she had not taken the trouble to discover he had no more love for his long-lost mother than he did for brass-faced encroachers.

Watching him from the safety of the door, the butler cleared his throat.

"Shall I have them sent away?"

"No." The handsome features hardened and the blue eyes narrowed in a manner that sent a chill through poor Roberts' heart. "I will handle this myself. I have had my fill of unscrupulous freeloaders who hope to hang on to my coattail. I will prove to the entire county that I am not the easy mark that they have supposed."

"I think I should warn you that she appears to be a rather fragile old woman," Roberts said in reluctant tones.

Julius waved an impatient hand. He did not care if she were crawling upon her knees.

"I will not harm her, for goodness sakes. I am not a monster."

Roberts gave a stiff bow. "Of course not."

"I do, however, intend to put an end to these tiresome pests."

Brushing past the servant, Julius headed grimly toward his chambers to change.

Who the devil could have known that a sudden inheritance would land him with every muckworm in England?

It was almost enough to make a gentleman wish himself back on the battlefields. The French at least had the decency not to smile in your face while sticking a knife in your back.

It had been a mistake to come.

Charity Smith had known it was a mistake before they had ever left Surrey.

She had known it when Mrs. Hanson had first begun to babble about mending the breech between herself and her beloved son.

And she certainly knew it the moment they had arrived at the sprawling estate set like a burnished gem upon the vast parkland and entered the black-and-white tiled foyer with its vaulted ceiling.

The poker-faced butler had regarded them as if they had crawled from beneath some particularly nasty rock despite the fact Mrs. Hanson was attired in a fine black bombazine gown and she herself had chosen a muted rose gown that draped nicely over her tall slender frame and put a new rose bonnet upon her dusky black curls. He had then abandoned them in this foyer, where he had left them to wait for nearly an hour.

Obviously Lord Rockworth was not overcome with delight at the announcement that his mother had arrived. She could only hope that the butler was not gathering footmen to have them hauled off the estate.

This last thought was unnerving enough to prompt Charity to reach out and grasp the hand of the woman seated next to her on the hard marble bench.

"Perhaps, Mrs. Hanson, you should reconsider," she said in soft tones. "To arrive here without warning is bound to be a shock. We should return to the inn and await word from Lord Rockworth."

Although a tiny woman with a puff of gray hair and sweet nature, Mrs. Hanson had proven to be uncharacteristically contrary when it came to seeing her son.

Now she gave a firm shake of her head. "Nonsense. I have put off this visit too long. I must see Julius today."

Charity heaved a sigh, knowing only too well what had prompted this sudden visit.

"I just do not wish you to be disappointed. It is very likely he will not even agree to see you," she warned with a pointed glance toward the ormolu clock set upon a pier table.

"Oh, he will not have changed that much. He was insatiably curious as a child. He will agree to see me if only to ease that curiosity."

"And no doubt proceed to toss us out upon our noses," Charity muttered.

Mrs. Hanson smiled in a complacent manner. "All will be well."

"I fear I do not share your confidence," Charity began, only to snap her lips closed at the sound of approaching footsteps that echoed through the vaulted foyer.

She watched with an unexplainable sense of dread as a pair of gleaming Hessians came into view. Her breath caught as the decidedly masculine legs encased in buff breeches could be seen and then a tailored blue coat that revealed shoulders impossibly wide. At long last she could view the unfashionably dark countenance with its bluntly chiseled features and ice blue eyes. Hair the color of fresh honey was tousled, as if he had run his fingers through the satin strands on more than one occasion. Coming to a halt at the bottom of the steps with his feet spread wide and his hands planted upon his hips, he looked as large and dangerous as a marauding Viking of old. Even the grim set to his expression added to the image of ruthless invincibility.

He was also without a doubt, the most enticingly handsome gentleman that Charity had ever encountered.

"Oh," she breathed softly.

At her side Mrs. Hanson gave a chuckle. "I knew he would grow to be a handsome man. But not even I could have hoped for such perfection."

Perfection.

Yes, Charity silently acknowledged.

He was utterly perfect from the tip of his gleaming honey hair to the champagne gloss upon his boots.

That was if she discounted the black scowl currently marring his noble brow.

"He does not appear particularly pleased to see us."

"Allow me to handle this, my dear."

"With pleasure," Charity muttered, reluctantly rising to her feet as Mrs. Hanson leaped up and crossed toward the middle of the tiled floor.

"Julius, how well you look," she said in bright tones, seemingly indifferent to the smoldering tension in the atmosphere.

Narrowing that frigid blue gaze, the large gentleman strolled forward, a sardonic smile twisting his full lips.

"Ah yes, it is amazing what an earldom can do for a gentleman. I did not look nearly so well when I was a common solider upon Napoleon's battlefield."

Charity flushed at the taunting edge to his deep, husky voice, but as usual Mrs. Hanson was impervious to the insult.

"I can not believe that. I would say you looked extraordinarily handsome in your regimentals."

"Indeed?" The honey brows shot upward. "And yet you did not seek me out until I had inherited a fortune. Is that not an odd coincidence?"

Mrs. Hanson gave a rather puzzled frown. "Well, I do not think I could have easily traveled to Spain. But, of course, I should no doubt have made the effort."

Unamused by her response, the man glared arrogantly down the length of his nose.

"No, you should not have," he retorted in clipped tones. "Since I would have told you then what I shall tell you now. Even supposing you are my mother, which I do not believe for a moment, I have no desire for you to be anywhere in my vicinity. My mother deserted me when I was but a child. Any claim she might have had upon me was lost the day she left. So whatever you hope to gain by coming here and perpetrating this fraud you can just forget. You will never see so much as a quid from me. Do I make myself clear?"

Sucking in an angry breath, Charity moved to stand beside her dear friend, her dark eyes blazing as he shot her an indifferent glance. Mrs. Hanson, however, merely smiled.

"I did not desert you, Julius. I was forced to leave by your father."

If possible the blue eyes chilled even further. "You dare to spread lies about my father?"

"It is no lie. I begged upon my knees to remain with you. Do you not recall I even left behind a locket with a clipping of my hair to remind you of me?"

There was a sharp silence and Charity caught her breath as Lord Rockworth took a step forward.

"How did you know of that?" he gritted.

Mrs. Hanson smiled with a sweet sadness. "I placed it beneath your pillow while you were sleeping before your father forced me into a carriage and ordered me never to return. My heart fair broke that day."

His hands clenched at his sides. "My mother left with a common actor in the hopes that a life as a harlot would prove more profitable than a respectable marriage to a mere vicar."

The sheer lack of emotion in his voice oddly touched Charity's soft heart. Beneath that icy anger was a lingering wound he was desperate to hide.

Mrs. Hanson was also swift to sense the bitter vulnerability and she gave a slow shake of her head.

"Poor Julius."

Abruptly realizing that he had revealed more than he intended, Lord Rockworth stiffened.

"Hardly poor."

"Only in spirit," Mrs. Hanson said in soft tones. "I can sense your bitterness and I am sorry for it. Your father was wrong to make you believe you had been abandoned. How could any mother willingly leave her son?"

"Enough," Lord Rockworth ground out. "I will not listen to your lies."

Mrs. Hanson gave a click of her tongue, remarkably indifferent to the danger that hung about the towering gentleman like a shroud. Charity could only wish she was as obtuse. As it was she was finding it increasingly difficult to ignore the frozen fury in those blue eyes.

"Ah, I remember that temper, too." The older woman shook a finger toward Lord Rockworth, as if he were still a child rather than a very large, very angry earl. "When other little boys would be in tears after skinning their knee or falling from a tree you would climb to your feet and bellow in rage. Even as a child you hated to reveal any hint of weakness."

Sensing that one of those famous bellows was about to erupt, Charity took Mrs. Hanson's arm and tugged her toward the door.

They had risked their luck far enough for one day.

"Perhaps we should leave, Mrs. Hanson," she muttered, warily keeping an eye on the large nobleman.

Thankfully the unpredictable woman allowed herself to be hustled away, although she did turn her head to call over her shoulder, "I am staying at the local inn, my dear. I should very much like to have you call upon me there."

"Just go," he roared.

With one last yank Charity had them over the threshold and tripping down the stairs.

Blast, the man was a devil, she seethed, as she relentlessly pulled her employer to the waiting carriage.

A handsome devil, a treacherous voice whispered, but utterly without the least amount of heart.

He had made it painfully clear he did not wish to discover the truth of his mother's disappearance. Or even to believe that Mrs. Hanson was indeed his mother.

He far preferred to condemn them as conniving rogues than to listen to the truth. Even if that truth could heal the wounds he still harbored.

Reaching the carriage, she glanced at the elderly coachman. "Back to the inn."

"Yes, miss."

The groom tenderly settled Mrs. Hanson against the squabs, then waiting for Charity to settle herself, he closed the door and they were off. Charity heaved a sigh as they raced down the tree-lined drive, thankful to be free of that icy blue glare.

Across from her, Mrs. Hanson smiled with an odd contentment.

"I think that went very well, do you not?"

"Well?" Charity choked out in disbelief. Not even this dear woman was that daft. "He was furious."

"Of course he was," the older woman said calmly. "For years he has convinced himself that his mother abandoned him. Now to discover that I have loved him all along is bound to be unsettling. We must give him time to adjust."

"If you say," Charity forced herself to mutter.

"Trust me, my dearest. My son may be stubborn, but he possesses a good heart. He shall be calling upon us within the week."

Charity recalled the near tangible disgust Lord Rockworth had not bothered to disguise.

"And cows will be dancing the waltz," she said beneath her breath.

Trembling with fury, Julius threw open the door to the library and moved to jerk upon the velvet rope, nearly dislodging it from the bell.

"Damn the impertinent jades," he muttered.

It was bad enough that they had dared to invade his home, but to have obviously investigated his childhood went beyond the pale.

It made his stomach clench to imagine them paying off old servants, or even neighbors, to discover the intimate details of his past.

How else could the old Jezebel have known of the locket? A locket that had suddenly appeared beneath the pillows the morning his mother had disappeared and that he still possessed.

He briefly closed his eyes, only to wrench them open again.

It was not the image of the tiny Mrs. Hanson that had risen to his mind, but the silent companion.

Gads, he had barely paid her any heed, but he had been able to conjure every detail with startling clarity. The tall, elegant form. The bold features and peach-kissed skin. The black eyes heavily fringed, and raven curls that had peeked beneath the ridiculous bonnet.

It was absurd.

She was clearly in the despicable plot with Mrs. Hanson.

So why was his body stirring at the mere thought of those elegant curves pressed against him?

"Yes, my lord?" The voice of Roberts thankfully brought him back to his senses and he turned to regard his butler with a smoldering fury.

"I wish you to send Brush to Dorset. There is an old groom that lives in the town of Mansonville by the name of Joseph Cower. I want him brought here."

"Very good."

"And, Roberts."

"Yes, sir?"

"Bring me brandy. Lots of brandy."

The butler gave a brisk bow. "At once."

Two

Although the gardens behind the inn were little more than a patch for vegetables, it was at least enclosed from the noisy stable yard and out of the cramped darkness of her chamber.

Charity breathed in deeply of the late April air. It had been four days since their disastrous visit to Westport, but while she had pleaded with Mrs. Hanson to return to Surrey, the older woman was adamant. She had convinced herself that her beloved Julius would arrive at the inn. And nothing was going to budge her. Not even the increasingly curious gazes of those who had overheard the older woman speak of herself as Lord Rockworth's mother.

Charity kicked a pebble in frustration.

Blast. She wished they had never come.

Mrs. Hanson's heart would never have been broken.

And she . . .

Well, she would not be spending her nights plagued with dreams of honey-haired Vikings.

She gave an impatient growl at her foolishness, knowing she should return to the inn and make sure that Mrs. Hanson had received her breakfast tray.

There was nothing to be accomplished by brooding upon what could not be changed.

Turning about, she suddenly spotted a small stable boy hurrying in her direction.

"Pardon me, miss."

"Yes?"

"Lord Rockworth is in the front parlor. He wishes to speak with you."

Charity felt her knees weaken before she ruthlessly gathered her shaken composure. She would not be intimidated by the cold, imperious man.

"I will tell Mrs. Hanson."

"Excuse me, miss, but he says that he is wishing for you to come alone."

"I see." Charity gave a tilt of her chin. "I shall be along in a moment."

"Yes, miss."

The boy darted away and Charity pressed a hand to her stomach.

Why the devil did he wish to see her alone?

Was he having second thoughts about his cold dismissal of his mother?

Or had he brought along the magistrate to have them charged with fraud?

Well, she would never discover his intentions by standing like a half-wit in the middle of the path, she chastised herself.

Ignoring the renegade urge to flee to her chamber, she forced herself to briskly return to the inn and make her way to the front parlor.

He was standing in the center of the floor, his bulk consuming an unfair portion of the cheerful room when she entered.

An odd rash of awareness raced over her skin as she forced herself to calmly remove her bonnet and toss it onto a nearby table.

What the deuce was the matter with her?

She had always been a sensible, well-ordered maiden. Nothing ruffled her composure, or overset her nerves. Not even overbearing gentlemen who were far too handsome for their own good, she told herself sternly.

"Good morning, my lord," she said as she reluctantly met the unnerving blue gaze.

"Thank you for agreeing to see me, Miss . . . ?"

"Smith," she supplied.

His lips curled in a mockery of a smile. "Of course."

Realizing he thought she had invented the common name, she felt her temper begin to simmer.

"What is it you desire, my lord?"

He folded his arms over the width of his chest. He was once again attired in buff breeches with a dark cinnamon coat that molded to his body with indecent perfection.

"The truth would be a pleasant change."

So much for her hope that he had reconsidered his harsh dismissal of them, she wryly acknowledged. If anything, he appeared even more furious this morning, although it was hidden behind an aloof disdain.

"And what truth would that be?" she demanded, her eyes flashing.

He seemed to still as he regarded her suddenly flushed features, then his nose flared with distaste.

"What do you hope to gain by this deceit? Is it money?"

Her brows snapped together. "Certainly not. Mrs. Hanson may not be a member of nobility, but she is very comfortably settled."

"Easy enough to claim."

"If you do not believe me then you may contact her solicitor in London. He will be able to assure you that Mrs. Hanson is in no need of your money."

His gaze narrowed. "Then she desires a position in society? No doubt the mother of an earl could see a number of doors previously closed suddenly thrown wide open."

Charity forced herself to count to ten, even as she contemplated smacking the superior expression from his countenance.

"Mrs. Hanson has never possessed the least interest in society. Indeed, she prefers to live very quietly."

"I am not the gullible fool you have marked me, Miss Smith. There is something that she wants."

"Yes," she agreed between stiff lips. "To know the son she has not seen in twenty-two years. Is that so terrible?"

"It is absurd." His hands dropped to clench at his side, his forceful presence seeming to fill the entire room. "Even supposing she was my mother, why would she wait twenty-two years to seek me out?"

Charity briefly faltered. She had promised Mrs. Hanson she would not reveal the truth of her sudden desire to seek out her son. Not even to turn away the vile suspicions of Lord Rockworth.

"I suppose she feared your reaction to her return."

His lips twisted. "But she managed to overcome her fear after discovering the news of my inheritance?"

Blast it all. The man was clearly demented. Why else would he be so obsessed with the thought they were after his damnable inheritance?

"Your inheritance had nothing to do with her decision."

"Of course not." Without warning, he allowed his gaze to roam openly over her slender curves. "And I suppose her decision to bring along a young, extraordinarily lovely maiden was coincidence as well?"

He thought her lovely?

There was a treacherous flutter in her stomach even as she stiffened at the provocative words.

"I beg your pardon?"

A disturbing glint entered his eyes as he stepped uncomfortably close to her rigid form.

"Did she hope I would be so dazzled I would not have the will to send you both packing?"

She sucked in an angry breath, only to wish she hadn't when the warm male scent of him made her head swim.

"I am Mrs. Hanson's companion," she gritted. "Of course she desired me to travel with her."

"And when did she hire you?" he demanded. "Before or after she decided to latch on to me?"

The man was impossible, she decided, wishing he were not wearing his riding boots so that she could stomp upon his toes.

"I have been with Mrs. Hanson for nearly six months."

"Ah. Precisely the length of time I have possessed the title of earl."

Her lips thinned as she met him glare for glare. "You are a very disagreeable man."

"Forgive me. I dislike being fleeced by common trollops. But if you desire me to be bewitched, who am I to quibble?" he mocked, his hand lifting without warning to cup the back of her neck. "I discover I have an unexpected taste for treacherous beauties."

"Sir . . ." she began to protest, only to be effectively silenced when he abruptly angled his head downward and claimed her lips in a bold, seeking kiss.

Julius had not intended to kiss the chit.

Oh, he had rather casually wondered if Miss Smith could be lured into revealing her true nature. But he had intended to make a subtle offer to become his mistress. Or even to tempt her with a promise of a reward if she confessed Mrs. Hanson was a fraud.

Surely a woman on the hunt for an easy handout would readily trade upon her obvious beauty, or even turn on her supposed employer?

Once she accepted his disreputable offer he would be in a position to force both of the jades back beneath the rock they had crawled out from.

But from the moment she had stepped into the room he

had been battling the most aggravating desire to have her in his arms.

A desire that had become a compulsion when those dark eyes had flashed in defiance, nearly daring him to gain command of her in the oldest, most primitive manner possible.

And from the moment his lips touched the satin heat of her mouth he could not regret his impulsive decision.

With a groan he wrapped his arms about her, tugging until she stumbled against his hard body. She fit against him perfectly, he decided with a shudder of pleasure. She was tall enough he did not have to crane his neck to deepen the kiss, while the slender form possessed a fluid strength that did not make him fear she might shatter as his hands ran a restless path down the curve of her spine.

Quicksilver heat flooded his body as he felt her betraying tremor. Gads, he wanted this woman. Regardless of her black heart and nefarious designs. He wanted her so badly he could willingly lay her upon the worn carpet and lose himself in temptation without giving a damn that someone might stumble in on them.

The realization of how close he was to losing control of his passions had him abruptly pulling back, but his arms remained stubbornly locked tightly about her delightful curves. Almost as if they had a mind of their own.

With a brooding bemusement he studied the flushed features and dazed black eyes.

"You taste of honey." He at last broke the pulsing silence.

She drew in an unsteady breath. "I had it on my toast."

He gave a low growl as he dipped his head to tenderly flick his tongue over her lips.

"I am especially fond of honey."

She trembled, but annoyingly she arched away from his caress.

"My lord, you must release me."

"In a moment. I am not yet properly bewitched."

Not nearly as eager as he had hoped for a delightful seduction, she planted her hands firmly upon his chest and pushed herself free of his embrace.

"You are mistaken," she said in furious tones. "I came because Mrs. Hanson requested that I do so. Any other reason is merely a figment of your foul imagination. Excuse me."

Whirling on her heel, she stormed toward the door, only to be forced to a halt when it was suddenly pushed open and the tiny form of Mrs. Hanson entered the room.

"Oh, there you are, Charity," the older woman exclaimed with a smile.

It took a moment for Miss Smith to reclaim her composure, although Julius could not help but admire her swift transformation from outraged maiden to the role of dutiful companion.

A born actress, he told himself cynically. Although he wished she played the part of temptress with less skill.

His body still ached with unfulfilled need.

"Good morning, Mrs. Hanson." Miss Smith gently took the older woman's arm. "Have you had your breakfast?"

"Yes, indeed. Some lovely ham and toast with honey."

Julius gave a smothered groan. "I can attest that the honey is quite delectable."

Miss Smith rewarded him with a dark scowl, but Mrs. Hanson glanced toward him with a sudden smile.

"Julius, I knew you would come."

Abruptly recalled to the reason for his visit to the inn, Julius folded his arms across his chest and glared down the length of his nose.

"Yes, I suppose you did. I could hardly stay away when the entire county is speaking of the sudden appearance of my mother and the fact she is residing at an inn rather than my home."

The older woman raised a flustered hand to her heart.

"Oh dear. I do hate gossipmongers. I fear I had not considered such unpleasantness. Forgive me."

Julius thinned his lips, knowing that was precisely what the old jade had intended.

"Whatever your purpose, you have put me in an untenable position. Unfortunately I can not force you to leave however I might wish to do so."

"I promise you we will be most circumspect from now on," Mrs. Hanson promised.

He gave an impatient wave of his hand. "It is too late for such promises. As long as you remain in the neighborhood there will be precisely the sort of talk and speculation I detest. Obviously I have no choice but to take you to Westport."

The older woman clapped her hands together while the younger one continued to scowl.

"What a lovely notion," Mrs. Hanson chirped.

Julius smiled sardonically. "You would, of course, think so."

Indifferent to his mockery, the woman heaved a pleased sigh. "We shall have ample opportunity to become better acquainted. I was so concerned, you know, that a handful of brief visits would never do."

"Perhaps you should see to your packing," he said sharply, deeply resenting the fact he had been manipulated into allowing the two charlatans into his home.

"Of course. I must find Betsy. Come along, Charity."

Julius took a step forward. "Actually, I would like a word alone with Miss Smith."

"Oh. Very well."

With a rather bemused expression Mrs. Hanson turned to leave the room, allowing him a measure of privacy with the woman, who clearly hoped to slay him with her smoldering glare.

"Yes?" she demanded with all the haughty dignity of a proper lady.

The fact that his body was still ready and painfully willing to possess the minx did nothing to ease his temper.

Gads, he hadn't felt this randy since he first discovered there was a difference between men and women.

He sternly focused his renegade thoughts upon his purpose. He intended to convince the treacherous beauty he was no easily swayed greenhorn. Not even if a certain part of his anatomy whispered it would not be that horrid to be beguiled for a few pleasurable nights.

"I may have been neatly cornered into allowing you and that woman into my house, but I assure you that nothing has changed. You shall be watched every moment you are beneath my roof."

"You believe we might escape with the silver?" she challenged.

His lips curled. "Oh no. You are far too clever to settle upon mere silver. I do not doubt you will demand nothing less than a fortune."

"And yet you freely invite us to reside with you?"

"Not freely," he corrected in cutting tones. "Indeed, it is very much against my will. But I refuse to be the fodder for the local gossips. And besides, it will only be of a short duration. In less than a fortnight this absurd charade will be at an end."

Ah, that captured her attention, he acknowledged, as she regarded him in suspicion.

"What do you mean?"

He slowly smiled. "It means, my dear Miss Smith, that I have already sent for my old groom. He was well acquainted with my mother and will swiftly prove your Mrs. Hanson is no more than a scheming adventuress."

Astonishingly, she planted her hands upon her hips and eyed him boldly.

"No, he will prove she is indeed your mother."

Although Julius had harbored only a vague hope that the

threat of exposure would be enough to end the ridiculous plot, he was not nearly as disappointed as he should have been.

Could he actually want this woman beneath his roof?

Sleeping close enough that he had only to take a few steps to join her?

He swiftly shoved the dangerous thoughts aside.

"In the meantime I intend to revert to my days as a soldier and keep my enemies well within sight," he informed her in biting tones, his gaze unwittingly lowering to the full softness of her mouth. "Which, when it comes to you, my minx, will not be entirely repulsive."

She took a hasty step backward, her dark eyes flashing. "You have made your threats annoyingly clear, my lord. We are to be carted to your house and regarded as little better than prisoners."

"Intelligent as well as beautiful," he drawled.

She was not amused.

"After which you no doubt hope to turn us over to the local magistrates?"

"That is always a possibility," he readily agreed.

Her chin abruptly tilted. "Well, I have a warning for you."

"Indeed?"

"Yes." She regarded him with a rather surprising courage. "Mrs. Hanson is the sweetest, kindest woman it has ever been my privilege to know. There is not a day that passes when her generosity is not improving the lives of others. And there is not a person who knows her who would not willingly lay down their life for her. If you break her heart, my lord, if you so much as bring a tear to her eye, you will answer to me."

Turning on her heel, the vixen flounced from the room before he could halt her retreat.

Once alone, Julius sucked in a deep breath.

Gads, but she was spectacular.

And he wanted her.

No, he had to have her.

Even if he had to allow every scheming, money-grubbing tart in England into his home.

"Damn."

Three

Three days later Charity sat with her employer in the back parlor. It was another beautiful spring day, but while Charity longed to be out exploring the vast parkland, she determinedly remained close to the older woman.

It was not that she feared Lord Rockworth would actually harm his unwanted guest, she reluctantly acknowledged. He might be arrogant, disagreeable, and unpleasantly cynical, but he was a gentleman. Since their arrival he had treated Mrs. Hanson with a chilly politeness, whenever he was not making a pointed attempt to avoid her altogether.

But as for his treatment of her . . .

Charity curled her hands into fists.

There was nothing precisely scandalous in his manner. He had not, for instance, grasped her and forced her to endure any more of his unwelcome kisses. And yet, not even she was innocent enough to mistake the manner his gaze followed her every movement. Or his determined habit of seeking her out whenever she was alone. To make matters worse, his casual touches were becoming less casual with every passing day.

His less-than-subtle attempts at seduction had not come as a surprise. He had already revealed that he considered her no better than she should be. Why would he not believe her open to a slip on the shoulder?

What had surprised her was the sharp, vivid awareness that his touch aroused within her body.

The man thought her a fraud and worse. He treated her beloved employer with barely concealed contempt.

She should hate the very sight of him, but that did not keep her from shivering when he was near, or dreaming of him long into the night.

His kiss had disturbed her, leaving her aching and restless in a manner she did not fully comprehend.

She was quite determined he would not catch her alone again.

She did not trust where those tingling shivers might lead her.

Setting aside her tea, Mrs. Hanson leaned back upon the satin ivory cushions with a satisfied sigh.

"Such a lovely home Julius has. How pleased I am to know he is surrounded by such beauty. And, of course, someday my grandchildren."

"It is a fine home," Charity was forced to concede. Not even the most exacting connoisseur could find fault in the elegant rooms furnished with delicate rosewood, pale green, blue, and yellow wall coverings, and a collection of Sevres that could rival the Prince's.

"So much nicer than that horrid vicarage he was raised in," the older woman said, then she gave a small gasp. "Oh, forgive me, my dear. I did not refer to all vicarages."

Charity gave a chuckle. "Do not fear of wounding my sensibilities. I assure you my father's vicarage was quite shabby, with roofs that leaked and chimneys that smoked. Thank goodness there were eight of us girls to sleep together or we would have frozen during the winters."

"Ah, but you had the comfort of love which allows any home, no matter how shabby, to seem a wonderful place."

"Yes, I suppose." Charity paused, then allowed her burning

curiosity to overcome her better sense. "Lord Rockworth was not loved?"

Mrs. Hanson gave a sad shake of her head. "His father was a very cold and distant gentleman. He found it very difficult to reveal his emotions."

Charity's lips twitched. "Not a trait shared by his son," she murmured, all too aware of the emotions that smoldered just beneath Lord Rockworth's surface. He might desire to appear frigidly aloof, but not even a looby could fail to sense he was a volcano about to explode.

"No, Julius has always been high-spirited. Goodness, the scrapes he could get himself into. And no one could toss a finer tantrum."

"I do hope you are not referring to me, madam."

At the sound of the dark, husky voice Charity grew cold, then turning to meet the brooding blue gaze, she felt an unwarranted flare of heat rush through her.

"But of course I am." Mrs. Hanson chuckled, not at all intimidated by the tall, broad form attired in dark breeches and a moss green coat. "I recall the morning I refused to allow you to wear your new riding boots to church and you tossed yourself onto the floor and kicked your heels until the entire household feared we were under attack."

Halting in the center of the Persian carpet, Lord Rockworth arched his honey brows.

"I fear you are mistaken. I never possessed a pair of riding boots until I was sent to school."

Mrs. Hanson's smile never faltered. "No, your father took them away when he heard of your . . . small display of displeasure. He claimed that you were clearly too young to appreciate his generosity, although I believe it was your grandfather who purchased the boots for you."

The handsome features hardened. "My father possessed a great dislike for my temper."

"I am relieved he did not break your spirit."

"No, much to his dismay he never managed to do so," he retorted in clipped tones. His eyes narrowed. "I hope you have settled in?"

"Yes, indeed. I was just telling Miss Smith what a lovely home you possess. Quite surprising really. I seem to recall the previous earl as being rather eccentric and not at all inclined to keep his estate in such fine form."

A wry smile twisted his lips. "I assure you the house was in a disreputable condition when I first arrived. I do not believe the rooms had been so much as cleaned, let alone refurbished in the past fifty years. It has taken me months to restore the house to a bearable condition."

Charity gave a choked noise of surprise. "You restored the house?"

She could have bitten her tongue as the blue gaze turned toward her, darkening as it made a leisurely survey of her trim buttercup gown and dark curls that she had loosely piled atop her head, leaving several to frame her oval face.

"I did not personally lay the carpets or sew the drapes, but I did choose the furnishings. Does that surprise you?"

It did, of course.

Surely such beauty could only be created by one with a sensitive, artistic nature.

She gave a lift of one shoulder. "I did not suppose most gentlemen took an interest in such things."

His lips twitched as if easily reading her true thoughts. "Since I am the one who will be living here it only seemed sensible to arrange the house to suit my tastes. I am currently in the process of redesigning the gardens."

"But how marvelous," Mrs. Hanson abruptly cried. "Charity is a great lover of gardens. You must show her your plans."

Charity gave a swift shake of her head. "Oh no, I . . ."

"Actually, it would be better if I took her to the gardens and discussed my ideas for alterations," Lord Rockworth interrupted, a bothersome glint in his eyes. "She will have a much better understanding of the overall view."

"An excellent notion," Mrs. Hanson agreed, reaching out to pat Charity's chilled hand. "Run along, my dear. I believe I shall have a short nap."

Charity was certain there were half a dozen excellent excuses that could release her from the unwelcome tour of the gardens. It was unfortunate that she could not conjure up a single one. Instead she gaped blankly at Lord Rockworth's sardonic smile until he at last held out his arm.

"Miss Smith?"

Cursing herself for a simpleton, she rose reluctantly to her feet and placed her hand upon his arm.

"I shall look in on you when I return," she assured her employer.

The unexpectedly treacherous woman merely smiled. "There is no hurry. You go and enjoy yourself."

Feeling decidedly smug, Julius led his elusive prize toward the back of the house.

He was well aware that she had been deliberately avoiding being alone with him. Since yesterday morning she had been a virtual shadow to Mrs. Hanson, not leaving her side until it was time for her to retire to her chambers.

The mere fact that she had so determinedly attempted to evade him only piqued his appetite.

What hunter did not prefer a wily prey?

Now, however, he had her firmly in his clutches.

He intended to take full advantage of their time together.

Glancing down at her set features, he gave a husky chuckle. She was obviously not as pleased as himself at their delightful interlude.

"You need not look as if I am escorting you to your own execution," he taunted softly.

"I would simply prefer to stay with Mrs. Hanson. I am paid to be her companion."

"And here I thought you would desire a few moments of privacy with me."

She shot him a suspicious glance. "I can not imagine why you would presume such a ridiculous thing."

He turned her toward the long flight of stairs.

"Why, to thank me for my exceedingly polite hospitality, of course."

He felt her predictably stiffen at his words. The chit might pretend to be a paid companion, but she had far too much spirit for a mere servant. She was opinionated, forceful, and quite willing to order others about. Gads, she had already gained command of his staff and altered his household to suit the needs of Mrs. Hanson. She might as well have been the mistress of Westport rather than an unwelcome guest.

And, ridiculously, he had not raised one protest.

"If by 'exceedingly polite' you mean ignoring Mrs. Hanson for the past three days and making only grudging appearances for dinner with no other purpose than to lure the dear old woman into a trap that will reveal her as a fraud, then yes, I suppose I have neglected to thank you."

He was not at all bothered by her sharp tongue. She added a definite spice to his days.

"I have not locked you in the dungeon nor forced you to exist on bread and water. Which, I assure you, was my first inclination."

"A rather difficult task considering you have no dungeon," she retorted wryly.

"True enough." His gaze stroked over the pure lines of her profile. There was none of the spun-sugar loveliness most gentlemen preferred in their maidens, he conceded. Her features were as bold and vivid as herself. But there was a beauty to them that would stand the test of time. He found himself increasingly curious to learn more about this mysterious woman. "Tell me, Miss Smith, what would you have me do? Throw my arms open to a complete stranger who lands upon my doorstep without warning, claiming to be the mother who abandoned me twenty-two years ago?"

She gave a faint shrug. "I would hope you would listen to her with an open mind."

"Why should I?"

"She is your mother."

"Highly doubtful," he retorted in dry tones. "But in any event, I did not ask her to come. Any need or desire I might have for a mother in my life is long past."

There was a brief silence before she turned to regard him in a somber fashion.

"Perhaps she has need of you."

Julius experienced a sharp, wholly unpleasant twinge in the region of his heart.

A twinge he was swift to smother.

"Oh no, you are wide of the mark if you think to stir my sympathies," he said in tones more harsh than necessary. "I have already turned off a loose-screw cousin who claimed the previous earl had promised him a large allowance, an obnoxious aunt who presumed that she could lay claim to the collection of Rockworth diamonds and a half a dozen distant acquaintances who hoped to hang upon my coattail. That is not even to mention the tenants, neighbors, and merchants who have all made demands upon my purse."

Expecting a biting condemnation of his cynical nature, Julius was unprepared as she came to a halt upon the bottom step and regarded him with an expression of sympathy.

"I am sorry."

"What?"

"I did not realize what it must be like to have suddenly inherited a fortune."

"Good God." He gave a startled laugh. "I have yet to have

received pity for my obvious windfall. Envy, greed, and outright chagrin that so unworthy a soul should have been blessed in such a fashion, but never pity."

The dark gaze searched his countenance, seeming to see far more than he would desire.

"It must have been very disconcerting to acquire a title you had not been expecting."

Julius grimaced at her perception. She would not be an easy woman to fool.

"Yes, as a matter of fact, it was," he grudgingly conceded. "One day I was tramping through the mountains of Spain and the next I was being hauled off to an estate I had never before clapped eyes upon, with nearly a hundred servants and tenants awaiting me to take charge. I nearly crawled back into the carriage and returned to Spain."

"And then came the sponges?"

"Precisely."

"Mrs. Hanson is not one of them," she said softly. "She desires nothing more than a bit of your attention."

He stiffened at her subtle attack. Gads, what did he have to do to convince her that she was betting on a losing hand? There was only one means she possessed to tempt him into generously sharing his wealth.

And for this woman he would be generous indeed.

"She at least is clever enough to disguise herself in a seeming illusion of innocence," he said with a faint sneer. "Although I prefer those who are forthright in their avarice. I possess a great dislike for covert treachery."

The brief softening of her expression was effectively banished as she snapped her brows together.

"You really are a detestable man."

"Because I refuse to be fleeced?" he demanded.

"Because you are determined to think the worst in others."

"I am rarely proven wrong." He reached up to gently stroke a raven curl that lay against her creamy skin. "Although I might be willing to be convinced of my error if the temptation was great enough."

A sudden heat sizzled in the air, making Julius consider sweeping her off her feet and carrying her up to his chambers. How perfect she would fit beneath him, he thought as the potent image began to brand itself upon his mind. Those long elegant limbs would wrap about him. . . .

"Were we not going to the gardens?" She sharply broke into his delicious thoughts and Julius heaved a rueful sigh. Unfortunately it did not appear that she was quite as anxious as himself to bring about the inevitable conclusion to their prickling awareness of each other.

Julius gave an inner shrug.

The wait would only make the final moment that much sweeter, he assured himself.

"Of course." Moving toward the nearby door, he pulled her onto the wide terrace, not halting until they reached the stone railing. "Here we are. A rather eyesore at the moment, I fear, but I shall soon have it set to rights."

"No doubt," she said dryly, but her gaze was closely surveying the overgrown beds and winding paths that had all but disappeared over the years of neglect. "What are your plans?"

He leaned against the railing, his gaze studying the lovely lines of her countenance rather than the familiar gardens.

"Being a soldier I naturally prefer the straight lines and symmetry of the European gardens. Far more tidy in my mind."

She gave a slow nod. "You will have it terraced?"

"Yes, with a long canal that leads to the grotto you can see in the distance. I also intend to enclose the rose garden and place a fountain in the center with a hedge maze where that tangle of fir trees blocks the view. Along the walks I will place several statues that I have already commissioned in Rome."

"It is a very ambitious undertaking," she murmured.

He gave a sudden laugh, recalling the gardener's disbelief when he had first begun sketching his ideas for the renovations.

"The old gardener has already lodged his protest. He is in the belief that his obvious neglect can be passed off as the notions of Capability Brown, who preferred the natural style."

"A notion you were no doubt swift to disabuse."

"Yes." His gaze lingered on the ripe satin of her lips. "What do you think?"

"It will be very elegant."

"Westport demands elegance."

"Yes."

"As do you, Miss Smith," he said softly.

She abruptly turned to regard him in wary suspicion. "What?"

"Surely you have been told that you are a very elegant woman? Long-limbed with a grace of movement that demands a gentleman's attention. And, of course, features that could easily grace an angel."

A surprising blush added a rosy tint to her smooth skin. "You are being ridiculous."

Julius slowly pushed away from the railing, his hand reaching up to gently trace the line of her stubborn jaw.

"So I have told myself, but that does not halt me from longing to seek you out, or finding my fingers itching to discover if that hair of ebony is as astonishingly soft as it promises. I often think of our kiss, do you?"

"I . . . no."

He gave a low chuckle, his hand shifting to cup the back of her neck.

"Then perhaps I should remind you of how utterly delicious it was."

With a sudden tug he had her pressed to his aching body, his head swooping swiftly downward to brand her with a possessive kiss.

He had waited three days for this moment, at times concerned that he had allowed himself to make far too much of a mere kiss. After all, a maiden was a maiden and a kiss was a kiss.

But his lips had barely touched hers when a shower of sparks shimmered through him.

No, this was no mere maiden and no mere kiss, he acknowledged in bemusement. This was a promise of paradise.

With a low groan he gathered her closer and urged her lips apart. He needed to taste of her sweetness, to feel her tremble in response to his touch.

And she did tremble. As tender as a new leaf in the spring breeze. But even as her hands briefly grasped the lapels of his coat, she was abruptly shoving herself away.

For a moment she regarded him with wide, dazed eyes. Then with a sharp cry she was turning upon her heel and fleeing back to the house.

Julius did not follow.

He could not.

He was far too shocked by the undeniable panic that had been etched upon her flushed countenance.

A panic that could only belong to a maiden who was completely and utterly innocent.

Four

Nearly a fortnight had passed since the unwelcome arrival of his guests and Julius discovered himself to be in an oddly restless mood.

Perhaps not so odd, he acknowledged as he crossed the library to snatch an almond cake from the tray that had been left there earlier. What gentleman would not be restless to have a lovely young Gypsy beneath his roof that he could not make his own?

Gads, it was nearly a torture to watch her float across the room, to see her seated at the pianoforte with the candlelight gleaming off her raven locks, and to smell the musky scent of her warm skin. She seemed to fill the entire house with her vivid presence.

It would be a wonder if she did not drive him to Bedlam with her seductive charms and blasted innocence. Or at least force him to reconsider his stern rule never to dally with virgins.

And perhaps, just as disturbing, was Mrs. Hanson.

It was a simple matter to dismiss her as a clever fraud.

It would not have taken a great deal of effort to discover that his mother had disappeared. And that his father in a cold fury had not only sought a divorce, but had destroyed every belonging that might have held any memory of his former wife.

Any sly female could lay claim to being his mother with the certainty he could not personally deny her authenticity.

But while he continued to assure himself it was all no more than a devious scheme, there were those startling moments when she managed to shake him to his very soul.

How had she known of the locket?

How could she speak so easily of servants he could barely recall?

How did she know how he had received the scar on his chin or that he hated custard?

Was it possible that his father had lied and that he had indeed driven his mother from their home? It certainly would not be beyond the cold, overly proud man.

Still, the bitterness that had been such a part of Vicar Sutton's character had spoken more of a betrayal than mere disappointment.

Annoyed by the treacherous uncertainty that had begun to plague him, Julius polished off the almond cake and reached for an apple tart. At the same moment there was a tinkling laugh and he turned to discover Mrs. Hanson had stepped into the room and taken a seat in one of the wide wing chairs.

"Dear Julius, I see that you still have that naughty sweet tooth," she teased with a glint in her eyes. "As a lad you were forever slipping into the kitchen to filch a tart or a slice of Mrs. Norman's cake. Not even the threat of being sent to bed without your dinner could keep you from temptation."

That sharp stab of unease assaulted him before Julius determinedly gathered his senses.

Mrs. Hanson might appear to be sweetly innocent, but that did not mean she did not have the heart of a viper.

"Nor my father's whippings," he drawled, returning the tart back to the tray.

"No." Mrs. Hanson gave a slow shake of her head. "I did attempt to warn him that striking you only made you more determined to have your own way. But you both were always so wretchedly stubborn."

"Indeed."

Her expression abruptly cleared. "Unlike your father, however, you have always possessed an unshakable sense of fairness and, of course, a sympathy toward those who were weaker than yourself. You were never a bully."

Moving to lean his elbow upon the mantel, he regarded her with a careful gaze.

He would not be swayed with soft words.

"Where did you go?" he demanded abruptly.

She gave a bemused blink. "Pardon me?"

"After you left the vicarage, where did you go?"

"Oh, well, I traveled toward London, but the carriage was overturned near Folkham and I was laid up for several weeks. In truth the doctors were quite convinced that I would never survive. It was there that I met Mr. Hanson, who ran a very prosperous business. At first he hired me as his housekeeper. It was nearly five years later before he could convince me to become his wife."

"You worked as a housekeeper?" he retorted in disbelief.

"I was given only a few pounds from your father before being bundled into the carriage and ordered to leave and never return. I had to support myself somehow."

She spoke with such a quiet dignity that Julius discovered it difficult to brand her a liar.

"You are now a widow?"

"Yes. Mr. Hanson was several years older than myself, which is why I suppose we were never blessed with children. He died nearly ten years ago, which is a great pity because I believe you would have liked him." She heaved a deep sigh. "I do miss him terribly."

Julius gave a restless shake of his head at the sadness in her tone.

"And now you have Miss Smith."

As expected, her expression swiftly brightened at the mention of her young companion. Regardless of the woman's true identity, there was no doubt she was deeply attached to Miss Smith.

"Yes, indeed. What a delight she has been."

Julius smiled wryly. Miss Smith might be a delight, but she was also a deuced torment for a warm-blooded male.

"Have you known her long?"

"Only since she came to me in November. Until then she was residing with her family a few miles from my home. Her father is a vicar, you know."

Julius swallowed a groan. It was not enough that she was as innocent as a babe? She had to be the daughter of a vicar as well?

"Is she?"

"Oh yes, although I do not believe him to be anything like your father," the older woman chattered, thankfully unaware of his frustrated thoughts. "From all accounts he seems to be a benevolent gentleman, although he has instilled the oddest belief in his eight daughters that they are to discover a means of being of service to others."

"Good God. Eight daughters?"

"Charity is the youngest," Mrs. Hanson readily explained. "She was set to travel to the Americas as a missionary when a dear friend of mine convinced her that I was in need of her companionship."

Julius discovered himself stiffening at the mere thought of the young woman traveling all the way to the Americas. Did her father have no care for her at all? Such a trip was dangerous for even a seasoned traveler, let alone a gullible innocent. Why, anything could happen to her. . . .

Abruptly realizing the absurdity of his thoughts, Julius forced his tense muscles to relax.

What did he care if the woman desired to fly into the teeth of danger?

It was none of his concern.

And goodness knew she was ruthlessly capable of taking care of herself.

"Miss Smith as a missionary?" he forced himself to mock. "The poor savages would not know what had happened to them. Gads, she would have them tamed, scrubbed, and reformed before they could recognize their danger."

"She is a very efficient maiden," Mrs. Hanson agreed in serene tones.

He gave an inelegant snort. "She is a managing bully who has already frightened my staff into bowing to her every whim rather than following the schedule I have established."

The pale eyes twinkled. "Oh, not precisely managing."

"She is stubborn, outspoken, shrewish . . ."

"She does possess the kindest heart," the older woman firmly interrupted. "And she is generous to a fault. She has already set about purchasing fresh bread and milk to deliver to the poorer folk about the neighborhood."

Julius was already aware of the young woman's efforts. The staff were all atwitter about the beautiful maiden who so diligently gave of herself to others. A ministering angel, they said in reverent tones, not seeming to concern themselves with the knowledge she might very well be scheming to steal his fortune.

Not that everyone was pleased with her interference, he acknowledged with a grimace.

"Yes, the vicar has already called upon me wondering if I am dissatisfied with his efforts. His nose was distinctly out of joint by Miss Smith's efforts."

Mrs. Hanson shrugged. "She simply can not help herself. As I said, she was raised to devote herself to others and their needs."

"And who will see to her needs?" Julius muttered before he could swallow the impulsive words.

"What?"

"Nothing." He abruptly straightened, needing a bit of fresh air to clear his tangled thoughts. Between Mrs. Hanson and Miss Smith he was surely destined for Bedlam. "I must be off."

As had become her custom, Charity rose early and made her rounds to the local cottages. It was a task she had performed since was a young child still being carried in her father's arms, and one she continued no matter where she might be. It gave her a sense of satisfaction that far outweighed the pleasure of remaining abed.

Returning to the house, she stepped into the foyer at the same moment Lord Rockworth moved down the stairs. She stumbled to a halt, wishing she had taken a side door. Although this gentleman had mysteriously halted his unnerving pursuit, she was still far from comfortable in his presence.

He had only to enter a room for her body to tingle with that peculiar sense of excitement, almost as if it possessed a special awareness of his male presence. And just as disturbing was the new, wholly unwelcome sympathy for his uncertain position.

It could not be easy for him to have been thrust into such a prominent role without warning. The responsibilities and endless demands on his time were difficult enough for a man groomed for such a position. And now to have a mother he had not seen for twenty-two years descend upon him only added to his troubles.

She could all too easily comprehend his wary distrust. And perhaps even forgive his harsh response to their abrupt arrival.

Such sentiments made her feel oddly vulnerable when he was near. And more than once she had discovered herself longing to reach out and soothe the troubled frown from his brow.

Dangerous thoughts that warned her to put a much-needed space between herself and this compelling gentleman.

Still, she could not forget her reason for being at Westport, she sternly chided herself as Lord Rockworth purposely crossed the foyer to join her.

Mrs. Hanson desperately desired a relationship with her son. She needed to know that he could forgive her for the years that she had been gone.

And it was Charity's duty to do whatever was necessary to ease the strain between them.

No matter how much her own nerves might be tangled into impossible knots.

Keeping the noble thought uppermost in her mind, she managed a small smile as he halted beside her.

"Good morning, my lord."

"Ah, Miss Smith, I was just on my way to the village. Would you care to join me?"

Her noble intentions wavered.

Already she could feel her stomach quivering and a warm heat coursing through her blood. It did not help that those blue eyes smoldered with a restless fire that was echoed deep within her.

Such sensations seemed utterly dangerous to a naïve innocent such as herself.

Then she was swiftly chastising herself for her absurdity.

Lord Rockworth was a handsome, intelligent, and occasionally charming gentleman. What maiden would not discover herself attracted to him?

The only danger was allowing herself to forget her true purpose for being in Kent.

"Thank you," she forced herself to agree.

If he was surprised by her ready capitulation, he hid it well and merely led her back out of the house and into the carriage that had pulled to a halt in front of the stairs.

With a brief word to the coachman he settled them upon

the leather seat and was now regarding her with a faint smile.

"You are appearing particularly lovely on this fine spring day."

Ignoring her flare of pleasure at his husky words, she primly folded her hands upon her lap.

"Have you spoken with Mrs. Hanson this morning?"

His lips thinned as she determinedly steered the conversation away from herself.

"She managed to corner me in the library."

The faint edge in his voice brought a frown to her brow. "I hope you did not say anything to upset her."

He gave a short laugh. "And it does not worry you that she might have said something to upset me?"

"Did she?" Charity demanded in surprise.

He shrugged. "It is not particularly comfortable to have my past unburied. Especially since it was not a pleasant childhood."

"Do you have no memory of your mother?"

"Not really. I was only five when she left. And since my father destroyed all portraits of her and forbade any mention of her in the house she swiftly faded from my thoughts."

Charity experienced that renegade flare of sympathy. It was far too easy to picture the heartbroken lad left in the care of a cold, disapproving father.

"Her memory may have faded, but not the loss of her, I think."

His lips twisted at her soft words. "You presume I have been crippled by some dark, brooding need for a mother?"

She refused to be turned aside by his taunting manner. She was slowly learning that it was no more than an instinctive defense.

"I think you have been made cynical and unwilling to trust others. Which no doubt explains why you have never wed."

A honey brow rose at her presumptive remarks. "And

what of you?" he charged in return. "According to Mrs. Hanson you are the product of a loving family. Why are you not married with the traditional batch of children?"

"My father was very set upon encouraging his daughters to devote their attentions to serious tasks rather than foolish entanglements of the heart," she said in calm tones. "Only a life lived in the service of others is worthy of heaven."

"Good gads, do you mean to say none of your sisters have wed?"

She gave a sudden laugh. "Actually all of them."

"Obviously your father possessed little control over his household," he said dryly.

She gave a lift of her shoulder. "What is a life of service when one is young and in love? I am his last hope for a sensible daughter."

For some unfathomable reason her light words made the dark features abruptly tighten.

"So you became a companion to Mrs. Hanson just to please your father?"

Her expression became defensive. "It was obvious she was in need of someone to oversee her affairs and ensure that she was taken proper care of. And it is hardly a life of drudgery. Mrs. Hanson treats me more like a daughter than a servant."

"You surely do not intend to remain a companion forever?" he said sharply.

Her chin instinctively tilted. "No, someday I shall travel to the Americas. I am quite fascinated by the natives there."

He made a disgusted noise at her crisp words.

"Heaven have mercy upon them," he muttered.

She stiffened in outrage. "Did you say something, sir?"

"Nothing of importance."

About to demand that he explain his less than flattering comment, Charity was halted when the carriage rolled to a stop. Lord Rockworth opened the window as a uniformed servant on horseback halted next to the carriage.

"Yes?"

"This just came by post, my lord. It is from Brush."

"Thank you."

Taking the folded letter, Lord Rockworth swiftly broke the seal and read the brief contents.

"Damn."

"Is something the matter?" she demanded.

"My old groom has traveled to Scotland to visit his daughter. It will be some time before he can be located and returned here."

Her lips pursed at his obvious frustration. "I suppose Mrs. Hanson and I are to bear the suspicion of having lured the man to Scotland just when you have need of him?"

"There is always the possibility," he said sourly. "You are terrifyingly efficient and quite in the habit of brushing aside whatever and whomever dares to stand in your way."

"That is a horrid thing to say."

Indifferent to the servant regarding them with open curiosity, he gave a shrug.

"Why? It is no less than the truth."

"You make me sound like a martinet, which I assure you I am not."

His lips abruptly twitched at her sharp tone. "No? I fear I shall have to take your word for that."

Aggravating man, she seethed as his anger suddenly fled and he regarded her with open amusement.

"I will have you know that I am very accommodating and entirely complacent."

He gave a shout of laughter. "Accommodating and complacent? You?"

"Yes."

"I suppose you also consider me sweet-tempered and utterly charming?"

"Do not be absurd," she retorted, although a part of her

could not deny he did possess the devil's own charm when he chose.

"Then do not try to sell me such a whisker. You are a managing shrew and I am a short-tempered brute. Which no doubt is the reason we are so well suited." An odd smile curved his lips as he reached up to gently trail a finger over the curve of her lower lip. Charity shivered, but with a sharp shake of his head he was pulling back and leaning out the window. "Drive on, Morgan."

Five

Julius cursed his foolishness even as he stood in the middle of the foyer.

Nothing good could come of seeking out Miss Smith, he had told himself sternly. Already she had deeply ingrained herself within Westport, from the fresh flowers that now filled every room with their pungent perfume to the sound of her quiet humming that brightened the entire household.

Just as undeniably she had deeply ingrained herself within him, he acknowledged wryly.

Not just because of the desire she had stirred to fever pitch within him, although that was potent enough in itself. But also because she fascinated him with her generous heart and devotion to others. From Mrs. Hanson to the poorest tenant, she spent every waking moment ensuring their comfort.

He was accustomed to women who concerned themselves with their gowns and parties and eligible men who happened to be within their vicinity. They might have care for others, but they certainly did not bestir themselves to deliver food to the hungry or spend an afternoon in the kitchen mixing potions for a stable boy who had fallen ill.

And then there was Miss Smith's obvious intelligence.

When she was not brangling with him she revealed a startling grasp of both politics and social reform. She was also well schooled in the classics, history, and even Latin.

Julius at times found himself debating with her as if she were one of his friends, rather than a beautiful woman.

Perhaps even a treacherous fraud.

A fact he forgot all too often.

Truth be told, he enjoyed her companionship, he ruefully acknowledged. And he was not nearly so aggravated at having to wait for his groom's return from Scotland as he should be.

Which was why he was currently waiting for her like a moonstruck looby rather than heeding his common sense, which warned him the less he saw of Miss Smith the better.

He was left standing for nearly a quarter of an hour before Miss Smith at last appeared with two large baskets in her hands.

She appeared fresh and sparklingly alive as she moved with her confident stride, although her expression dimmed at the sight of his tall form.

"My lord," she said uneasily.

"Good morning, Miss Smith. Off on your errand of mercy, I see." He offered her a smile.

"Yes."

"May I join you?"

"Why?" she demanded bluntly.

"If there are those in need upon my estate, then as their earl it is surely more my duty than yours to offer them support," he pointed out, firmly moving forward to take the baskets from her hands before she could protest.

There was a long silence as she regarded him with a searching gaze, then with a faint shrug she moved toward the door being held open by Roberts.

"You take your position very seriously, do you not?" she demanded as they moved down the stairs and toward the path that would lead them to the outskirts of the estate.

"Of course." He flashed her a bemused glance, wondering why she should sound so surprised. Did she think him a fribble with no thought beyond his own pleasures? "Despite my obvious lack of experience I am determined to make a success of Westport. Not an easy task considering the previous earl was a clutch-fisted recluse who allowed the entire estate to fall into disrepair. It is fortunate that I possess the funds to begin restorations. Otherwise you would have arrived to discover your beds damp and your food inedible."

She gave a dry chuckle, easily able to keep up with his long strides.

"It would not have been the first damp bed that I have slept in."

"Nor I," he swiftly agreed. "But Westport deserves better."

"Yes. It is a beautiful home."

His heart gave an odd jolt at the clear admiration in her tone.

Why should it matter that she approved of his home?

He gave a sudden shake of his head, not at all willing to ponder the leading question.

"Unfortunately I still have much to learn," he said in an effort to distract his wayward thoughts.

Surprisingly she allowed a smile to curve her full lips. "You are better than most landlords by the mere fact you desire to learn. It is a shame how many nobles prefer to live off the profit of their land while not being bothered with the tedious details."

Julius shuddered at the mere thought of handing control to another.

"Only a fool entrusts his future to the hands of others."

"Ah, of course. The voice of a cynic."

"A realist," he corrected firmly. "What tenant or steward would not be tempted to fadge the books if the earl was absent?"

She did not appear overly impressed with his rational explanation. Indeed, she regarded him with a commanding expression that made his lips quiver. The chit hadn't the least notion of how to treat a gentleman of his position.

Thank God.

"I do hope you will attempt to hide your suspicious nature while we are making our visits," she warned. "You will have the poor souls quaking in terror."

He resisted the urge to reach down and kiss the smile back to those maddeningly tempting lips.

The danger to do far more than merely kiss her was all too real.

"I am not an ogre. I assure you that no one possesses more concern for tenants than myself."

"Perhaps, but like most people you are no doubt the sort who believes that God helps those who help themselves." She turned them onto a side path that wound through a small meadow. "Those we are visiting today, I fear, possess no such ambition."

He lifted his brows at her ominous words, wondering what the devil he had gotten himself into.

"What do you mean?"

"Well, to start with, Mr. Burton is hopelessly attached to his gin. Mrs. Richardson has a great love for playing the invalid despite the fact the doctor has declared that she is perfectly healthy, and Mr. Conner has hidden himself in his cottage and refuses to leave, even at the danger of starving to death."

"Good gads," he retorted before he could halt the words.

"Precisely," she agreed. "The vicar has obviously washed his hands of them, but while I sympathize with his impatience I believe my father would say that we are all God's children and all deserving of his goodwill."

Julius wryly considered his own father's reaction to such tenants. Vicar Sutton believed the will of God was reserved for only a select handful that could meet his own exacting standards. A very small handful, indeed.

"It does not disturb you that they prey upon the sympathies of others?" he demanded.

She met his gaze steadily. "What is in their heart is between God and themselves."

The immeasurable generosity of her soul brought a glint to his eyes.

"And yet you can not miss an opportunity to chastise me for the hardened state of my own heart."

She possessed the grace to blush as she abruptly averted her face.

"Only because I worry for Mrs. Hanson."

"She appears perfectly content."

"She would never complain no matter how you choose to treat her. It is enough that she is allowed to see you each day."

He gave a resigned shake of his head. It appeared her pity did not extend to a lonely earl who suddenly felt as uncertain and confused as a schoolboy.

"No, I refuse to be at cross words with you on such a lovely day," he forced himself to say in light tones. "We shall instead concentrate on these poor, pathetic wretches of yours."

It was nearly two hours later that Charity at last turned back toward Westport.

It had taken a considerable amount of time to awaken Mr. Burton, who had been discovered sleeping on his threshold, then naturally Mrs. Richardson had complained she was far too ill to wash the dishes piled about the cottage, or to bring in the wood for her fire, so that Charity was forced to devote nearly an hour to restoring a bit of order to the cottage. And Mr. Conner had taken exception to the tall, forbidding earl at her side and had to be gently coaxed into opening his door so that she could give him his food.

Through it all, Lord Rockworth had been nearly silent, although nothing had missed that shrewd blue gaze. Not the empty gin bottles piled about Mr. Burton, not the manner Mrs. Richardson was well enough to gobble down the food set before her, nor the gun Mr. Conner had kept pointed at them until they were well out of sight.

Returning to the path that led through the meadow, Lord Rockworth at last heaved a harsh sigh.

"Good God."

Charity smiled wryly. "I did try to warn you."

"It is no wonder that the vicar has given up hope."

"They can be rather trying on the nerves, but surely they are the ones most in need of our sympathy? Their lives must be a misery, indeed," she said, lifting her gaze to discover him regarding her with an oddly somber expression. "Is something the matter?"

He gave a slow shake of his head. "I do not believe that I have ever met anyone quite like you, Miss Smith."

Her heart gave a betraying quiver as the smoky huskiness of his voice feathered down her spine.

"What do you mean?"

"Do you never concern yourself with your own needs?"

She gave a vague lift of her hands at his absurd question. "I have no needs. I have a very comfortable position with a lovely lady who pays me more than a generous wage."

He impatiently waved aside her words. "But what of enjoyment? Do you never long to attend dances or flirt with handsome young gentlemen?"

"Not particularly," she retorted in all honesty. "I am not really of a frivolous nature."

"How would you know if you have never tried a few frivolous entertainments?" he persisted.

She regarded him with an expression of amused exasperation. Really, did the man think that she had been browbeaten and mistreated like some tragic heroine in a novel?

"My father was not so Gothic as to lock his daughters in the vicarage. I have attended assemblies, any number of dances, and even a ball, but to be honest I found them a tedious bore. I suppose the dancing was pleasant enough, but the handsome young gentlemen devoted most of their time to boasting of their endless skills while their gazes never lifted above my neckline. And the other maidens were far too conscious of their self-worth to be seen with a poor vicar's daughter."

His brows drew together, as if he were displeased by her offhanded explanation.

"You prefer pandering to an old lady or saving the souls of wild savages?"

She came to an abrupt halt, turning to regard him with her hands planted upon her hips.

"Why should my chosen career bother you?" she demanded.

His lips tightened as if he might refuse to answer her question, then he gave a restless grunt.

"It is a waste."

"Helping others is a waste?" She gave a lift of her brows. "I fear I must disagree, my lord."

"You are beautiful, intelligent, and possess a warmth of nature that is all too rare. You should have a husband to care for you."

Absurdly, his words sent a shaft of pain through her heart.

Utter nonsense, of course.

What need did she have for a husband?

Although her sisters had all wed kind, worthy gentlemen, Charity did not envy their lives. She enjoyed her sense of independence as well as the notion of helping others. That was more fulfilling than being at the constant demand of a husband.

Still, she could not deny that there had been occasions lately when her life was not quite so satisfying as she had hoped. There was a vague discontent that had only become more pronounced since arriving in Kent.

She desired . . .

What?

That was the question.

Sensing she was revealing her very private unease to the gentleman regarding her closely, she lowered her gaze.

"In my experience husbands are far more likely to be in need of care than to offer it."

She felt his fingers lightly brush over her cheek and then boldly move to trace the outline of her lips.

"Not a husband who truly loved you," he said in husky tones.

A sudden panic seized her, as much from the searing pleasure of his touch as from the low words. Abruptly turning, she continued up the path at a brisk pace.

"We should return to the house. Mrs. Hanson will be expecting tea."

"I do have any number of maids who are capable of carrying a tea tray," he retorted in dry tones, easily keeping pace at her side.

She was not about to admit that it was more a need to be free of his disturbing presence than duty to her employer that explained her sudden haste.

"Yes, but she always enjoys having me read her the paper so that she can learn of the latest scandals from London."

"A waste," he muttered in disgust.

Her eyes flashed with sudden annoyance. Why could he not leave well enough alone?

"Please allow me enough sense to arrange my own life, my lord."

His lips snapped together, and with an obvious effort he swallowed his hasty words. He had at least discovered that she was not a woman to easily bully.

They walked in prickling silence for some time, then, at

last recovering his temper, Lord Rockworth turned his head to regard her with a faint smile.

"Are you going to sulk for the rest of our walk?" he teased.

Her own lips twitched with a reluctant humor, realizing that she had been absurd.

"I am not sulking."

"Pouting? Blue-deviled? Out of curl?"

She gave a sudden laugh. "Enough."

"There." His eyes glowed with a sudden satisfaction. "You should always smile. You are quite astonishingly beautiful."

Her lashes fluttered downward in pleased confusion. Blast. She had been flattered before. Any number of gentlemen had claimed she was beautiful. But none had managed to make her feel this delicious warmth flow through her body.

Tongue-tied for perhaps the first time in her life, Charity struggled to think of something clever to say. Thankfully, since her mind remained stubbornly blank, she was saved from her awkward dilemma when a maid suddenly appeared on the path.

"Oh, Miss Smith, I am so glad you have come back," the girl said in obvious agitation.

Charity's heart froze in fear. "What is it?"

"Mrs. Hanson."

"Where is she?"

"In the garden."

Hiking up her skirts, Charity dashed toward the nearby house, disregarding the impropriety of her hasty flight. Her only thought was reaching her beloved employer and discovering what was amiss.

Barely aware of Lord Rockworth still close by her side, she angled toward the side of the house and entered the overgrown gardens. It took several long, nerve-wracking moments to discover the tiny woman standing beside a crumbled fountain.

Charity deliberately slowed her pace as she realized that the woman did not appear in physical harm. She did not wish to frighten her by charging upon her unawares.

Taking a deep breath, she moved to stand before the woman, who regarded her with a bemused gaze.

"Hello, Mrs. Hanson."

Mrs. Hanson gave her a vague smile. "Oh, hello. Do I know you?"

Having endured the strange spells that occasionally afflicted the older lady, Charity was not caught off guard by her obvious confusion. Lord Rockworth, however, sucked in a sharp breath.

"Yes, Mrs. Hanson," she said in gentle tones. "I am your companion, Miss Smith."

"I see." Mrs. Hanson frowned in puzzlement. "I seem to be lost. Could you tell me where I am?"

"We are in Kent, my dear." Charity firmly took the woman's arm, acutely aware of Lord Rockworth's hard, glittering gaze. "Why do you not come along with me and I will help you settle into your chamber?"

"Very well."

Pulling the woman firmly toward the house, Charity was abruptly halted as Lord Rockworth grasped her shoulder.

"I will call for a doctor."

Charity felt her stomach knot in dread. Blast. Why was he not in his study or overseeing the tenants as was his custom during the day? The last thing Mrs. Hanson desired was for this gentleman to learn of her odd illness.

"No, it is not necessary," she denied in sharp tones. "She only needs a brief rest."

His gaze abruptly narrowed, as if he sensed she was attempting to hide something from him.

"I fear I must insist. Mrs. Hanson is currently a guest beneath my roof. I will decide what is best for her welfare."

The stubborn set of his jaw warned her that it would be

futile to argue. With a toss of her head she resumed leading Mrs. Hanson toward the house.

Soon enough he would learn the truth.

She could only hope that Mrs. Hanson could forgive her for failing so miserably.

Six

Charity remained at Mrs. Hanson's bedside for hours.

Gently holding her hand, she had spoken to her in comforting tones and even managed to coax her into swallowing the warm soup she had ordered to be sent up from the kitchen.

It was well past sundown when the older woman's confusion began to lift and she was once again in full control of her faculties. Charity breathed a sigh of relief, even as her stomach remained tied in knots of unease.

Lord Rockworth had made good upon his promise to send for a doctor. Charity had barely managed to settle Mrs. Hanson in her bed when the thin, silver-haired gentleman had bustled into the room. With annoying thoroughness he had demanded to know every detail of the older woman's odd behavior and easily surmised that it was not her first, nor was it destined to be her last spell of confusion. He had remained for nearly an hour before leaving the chamber and no doubt heading directly for Lord Rockworth to give a full account.

What would the Earl of Rockworth do when he learned the truth?

Deep in her heart Charity longed to believe he would be compassionate. Over the past few weeks she had discovered that beneath his brittle wariness was a warm, caring gentleman who was deeply devoted to restoring his estate and ensuring the future of his tenants. There was also a vulnerability that could occasionally be glimpsed that strangely touched her heart.

But she was all too aware that his life had made him cynical. First by the loss of his mother at such a young age, and being raised by a rigid, coldly aloof father. And then by being besieged by a host of fortune hunters the moment he had been thrust into his inheritance.

It was not easy for him to trust anyone, let alone a strange woman claiming to be his mother, who now revealed she could become desperately befuddled.

Would he turn from Mrs. Hanson in disgust? Would he condemn her as a crazed old woman? Would he have them tossed from the estate?

The questions gnawed at her as she absently patted Mrs. Hanson's thin hand and it was almost a relief when a maid entered the room to say that Lord Rockworth desired a word with her in the library.

She preferred to know the truth of his feelings, no matter how furious he might be, to being left to brood upon the uncertainty of their future.

"Best face the worse and be done with it," as her father would say.

Taking only a moment to wash her face and ensure that her curls were tidily pulled atop her head, Charity made her way through the candlelit corridors to the library. She entered to discover Lord Rockworth leaning against the mantel with a glass of brandy held in his hand.

She felt an odd tingle inch down her spine at his state of dishabille. The honey hair was tousled and his coat had been tossed onto a nearby chair. Even the crisp cravat had been pulled loose to dangle down the front of his shirt. He was no longer the commanding Earl of Rockworth, but a man who smoldered with a restless energy that seemed to fill the room.

Faltering to a halt, Charity met the glittering blue gaze with a gathering unease.

"You wished to speak with me, my lord?"

He allowed himself a thorough survey of her tense form and the manner her hands were clenched at her side before at last breaking the taut silence.

"Yes. Will you have a seat?"

"No, thank you. I do not wish to be gone from Mrs. Hanson for long."

He took a swallow of brandy. "She is better, I trust?"

"Yes, but she is very tired. I have ordered her to stay in bed."

"No doubt a very sensible suggestion. I will not keep you for long."

Another uneasy silence descended and Charity was hard put not to shift beneath that brooding gaze.

"Yes?" she nervously prompted.

"Why did you not tell me of these mysterious spells of Mrs. Hanson's?" he demanded abruptly.

She sternly kept her expression unreadable. It was important that she make the brief episode seem as meaningless as possible.

"Why should I?" She gave a shrug. "They happen infrequently and only for a brief measure of time."

His nose flared at her dismissive tone. "Dr. Marlow tells me that they will only become worse and more frequent."

Blast the meddling doctor, she silently cursed. What right did he have to announce Mrs. Hanson's illness to all and sundry?

"Yes," she admitted reluctantly.

"How bad is it?"

"This is only the third occasion it has occurred since I have been with her."

"The third occasion?" His brows snapped together. "And yet you did not think it worthy of mentioning to me?"

Charity squared her shoulders, her temper bristling at the sharp edge in his tone.

"Why? So that you could brand her an addled old woman and toss her out before you could ever hear her words of regret?"

He abruptly set his glass onto the mantel, his expression tight with annoyance.

"I have told you that I will make my decision regarding Mrs. Hanson when my groom arrives. There was no reason to lie to me."

"I did not lie," she instinctively protested.

"Oh come, Miss Smith, you deliberately hid the truth. That is quite the same as lying."

The fact that he was right only put her more on the defensive. "And if I had told you that Mrs. Hanson was ill you would have thought it was a ploy to gain your sympathy," she charged.

He pushed away from the mantel and regarded her with a dangerous glint in his eyes.

"Please halt your attempts to lay the blame for your deceit upon my shoulders, Miss Smith," he commanded in clipped tones. "Why did you not tell me?"

She licked her lips, knowing that she could no longer keep the truth from him. Despite her promise to her employer.

"Mrs. Hanson did not wish you to know."

"Why?"

"Because she did not want her time with you to be clouded by worry over her ailment."

He gave a wave of his slender hand. "Surely she realized I would eventually learn the truth?"

Charity took an unwitting step forward, knowing that she had to somehow convince this suspicious gentleman that they had meant no harm.

"She just wished to be with her son while she was still

able to enjoy your companionship. And more importantly, she wanted the opportunity to ensure you knew that she had always loved you, before it was too late."

The blue eyes darkened, then without warning he jerkily turned to stride toward the shadowed window. Charity regarded the stiff lines of his body with wary puzzlement.

He appeared more distressed than angry, as if she had somehow wounded him.

"And it never occurred to either of you how your deceit might affect others?" he demanded in strained tones.

Charity frowned. "What do you mean?"

"I lost my mother twenty-two years ago. Now you bring her back to me so that I can lose her all over again?"

Charity felt as if she had been slapped.

Dear heavens, it was true.

She had not considered the pain Lord Rockworth might suffer at discovering his mother, only to learn she was becoming increasingly ill.

Her only thought had been to ease the suffering of Mrs. Hanson. Now she realized that they had been utterly selfish.

Blast.

She was not usually so indifferent to the needs of those about her.

Filled with regret, Charity moved swiftly forward, halting only when she reached Lord Rockworth's side. Then taking his hand in her own, she gently squeezed his fingers.

"No, Julius," she said softly, unaware she had used his given name, even when his head shifted to regard her upturned countenance with an oddly brilliant gaze. "The doctor can only speculate about these strange spells. There is no certainty that they will become worse for several years to come."

"And no promise that she will not awaken tomorrow and not know me."

Her heart squeezed and she impulsively lifted his hand to her cheek.

"I am sorry. You are right. I only thought of Mrs. Hanson."

He seemed to still as their gazes locked, then with a strangled moan he was pulling free and turning his back upon her.

"You should go," he said roughly.

Stung by his sharp rejection of her sympathy, Charity determinedly moved to stand before him.

"Why do you do that?" she demanded in exasperation.

His own features were tight with strain. "Do what?"

"Turn from those who desire to help you?"

His lips twisted in a self-derisive smile. "You do not know the danger you so naively court, my dear."

Charity shivered as a new, deliciously dangerous tension entered the air.

"Tell me," she urged, even as she knew she should be fleeing for the safety of her room.

His eyes darkened as his hands raised to tenderly frame her face.

"I do not desire your sympathy or your help. I desire this."

With a slow, deliberate motion his head lowered. There was ample opportunity to pull away, but Charity made no attempt to free herself. Indeed, she was already swaying forward when his lips met her own.

Why should she deny the inevitable? she mused as his lips teased her own apart and his arms closed about her. She had ached for this moment. To feel the soft flutters in the pit of her stomach, the race of her heart, and the honey heat that flowed through her blood. This sweet passion had bewitched her to the point she no longer cared what was right or wrong. Just that she could be held like this forever.

"Julius," she murmured as his kiss eased and the tormenting mouth stroked down her cheek and along the line of her jaw.

"Dear Lord, you are driving me mad," he muttered, his

hands restlessly moving over her back. "Do you know the nights I have paced the floor? The long hours I work like a crazed man in the fields just to purge this aching need from my body?"

A thrill of excitement shuddered through her as she clutched at the fine lawn shirt to keep herself upright. The warm scent of him filled her senses and left her knees oddly weak.

"I have had my own share of sleepless nights, my lord," she admitted in uneven tones.

"You should not tell me such things." His mouth returned to plunder the softness of her own, briefly promising an end to their shared torment before he was reluctantly pulling back and sucking in a rasping breath. "Gads, you must go before I do something we will both regret."

The mere fact that she would have gladly followed wherever he might have led, warned Charity that it was indeed time to flee.

The love for this gentleman that had steadily, irrevocably been growing within her heart made her more vulnerable than she had ever dreamed possible.

Stepping back, she offered a sad smile, inwardly regretting the staunch nobility that had made it impossible for him to take her innocence.

"Very well."

With heavy steps she turned and made her way toward the door.

"Charity?" he called softly.

She paused, although she did not trust herself to turn around and face him. With only a glance he could have her flying back to his arms, where she so desperately longed to be.

"Yes?"

"Dream of me," he commanded in husky tones.

She gave a choked laugh as she hurried from the room.

She very much feared that she would be dreaming of this honey-haired gentleman until the day she died.

Julius heaved a sigh of regret as Charity hastened from the room.

Bloody hell.

He had not meant to seduce her.

He had not meant to so much as touch her.

But with his emotions rubbed raw with his concern for Mrs. Hanson, and his thoughts in turmoil, his passions had swiftly flared out of control.

How desperately he desired to drown in the pleasure of her tempting innocence. To forget his troubles in her sweetness.

Thank God he had come to his senses before it was too late, he acknowledged, even as his stomach twisted with unsatisfied need. He would not take Charity in a flurry of frustration. She deserved far better than that.

Raising a hand, he massaged the tense muscles of his neck.

He longed to polish off his brandy and sink into his bed in a haze of pleasant indifference. But he resisted temptation.

He needed to check on Mrs. Hanson before he could think of retiring for the night.

It had come as an unpleasant shock to realize how concerned he had been that she was ill.

He had told himself that becoming better acquainted with the woman was only a means of proving her false. Even when she stirred memories long buried and offered a warmth that had been all too absent from his life since he was a small child, he had not sensed the danger he was in.

With the same subtle magic that Charity possessed, the older woman had managed to slip into his heart, making him vulnerable to emotions that he would have sworn he did not possess.

Suddenly it did not matter if she was his mother or not. His only concern was that she be given the best care possible.

Unable to pinpoint the precise moment he had become an utter fool, he heaved a sigh. All he knew for certain was that it was too late to rid his heart of these two enchanting women.

Leaving the lure of the brandy behind him, Julius moved out of the library and up the steps to Mrs. Hanson's chambers. After knocking on her door he was bidden to enter and he crossed the room to gaze upon the tiny form nearly lost in the vast bed.

He felt a pang in his heart at her obvious frailty, but the warm happiness that glowed in her eyes at his arrival brought a smile to his lips.

"Good evening, Mrs. Hanson."

"Oh, Julius, how glad I am you stopped by."

"How do you feel?"

"Rather foolish." She gave a rueful grimace. "I hope that I did not frighten you?"

He reached out to firmly clasp one of her tiny hands. "Only when I feared you had suffered an accident."

There was a small silence before she cleared her throat.

"I suppose the doctor has told you of my ailment?"

"Yes."

Her eyes dimmed with sudden anxiety. "And now you think me a doddy old woman?"

"Of course not," he said in stern tones, angered by the thought that there were those who would think her strange illness a sign of madness. "I think you very kind and very courageous. Your life has not been an easy one and yet you face it bravely."

A tentative smile curved her lips. "Do you truly believe so?"

"Yes."

She heaved a faint sigh. "I have always hoped that I could be a mother you would be proud of. Even if we could not be together."

"You need not worry," he said gently. "I shall always be proud of you."

"Thank you, my dearest."

Unable to halt himself, Julius abruptly leaned downward and brushed his lips over her brow.

"Try to get some sleep."

Her expression was one of deep contentment. "Yes, I believe I will be able to sleep now."

"Good night."

Julius turned and left the room, making his way toward his own chambers. For a brief, tempting moment he halted before Charity's door.

Was she already in her bed, perhaps even now dreaming of him?

Or was she seated before the dresser as she brushed those satin raven curls?

The image of her attired in a thin night rail with her curls spilled over her breasts made him groan in pain.

Gads, he could bear the agony no longer.

Charity was destined to belong to him.

Now all he had to do was convince the stubborn minx of her fate.

Seven

With a restless unease Julius paced the floor of his library.

After a sleepless night he had arisen to discover that his old groom had at long last arrived at Westport and was even now speaking with Mrs. Hanson in the garden.

Julius had been stunned by the announcement.

After waiting weeks for precisely this moment, he had been struck by a sudden urge to run Cower from the estate and allow the charade to continue.

Did he truly desire to know the truth?

And more importantly, what would he do when that truth was revealed?

It was a question he could not yet answer, so instead of seeking out the two in the garden, he had instead locked himself in the library to pace like a cornered animal.

Gads, what a damnable mess, he thought as he abruptly reached out to tug on the bell that would call his butler.

One moment he had been wishing to be done with the blasted females who had so rudely intruded into his world, and the next he was longing to keep them closely guarded next to him.

What had happened to the clear-thinking, methodical soldier?

He sorely missed the days when all had seemed either white or black.

Returning to his pacing, Julius was relieved when the door was at last pushed open and Roberts stepped into the room. He was a gentleman accustomed to knowing precisely what was to be done. He did not like this sudden tendency to stew and debate until his thoughts were twisted into knots.

"Yes, sir?" the butler demanded with a low bow.

"Is Cower still speaking with Mrs. Hanson?" he asked in sharp tones.

"He is indeed, sir." A surprising smile curved the usually pursed lips. "Chattering like magpies, they are."

Julius frowned, not willing to read too much into the fact that Cower was still with the older woman. The old groom was a gregarious soul and would talk freely with whomever he could get to listen.

"I see."

"Is there anything I can get you?"

Julius briefly thought of a nice plate of almond cakes, or perhaps some pudding. Then he gave a sharp shake of his head.

"No, thank you, Roberts. That will be all."

"Yes, sir."

The butler backed from the room, leaving Julius once again at the mercy of his tangled thoughts.

There were, of course, any number of tasks that awaited his attention.

The tumble of estate books remained stacked upon a nearby shelf. There were the latest household bills and quarterly reports on his desk. But he made no effort to even glance in their direction.

Instead he returned to his pacing and disjointed thoughts that refused to be dismissed.

Thankfully, for the sake of his delicate carpet, it was less than a half an hour later when there was another knock on the door and his old groom stepped into the room.

Dressed in rough clothing, his battered hat in his hand, Cower moved forward to offer Julius a bow. Although bent with age he remained alert and surprisingly spry for a man of his advanced years.

"A good day to you, my lord."

"Cower, it is good to see you. I thank you for traveling so swiftly to Westport."

The older man gave a shrug. " 'Twas no hardship to leave Scotland. Even if I dearly love my lass, she has a sharp eye and even sharper tongue. A poor sod can't have a decent drink or a bit of a smoke without her cutting up rough."

"A terrible thing, indeed," Julius readily sympathized.

"Aye."

Unable to bear the strain a moment longer, he squared his shoulders. "I understand you have met with Mrs. Hanson. Did you recognize her?" he demanded bluntly.

The weathered face softened with a sudden smile. "I did, indeed. It's been years but there is no mistaking."

"Then she is my mother?" he demanded swiftly.

"No."

Julius momentarily reeled at the blunt denial. Somehow, despite all of his protests to the contrary, he had managed to harbor a small, utterly absurd hope that Mrs. Hanson had not been lying. A hope that his mother had not abandoned him like a bit of rubbish all those years ago.

Now he clutched at the edge of the desk and cursed himself for a fool.

"But you just said that your recognized her."

"T'aint your mother, but Mary Stallings, yer old nurse," the groom explained.

"My nurse?" That made Julius slowly straighten, a baffled frown upon his brow. "Good God."

Cower scratched his head, his expression rather bemused. "Don't rightly know what's the matter with Mary, but she's a good woman, my lord. I mean she wouldn't be wanting to hurt you or nothing. She loved you when you was a lad. Loved you more than anyone else in that house. It flat made her miserable when yer father went to blaming her for his wife's disappearance and ordered her from the vicarage. She begged upon her knees to be allowed to remain with you."

Distant, vague memories of the woman who had kissed him good night and held him close after he had been beaten by his father elusively fluttered at the edge of his mind. Over the years he had confused them with the image of his mother, but now he gave a slow nod of his head.

It all made much more sense now.

"My father forced her to leave?"

"Yes, sir." The groom grimaced. "He claimed that Mary knew of that rotter of an actor what was slipping about with Mrs. Sutton. What he thought poor Mary was to do even if she did know is beyond me. But then the vicar wasn't thinking clearly at the time. Wanted someone to blame and chose Mary."

Julius had no difficulty in believing his father could shift his anger from his wife to a helpless servant. The good Lord knew that Vicar Sutton had continued to dislike his own son for the unforgivable sin of being a constant reminder of his faithless wife.

Still, Julius remained confused.

"But why would she pretend to be my mother?" he muttered.

"Pardon me, sir, but I don't think she be pretending."

"What?"

"She seems to have convinced herself that she is rightly yer mother."

Julius gave a bemused shake of his head. "How odd."

Cower regarded him steadily, his eyes filled with sympathy for the confused old woman.

"Well, truth be told, she was more a mother to you than

yer own, if you will forgive me for saying so. T'was Mary who watched over you and played with you and taught you to read and write. It was her that wiped yer tears when you were sad and made you laugh with her silly songs. And it was only Mary who dared to stand up to the vicar when he so readily raised his hand to strike you."

His simple words deeply touched Julius.

Although his memories were vague, he did not doubt that Mary had been the one to love him, to care for him. What else made a mother?

"Yes," he breathed.

"The vicar should never have sent her away." Cower gave a shake of his head. "A sad day."

Julius gave a sharp bark of laughter at the thought of his father. "My father rarely concerned himself with the needs of others."

"That be a fact." The groom heaved a sigh. "Will you be wanting me for anything else, sir?"

"No, I thank you." Julius moved forward to place a hand upon the man's shoulder. "Thank you for what you have done, Cower, and be assured you are very welcome to remain as long as you desire. Of course, if you prefer, my carriage is at your disposal to return home."

The groom gave a sudden smile. "Well, if it be all the same to you, my lord, I believe I shall remain a bit. Mary was as good a friend as I ever had. I should like to spend some time with her."

Julius gave a lift of his brows. "I hope that you will have some time for me as well. It has been several years since we last rode together."

A twinkle returned to the faded eyes. "Aye. Although I have never ridden with a real earl afore."

Julius chuckled, his heart lighter than it had been in years. Perhaps since the day his mother had left and his devoted nurse had been wrenched from his side.

"I assure you that it is no different from riding with a vicar's brat."

"Then I shall be pleased to join you."

With a bow the groom turned and left the room. Standing in the center of the library, Julius allowed a smile to curve his lips.

He was a gentleman who had thought himself alone in the world.

Now he had the mother who had been taken from him all those years ago, and even more astonishingly, he had discovered the maiden destined to become the Countess of Rockworth.

Unaware that her fate had already been decided for her, Charity returned to Westport after her morning visit to the tenants.

It took only a moment after entering the foyer for her to realize that the household was atwitter, and tracking down the housekeeper she soon discovered that the muted excitement was from the sudden arrival of Lord Rockworth's old groom.

She felt her heart grow cold when she learned that Cower had already spoken with Mrs. Hanson and was even now closeted with the earl in the library.

It was absurd, she told herself sternly.

What did she have to fear?

She knew beyond all doubt that Mrs. Hanson was a sweet, utterly guileless woman. She would never attempt to cheat or deceive another.

Never.

And yet, Charity could not wholly shake off her gathering unease, and barely aware that she was moving, she discovered herself standing before the door to the library.

She had to reassure herself that all was well.

Without even bothering to knock, she pushed open the door. Slipping inside, she discovered Julius standing beside the window. At her entrance he slowly turned, his dark countenance giving nothing away.

Her heart faltered, but with a grim determination she lifted her chin.

For good or ill she needed to know the truth.

"Forgive me for intruding, my lord."

"You are not intruding. Please, come in."

She moved reluctantly forward, her skirts rustling loudly in the still silence.

"I was told your groom had arrived," she said as she came to a halt in the center of the room.

"Yes, he did."

"And he has seen Mrs. Hanson?"

"Yes."

His voice was unreadable and she was seized by a flare of impatience.

"And did he reassure you that she is your mother?"

"No."

Charity's breath was squeezed from her body as she regarded him in horror.

No.

She refused to believe she had been so mistaken in her employer. Or that she had been used in a devious attempt to fool this man.

"What?" she demanded in dazed tones.

He stepped toward her, appearing as much the conquering Viking as the day she had first encountered him.

"She is not my mother."

"That is impossible," she breathed.

"I fear that is the truth. She is Mary Stallings, my old nurse."

"But . . ." Charity gave a disbelieving shake of her head. "Mrs. Hanson would not lie about such a thing."

At last a faint smile curved his lips and the dark features softened.

"Cower is convinced that she truly believes herself to be my mother. Whether it is because of her accident years ago, or a symptom of her current illness is impossible to say. Whatever the case, she is not my mother."

Sudden tears filled Charity's eyes. She had known the older woman was confused, but she could never have suspected just how badly.

"Oh, poor Mrs. Hanson."

"Yes, it is very sad," he said in low tones.

Charity attempted to gather her badly scattered wits. She would have to consider what was to be done for Mrs. Hanson later. For now she realized she owed this gentleman her regrets. He had been right to question the older woman's claim.

Drawing in a slow breath, she forced herself to meet his steady gaze.

"I suppose I owe you an apology."

A honey brow flicked upward. "An apology?"

"Although it was not my intention, we did deceive you."

"Yes, you did."

She experienced a prick of annoyance at his brief words. She had, perhaps ridiculously, thought that they had discovered a deeper bond between them. Obviously she had foolishly misunderstood his kisses of the night before.

"Well, you needn't worry. I can soon have our bags packed and we will return to Surrey. I would prefer to be the one to explain the truth to Mrs. Hanson if you do not mind."

"No."

She gave a startled blink. "What?"

"Mrs. Hanson will be staying here."

She briefly wondered if Mrs. Hanson's illness was contagious. She could not seem to make sense of the man's words.

"But you have discovered she is not your mother."

He gave a firm shake of his head. “Perhaps she did not give birth to me, but as Cower was so swift to point out, she was more a mother to me than my own. She was the one to care for me, the only one to truly love me. She mourned my loss far more, I suspect, than the woman who walked away from her husband and child.”

The confusion faded and a welcome warmth filled her heart. This was the Julius she had always known lurked behind his cold demeanor. A man of gentle compassion.

“You are not angry?” she said in wonder.

“How could I be?” He gave a smile that made her toes curl. “I am very happy to have her with me.”

Charity smiled in return, then without warning she was struck by a new, wholly unwelcome realization.

Mrs. Hanson was now where she belonged. She would be well cared for and given all the attention she could possibly need.

There was no longer any reason for Charity to remain her companion.

A pain wrenched her heart. Not only at the thought of being parted from the woman she had grown to love, but at the knowledge that once she left Westport she would never see Julius again.

Dear heavens, until this moment she had not realized what a horrid wrench it would be.

Feeling decidedly ill, she struggled to keep her smile intact. “That is wonderful.”

He stepped closer, his gaze closely regarding her countenance.

“You do not appear particularly pleased.”

She breathed in deeply, inhaling the warm, precious scent of him.

“Of course I am.” She attempted to hedge. “But it will be difficult to leave Mrs. Hanson. I have grown very fond of her.”

His hand suddenly rose to brush her cheek in an achingly familiar manner.

"And who mentioned anything of your leaving?" he asked in low tones.

The air seemed to thicken as she struggled to keep her thoughts in order. Not an easy task when her heart was thumping with a poignant need.

"If Mrs. Hanson is to be in your care then she will have no further use of my services."

"There is that," he murmured, his fingers now teasing her lips. "And your duty, of course, is to seek out those in need."

"Yes," she breathed.

"Then I believe I may be of help. I happen to know of a person who is in desperate need, indeed."

Her thoughts were slipping away as a shiver of awareness raced through her.

Blast.

It was difficult enough to be in the same room with the man. To have him touching her in such an intimate fashion was driving her mad. Especially when he was blithely discussing sending her to another.

"Who is that?" she managed to choke out.

"Me."

She stilled, certain that she had not heard correctly. "That . . . is absurd."

He swiftly moved to wrap her in his arms, gazing deeply into her startled eyes.

"No, it is the simple truth. For too long I have allowed myself to believe that I was above the need for love. But then you arrived, turning my household into your own domain, challenging my determined refusal to allow Mrs. Hanson into my life, and suddenly forcing me to realize how desperately lonely I have been."

Her heart came to a complete, perfect halt as she frantically searched his face for any hint he was merely teasing with her.

Could he truly be implying that he felt as she did?

That the mere thought of parting was so painful it could not be endured?

The answer was in the blue eyes that no longer glittered with ice, but glowed with the warmth of a summer sky.

A flood of happiness rushed through her and she was forced to grasp at his shoulders to keep from sinking to the floor.

"Julius."

He reached down to kiss her with a lingering tenderness before leaning his forehead against her own.

"I have fallen madly, desperately in love with you, Charity Smith. If you leave I shall not survive. Surely there is no greater need than saving the life of an earl?"

She gave a low chuckle, knowing that she had in truth discovered the reason for her existence. Certainly she would always devote a portion of herself to caring for those in need, but a far larger portion would be devoted to this gentleman.

Still, she could not resist teasing him just a bit.

"And what of my savages?"

In answer he pulled her even tighter to his hard frame, making her deliciously aware that she would soon be far better acquainted with that warm male body.

"I fear that you will have to concentrate on reforming a headstrong, quick-tempered brute for now."

Her hands lifted to plunge into the honey silk of his hair.

"Well, I suppose someone must take on the burden."

"Not someone. Just you," he murmured as his lips lowered in a purposeful manner. "Only you."

Charity gave herself willingly to his kiss.

For a gentleman determined to live his life alone, he did not appear overly concerned at being landed with an almost mother and a soon-to-be wife.

Indeed, if his enthusiasm was any indication, he was one

of the most satisfied gentlemen in all of England, she acknowledged dizzily.

Which was just as well.

She was quite certain she was by far the happiest maiden.